The Frosted Felony

Excerpt

O livia descended the creaky wooden stairs to the bakery's basement, her flour-dusted apron a testament to the morning's baking frenzy. She flicked on the dim overhead light, casting long shadows between the stacks of boxes and renovation tools. The scent of sawdust mingled with the lingering sweetness of sugar and cinnamon from upstairs, an odd yet comforting combination.

"Right," she muttered to herself, eyeing the chaos. "Let's make you pretty for the Winter Festival."

The festival was the talk of Bayside Cove, but more so were Mayor Bennett's plans to modernize their quaint town. Olivia couldn't help the furrow of her brow as she thought of his latest speech, the words 'progress' and 'future' echoing in her head like a mantra she didn't remember choosing.

"Progress isn't always paved roads and new condos," she huffed, pushing aside a stack of empty flour sacks with a practiced nudge of her hip.

As she shuffled through the clutter, organizing paint cans into rainbow order—a habit born out of a love for aesthetics—her elbow caught the corner of an old wooden crate tucked away under a workbench. It wobbled precariously before tipping over with a thud that seemed too loud in the confined space.

"Whoops! Sorry, ghosts of pastries past," she quipped, hoping the spirits of failed eclairs wouldn't hold a grudge.

She knelt beside the fallen crate, patting it apologetically. But as she lifted it, her eyes fell upon a curious sight. A false bottom had come loose, revealing a hidden compartment beneath.

"Well, now, what secrets are you hiding?" Olivia's voice was low, imbued with intrigue as she peered closer. Her fingers, still dusted with flour, brushed against the edge of the concealed space.

"Let's have a look at you then," she whispered, more to herself than anyone or anything that might be listening. With the gentle prodding of her fingertips, she pried open the secret nook, her heart drumming a beat of anticipation in her chest.

Olivia's fingers trembled slightly as she gripped the edge of the wooden lid, her breath catching in the musty air of the basement. With a gentle tug, the compartment creaked open like a whisper from the past, revealing its secret—a journal whose leather cover was dulled by time, entombed in a shroud of dust and cobwebs that clung to it like remnants of forgotten memories.

"Hello there, old friend," she murmured, her voice soft with reverence. Carefully, Olivia lifted the journal from its resting place, the weight of history apparent in its heft. Tracing the faded gold lettering on its cover with a flour-caked finger, she felt the pulse of stories untold thrumming beneath her touch.

"Looks like you've got quite the tale to tell," Olivia said, her curiosity now aflame like the ovens upstairs. She blew gently over the cover, sending a cloud of dust dancing into the dim light filtering through the high windows. The particles sparkled briefly before dissipating into the stale air.

"Meow."

The sudden sound ricocheted around the room, slicing through the silence. Olivia's head snapped up to see Basil perched at the top of the rickety stairs, his amber eyes fixed on her with an intensity that seemed almost human. His tail swished back and forth in a metronome of feline concern.

"Basil, what is it?" Olivia asked, standing up with the journal cradled against her chest. The tabby cat let out another plaintive meow, his gaze never wavering from the book in her arms. "You're not usually one for dramatic entrances."

With cautious steps, Basil descended the stairs, each move deliberate, calculated. As he neared Olivia, his tail continued to twitch, betraying an unease that Olivia found disconcerting. Cats, after all, had a reputation for sensing things beyond the scope of human understanding.

"Is this journal more than just a piece of Bayside Cove's history?" she wondered aloud, meeting the cat's eyes.

Basil leaped down from the last step, his paws silent on the concrete floor. He brushed against Olivia's leg, a reassuring gesture, as if to say, 'Whatever secrets lie within, we'll face them together.'

"Alright then," Olivia said with a determined nod, her tone playful yet edged with resolve. "Let's see what this dusty old book has to say. But first, how about some fresh milk to calm those nerves, huh?"

The Frosted Felony

Basil purred, the vibration mingling with the hum of the refrigerator upstairs, a symphony of bakery life that anchored Olivia to the present amid the whispers of the past.

Olivia hesitated for a mere heartbeat, the weight of history in her hands. The journal, with its time-worn cover and secretive allure, seemed to beckon her further into its mysteries. With the warmth of Basil' presence at her ankles, she made a decision that was part pastry chef, part amateur historian. "Renovations can wait," she muttered to herself, brushing off the last of the cobwebs clinging to her apron.

She ascended the stairs, each step creaking underfoot, a reminder of all the footfalls these floors had endured over the years. In the bakery above, the air was sweet with the scent of cinnamon and sugar, a stark contrast to the mustiness of the basement. The golden glow from the hanging lights offered an inviting atmosphere, one that Olivia had carefully cultivated over the years.

"Alright, my mysterious friend," Olivia addressed the journal as if it could hear her, "let's see what tales you've kept hidden from us." She settled into her favorite corner booth, the cushions worn to perfection from countless hours of planning and dreaming. The bakery was quiet now, save for the soft hum of the oven—a lullaby for loaves and a backdrop to her unfolding adventure.

The journal's pages resisted at first, as though reluctant to divulge their secrets after so long. Olivia handled them with a reverence typically reserved for her most delicate pastries, gently coaxing them open. She was met with looping script that danced across the yellowed paper, each entry a breadcrumb on a path through time.

"Goodness, you're quite the enigma, aren't you?" she whispered, tracing a finger along the lines of ink, her brows knitting together as she deciphered the antiquated handwriting. The faint smell of old parchment mingled with the ever-present aroma of baked goods, an olfactory bridge between the here-and-now and days long gone.

With every page turned, the journal revealed another fragment of its story, drawing Olivia deeper into its embrace. She chuckled softly to herself, imagining the bakery's regulars trying to make sense of her current predicament—trading rolling pins for relics, cookie cutters for conundrums.

"Seems like I've got more than just recipes baking tonight," she said, her voice tinged with the warmth of intrigue. The cozy corner of the bakery, her haven for creation, had transformed into a detective's den where pastries and puzzles were equally savored.

As Olivia's fingertips grazed the aged pages, a faint shiver ran up her spine. The cryptic entries sprawled before her were penned with an urgency that time had not dulled. She leaned closer, the soft glow of the overhead lamp casting a halo around her as she read about a generations-old curse, whispered betrayals, and a recipe that seemed to be at the heart of it all.

1. Vanilla Bean Cupcakes with Cream Cheese Frosting

Ingredients for Cupcakes:

- 1 1/2 cups all-purpose flour
- 1 1/2 tsp baking powder
- 1/4 tsp salt
- 1/2 cup unsalted butter, softened
- 1 cup granulated sugar
- 2 large eggs
- 2 tsp vanilla bean paste (or vanilla extract)
- 1/2 cup whole milk

Ingredients for Cream Cheese Frosting:

- 1/2 cup unsalted butter, softened
- 8 oz cream cheese, softened
- 4 cups powdered sugar
- 1 tsp vanilla extract

Directions:

1. Preheat oven to 350°F (175°C) and line a cupcake tin with paper liners.
2. In a medium bowl, whisk flour, baking powder, and salt.
3. In a separate large bowl, cream butter and sugar until light and fluffy. Add eggs one at a time, then stir in vanilla.
4. Add dry ingredients to the wet mixture alternately with milk, beginning and ending with dry ingredients.
5. Fill cupcake liners 2/3 full and bake for 18-20 minutes. Let cool.
6. For frosting, beat butter and cream cheese until smooth. Gradually add powdered sugar and vanilla. Frost the cooled cupcakes.

2. Chocolate Espresso Cupcakes with Mocha Buttercream

Ingredients for Cupcakes:
- 1 cup all-purpose flour
- 1/2 cup cocoa powder
- 1 tsp baking powder
- 1/2 tsp baking soda
- 1/4 tsp salt
- 1/2 cup unsalted butter, softened
- 1 cup sugar
- 2 large eggs
- 1 tsp vanilla extract
- 1/2 cup brewed espresso (room temperature)
- 1/4 cup sour cream

Ingredients for Mocha Buttercream:
- 1 cup unsalted butter, softened
- 2 cups powdered sugar
- 1/4 cup cocoa powder
- 2 tbsp brewed espresso (room temperature)
- 1 tsp vanilla extract

Directions:
1. Preheat oven to 350°F (175°C) and line a cupcake tin with paper liners.
2. In a medium bowl, whisk flour, cocoa powder, baking powder, baking soda, and salt.
3. In a separate bowl, cream butter and sugar until fluffy. Add eggs one at a time, then vanilla.
4. Mix in dry ingredients alternately with espresso and sour cream.
5. Fill cupcake liners 2/3 full and bake for 18-20 minutes. Let cool completely.

6. For frosting, beat butter until creamy, then add powdered sugar, cocoa powder, espresso, and vanilla. Beat until smooth and frost the cupcakes.

---

3. Lemon Blueberry Cupcakes with Lemon Buttercream

Ingredients for Cupcakes:
- 1 1/2 cups all-purpose flour
- 1 tsp baking powder
- 1/2 tsp baking soda
- 1/4 tsp salt
- 1/2 cup unsalted butter, softened
- 1 cup granulated sugar
- 2 large eggs
- Zest of 1 lemon
- 1/4 cup fresh lemon juice
- 1/2 cup buttermilk
- 1 cup fresh blueberries

Ingredients for Lemon Buttercream:
- 1/2 cup unsalted butter, softened
- 3 cups powdered sugar
- Zest of 1 lemon
- 2-3 tbsp fresh lemon juice

Directions:
1. Preheat oven to 350°F (175°C) and line a cupcake tin with liners.
2. Whisk together flour, baking powder, baking soda, and salt in a bowl.
3. Cream butter and sugar until fluffy. Add eggs one at a time, then lemon zest and juice.

4. Gradually mix in dry ingredients and buttermilk. Fold in blueberries.
5. Fill liners and bake for 18-20 minutes. Let cool completely.
6. For frosting, beat butter and powdered sugar until smooth. Add lemon zest and juice. Frost the cooled cupcakes.

---

4. Caramel Apple Cupcakes with Salted Caramel Frosting

Ingredients for Cupcakes:
- 1 1/4 cups all-purpose flour
- 1 tsp baking powder
- 1/2 tsp cinnamon
- 1/4 tsp nutmeg
- 1/4 tsp salt
- 1/2 cup unsalted butter, softened
- 1 cup brown sugar
- 2 large eggs
- 1 tsp vanilla extract
- 1/2 cup milk
- 1 cup peeled and diced apples (Granny Smith or Honeycrisp)

Ingredients for Salted Caramel Frosting:
- 1/2 cup unsalted butter, softened
- 1/2 cup caramel sauce (store-bought or homemade)
- 3-4 cups powdered sugar
- 1/4 tsp sea salt

Directions:
1. Preheat oven to 350°F (175°C) and line cupcake tin with liners.
2. Whisk flour, baking powder, cinnamon, nutmeg, and salt in a bowl.

3. In another bowl, cream butter and brown sugar until fluffy. Add eggs one at a time, then vanilla.
4. Mix dry ingredients and milk alternately into the batter. Fold in diced apples.
5. Fill cupcake liners 2/3 full and bake for 18-20 minutes. Let cool.
6. For frosting, beat butter until creamy. Add caramel sauce, powdered sugar, and salt. Frost the cooled cupcakes.

---

5. Red Velvet Cupcakes with Cream Cheese Frosting

Ingredients for Cupcakes:
- 1 1/4 cups all-purpose flour
- 1 tbsp cocoa powder
- 1/2 tsp baking soda
- 1/4 tsp salt
- 1/2 cup unsalted butter, softened
- 1 cup sugar
- 2 large eggs
- 1 tsp vanilla extract
- 1/2 cup buttermilk
- 1 tbsp red food coloring
- 1 tsp white vinegar

Ingredients for Frosting:
- 1/2 cup unsalted butter, softened
- 8 oz cream cheese, softened
- 4 cups powdered sugar
- 1 tsp vanilla extract

Directions:
1. Preheat oven to 350°F (175°C) and line a cupcake tin with liners.
2. In a bowl, whisk flour, cocoa powder, baking soda, and salt.

3. In a large bowl, cream butter and sugar until light. Add eggs one at a time, then vanilla and food coloring.
4. Mix dry ingredients and buttermilk alternately into the batter. Stir in vinegar last.
5. Fill liners 2/3 full and bake for 18-20 minutes. Let cool completely.
6. For frosting, beat butter and cream cheese until smooth. Gradually add powdered sugar and vanilla. Frost the cupcakes.

The Frosted Felony

Patti Petrone Miller

Copyright ©2024 by Patti Petrone Miller

All rights reserved.

No part of this publication may be reproduced, distributed, or transmitted in any form or by any means, including photocopying, recording, or other electronic or mechanical methods, without the prior written permission of the publisher, except as permitted by U.S. copyright law. For permission requests, contact [include publisher/author contact info].

The story, all names, characters, and incidents portrayed in this production are fictitious. No identification with actual persons (living or deceased), places, buildings, and products is intended or should be inferred.

Book Cover by TMT Book Cover Designs

1 edition

Printed in the United States of America

Book List

The Frosted Felony

Accidental Vows

Best Served Dead

Cabinet of Curiosities

Pies and Perps

Sin Takes a Holiday

Hex and the City

The Gingerdead Men

Mama Mia It's Murder

Dedication

For Tessa

Patti Petrone Miller

The Frosted Felony

By Patti Petrone Miller

Patti Petrone Miller

Prologue:

Whispers in the Mist

Olivia descended the creaky wooden stairs to the bakery's basement, her flour-dusted apron a testament to the morning's baking frenzy. She flicked on the dim overhead light, casting long shadows between the stacks of boxes and renovation tools. The scent of sawdust mingled with the lingering sweetness of sugar and cinnamon from upstairs, an odd yet comforting combination.

"Right," she muttered to herself, eyeing the chaos. "Let's make you pretty for the Winter Festival."

The festival was the talk of Bayside Cove, but more so were Mayor Bennett's plans to modernize their quaint town. Olivia couldn't help the furrow of her brow as she thought of his latest speech, the words 'progress' and 'future' echoing in her head like a mantra she didn't remember choosing.

"Progress isn't always paved roads and new condos," she huffed, pushing aside a stack of empty flour sacks with a practiced nudge of her hip.

As she shuffled through the clutter, organizing paint cans into rainbow order—a habit born out of a love for aesthetics—her elbow caught the corner of an old wooden crate tucked away under a workbench. It wobbled precariously before tipping over with a thud that seemed too loud in the confined space.

"Whoops! Sorry, ghosts of pastries past," she quipped, hoping the spirits of failed eclairs wouldn't hold a grudge.

She knelt beside the fallen crate, patting it apologetically. But as she lifted it, her eyes fell upon a curious sight. A false bottom had come loose, revealing a hidden compartment beneath.

"Well, now, what secrets are you hiding?" Olivia's voice was low, imbued with intrigue as she peered closer. Her fingers, still dusted with flour, brushed against the edge of the concealed space.

"Let's have a look at you then," she whispered, more to herself than anyone or anything that might be listening. With the gentle prodding of her fingertips, she pried open the secret nook, her heart drumming a beat of anticipation in her chest.

Olivia's fingers trembled slightly as she gripped the edge of the wooden lid, her breath catching in the musty air of the basement. With a gentle tug, the compartment creaked open like a whisper from the past, revealing its secret—a journal whose leather cover was dulled by time, entombed in a shroud of dust and cobwebs that clung to it like remnants of forgotten memories.

"Hello there, old friend," she murmured, her voice soft with reverence. Carefully, Olivia lifted the journal from its resting place, the weight of history apparent in its heft. Tracing the faded gold lettering on its cover with a flour-caked finger, she felt the pulse of stories untold thrumming beneath her touch.

"Looks like you've got quite the tale to tell," Olivia said, her curiosity now aflame like the ovens upstairs. She blew gently over the cover, sending a cloud of dust dancing into the dim light filtering through the high windows. The particles sparkled briefly before dissipating into the stale air.

"Meow."

The sudden sound ricocheted around the room, slicing through the silence. Olivia's head snapped up to see Basil perched at the top of the rickety stairs, his amber eyes fixed on her with an intensity that seemed almost human. His tail swished back and forth in a metronome of feline concern.

"Basil, what is it?" Olivia asked, standing up with the journal cradled against her chest. The tabby cat let out another plaintive meow, his gaze never wavering from the book in her arms. "You're not usually one for dramatic entrances."

With cautious steps, Basil descended the stairs, each move deliberate, calculated. As he neared Olivia, his tail continued to twitch, betraying an unease that Olivia found disconcerting. Cats, after all, had a reputation for sensing things beyond the scope of human understanding.

"Is this journal more than just a piece of Bayside Cove's history?" she wondered aloud, meeting the cat's eyes.

Basil leaped down from the last step, his paws silent on the concrete floor. He brushed against Olivia's leg, a reassuring gesture, as if to say, 'Whatever secrets lie within, we'll face them together.'

"Alright then," Olivia said with a determined nod, her tone playful yet edged with resolve. "Let's see what this dusty old book has to say. But first, how about some fresh milk to calm those nerves, huh?"

Basil purred, the vibration mingling with the hum of the refrigerator upstairs, a symphony of bakery life that anchored Olivia to the present amid the whispers of the past.

Olivia hesitated for a mere heartbeat, the weight of history in her hands. The journal, with its time-worn cover and secretive allure, seemed to beckon her further into its mysteries. With the warmth of Basil' presence at her ankles, she made a decision that was part pastry chef, part amateur historian. "Renovations can wait," she muttered to herself, brushing off the last of the cobwebs clinging to her apron.

She ascended the stairs, each step creaking underfoot, a reminder of all the footfalls these floors had endured over the years. In the bakery above, the air was sweet with the scent of cinnamon and sugar, a stark contrast to the mustiness of the basement. The golden glow from the hanging lights offered an inviting atmosphere, one that Olivia had carefully cultivated over the years.

"Alright, my mysterious friend," Olivia addressed the journal as if it could hear her, "let's see what tales you've kept hidden from us." She settled into her favorite corner booth, the cushions worn to perfection from countless hours of planning and dreaming. The bakery was quiet now, save for the soft hum of the oven—a lullaby for loaves and a backdrop to her unfolding adventure.

The journal's pages resisted at first, as though reluctant to divulge their secrets after so long. Olivia handled them with a reverence typically reserved for her most delicate pastries, gently coaxing them open. She was met with looping script that danced across the yellowed paper, each entry a breadcrumb on a path through time.

"Goodness, you're quite the enigma, aren't you?" she whispered, tracing a finger along the lines of ink, her brows knitting together as she deciphered the antiquated handwriting. The faint smell of old parchment mingled with the ever-present aroma of baked goods, an olfactory bridge between the here-and-now and days long gone.

With every page turned, the journal revealed another fragment of its story, drawing Olivia deeper into its embrace. She chuckled softly to herself, imagining the bakery's regulars trying to make sense of her current predicament—trading rolling pins for relics, cookie cutters for conundrums.

"Seems like I've got more than just recipes baking tonight," she said, her voice tinged with the warmth of intrigue. The cozy corner of the bakery, her haven for creation, had transformed into a detective's den where pastries and puzzles were equally savored.

As Olivia's fingertips grazed the aged pages, a faint shiver ran up her spine. The cryptic entries sprawled before her were penned with an urgency that time had not dulled. She leaned closer, the soft glow of the overhead lamp casting a halo around her as she read about a generations-old curse, whispered betrayals, and a recipe that seemed to be at the heart of it all.

"Would you look at this," she murmured, her voice a blend of awe and disbelief. "A fateful recipe? What could possibly be so important..." Her words trailed off as the implications began to dawn on her, the quaint history of Bayside Cove unraveling to reveal a shadowed past.

The tell-tale thump-thump of paws on wooden stairs heralded Basil' arrival. Olivia didn't need to look up to know her intuitive tabby was making his entrance; his presence was always felt before seen. With a graceful leap, Basil landed on Olivia's lap, the force of his little body surprisingly grounding.

"Feeling the magic too, huh?" Olivia chuckled, scratching behind his ears. His purring rumbled like a miniature engine, vibrations syncing with the pulsating energy of the journal. She couldn't help but smile, warmth spreading through her as she considered her four-legged companion's unerring knack for the supernatural. "You're quite the charm against curses, aren't you, whisker-face?"

Basil simply blinked back at her, his eyes reflecting a wisdom that seemed almost otherworldly. He settled in, making a nest out of Olivia's apron, content to be part of her investigation into the eerie annals of their beloved town. It was as if he knew they were on the cusp of uncovering something monumental, and he wasn't about to let Olivia venture there alone.

The Frosted Felony

Olivia flipped open a fresh page of her notepad, the crisp sound slicing through the stillness of the bakery. Pen poised, she began to scrawl down the key details from the journal's cryptic entries. The looping handwriting of the past whispered secrets in ink, and Olivia leaned into the mystery, her brows knitting together with focus.

"Betrayal... Curses... And this recipe," she murmured to herself, tapping the pen against her chin. "What were you up to, Bayside Cove?"

Basil' purring had quieted to a soft thrum, yet his green eyes remained fixed on the pages as if he could read the ancient script himself. Olivia chuckled, shaking her head. "If only you could talk, my furry little detective."

She jotted down dates, names that rang like echoes of the town's history, and any mention of ingredients that seemed out of place for a simple bakery recipe. Her notepad was quickly becoming a map, one that charted a course through the foggy legends of Bayside Cove.

The comforting aroma of cinnamon and nutmeg wafted around her, the bakery's usual soundtrack of oven timers and the soft murmur of customers offering a grounding backdrop to the surreal task at hand. Yet even here, in her sanctuary of sugar and flour, reality intruded in the form of Mayor Bennett's latest plans for the town.

"Have you heard what the mayor wants to do now?" came a voice from the front of the shop, tinged with incredulity. It belonged to Mrs. Hargrove, a regular whose penchant for gossip was as strong as her love for Olivia's cherry scones.

"Turn the old mill into a shopping mall, I hear," replied Mr. Fletcher, another loyal patron, his tone laced with disapproval. "Tearing down history to put up consumerism, is it?"

"Imagine, a mall!" Mrs. Hargrove clucked her tongue. "And right before the Winter Festival. He's got some nerve."

Olivia's ears perked up, her pen ceasing its dance across the paper. She tried to shake off the chill that slithered down her spine at the thought of Mayor Bennett's relentless push for modernization, but it clung stubbornly, like dough to fingers.

"Can't say I'm a fan," said Olivia, without looking up from her notes. "But change has a way of creeping up, whether we welcome it or not." She glanced at Basil, who seemed to agree with a slow blink.

"Creeping up like ivy," Mr. Fletcher agreed. "Or like mold on good cheese."

Laughter rippled through the bakery, a brief respite from the weight of progress and the shadows of the past. Olivia smiled, allowing herself a moment of levity before diving back into the enigma nestled within the journal's pages.

"Back to it, then," she said softly to Basil, who responded by nuzzling her hand. Together, they would peel back the layers of Bayside Cove's hidden tale, one dusty page at a time.

Olivia traced the spine of the ancient journal with a finger, her mind a battlefield of conflicting emotions. The cozy corner of the bakery, usually her sanctuary of sugary scents and warm ovens, now felt like the eye of a storm. With every flip of the yellowed page, the weight of Bayside Cove's secret history pressed heavily on her shoulders.

"Share the truth or protect the town's peace?" she murmured to herself, the question hanging in the air amid the aroma of cinnamon and vanilla.

Basil, curled up beside her, twitched an ear as if contemplating the dilemma alongside her. Olivia scratched behind his whiskered cheeks, finding a small comfort in the rhythmic purring that ensued.

"Imagine," she continued, whispering to her feline confidante as much as to herself, "what could happen if the Winter Festival turned into a stage for ancient grudges instead of gingerbread contests and hot cocoa stands."

She envisioned the cheerful decorations around the town square, the children's laughter as they chased each other with snowflakes tangling in their hair, and the community coming together, united in celebration. Then, her thoughts darkened with the potential discord that her revelation could incite. It was a recipe for disaster, one not even her best baking could sweeten.

"Time isn't exactly waiting for us, Basil," she said, her voice tinged with urgency. The Winter Festival, the highlight of the year for Bayside Cove, was mere weeks away. She could almost hear the clock ticking down, each second a nudge towards a decision she wasn't sure she had the right to make.

"Should I stir the pot, or let sleeping cats lie?" Olivia glanced at Basil, who offered no opinion, his tail flicking contentedly. "Much help you are," she teased, though her smile didn't quite reach her eyes.

Rising from her chair, Olivia paced the length of the bakery, her apron swishing against her legs. Each step was punctuated by the creaking of the wooden floorboards as if they too were urging her to choose a path. Outside, the wind whispered through the eaves, carrying with it the distant murmur of the townsfolk, their voices interwoven with concern over Mayor Bennett's plans.

"Come on, Livvy, think," she urged herself, pausing to gaze at the trays of pastries lining the counter, each one crafted with care and attention to detail—her signature style. Perhaps, just like kneading dough until it's ready to rise, she needed to let the decision rest, to give it time before the reveal.

But time was a luxury she didn't have.

"Alright," Olivia decided, steeling herself with a deep breath that tasted like powdered sugar and resolve. "The secret has been buried long enough. It's time to bring it into the light, festival or not."

With a nod more to herself than to Basil, who watched her with wide, knowing eyes, Olivia knew that the story hidden within the journal's pages was about to become a part of Bayside Cove's living history. And she would be the baker who served it up.

Olivia's fingers lingered on the journal's worn leather cover before she gently closed it, a puff of ancient dust rising into the air like a silent exclamation point to her quandary. She set the tome beside a plate of half-eaten lemon bars, their tangy scent a stark contrast to the mustiness of the secrets she had just unearthed.

"Okay, Livvy," she whispered to herself, "you've got this." Taking a deep breath, she let it out slowly, as if with it she could expel the turmoil that churned inside her. Her eyes, always so keen to spot the golden hue of perfectly baked croissants, now searched inward for the courage to decide what to do with the knowledge that pressed against the confines of the journal.

She stood up, brushing off flour from her apron—a futile gesture, really, considering it was perpetually dusted like a fine winter snow. The bakery around her hummed with the warmth of the ovens, the air sweet and heavy with the promise of sugar and spice.

"Basil, old boy," she mused aloud, though the cat had sauntered off, likely in pursuit of a rogue moth or his next cozy napping spot. "What would you do, hm? Alert the press or just nap on the news?"

Her gaze drifted toward the large window that framed the bakery's front. It was a picturesque view, usually, but today it held a different kind of magic. As Olivia watched, the thick, morning fog that had blanketed

Bayside Cove began to retreat, revealing the quaint storefronts and cobblestone streets beyond.

"Clarity," she murmured, the word hanging in the air as if it were a tangible thing she could grasp and pocket. The lifting fog seemed to peel back the layers of uncertainty that had shrouded her thoughts, offering a glimpse of the path forward. And perhaps, she considered with a fluttering heart, it was a sign.

"Time to turn the page, Bayside Cove," Olivia said, a resolve firming in her voice, one born of love for her town and its people. "Let's see where the story leads us."

With a final look at the journal, its secrets now her burden to bear, Olivia turned away from the window. She rolled up her sleeves, ready to face whatever the day might bring, her spirit as resilient as her ever-rising bread.

Chapter 1

A Slice of Bayside Life

The air in the bakery was thick with the sweet aroma of sugar and spice, the warmth from the ovens mingling with the crisp chill that seeped in every time the door opened to admit another customer seeking shelter from the winter's bite. Amidst the hum of mixers and the clatter of rolling pins, Olivia Pierce stood with her sleeves rolled up, her hands a snowy landscape of flour as she worked in tandem with Sam Turner, her childhood friend turned right-hand man.

"Can you pass me the vanilla?" Olivia asked without looking up, her focus locked on the precise task at hand. Sam slid the bottle across the marble countertop, a small cloud of flour puffing into the air between them.

"Got it," Sam confirmed, his voice light with the ease of their well-worn camaraderie.

Olivia nodded, carefully pouring the extract with the steadiness of a surgeon. Each pie had to be perfect – it was not just her reputation on the line; it was the spirit of the Winter Festival itself. The townsfolk of Bayside Cove took pride in their annual celebration, and Olivia's lemon meringue pies were a tradition that heralded the season as much as the first snowfall.

"Did you triple-check the lemon zest?" Sam queried, peering over her shoulder with mock solemnity. "You know how Mrs. Henderson gets if it's not zesty enough."

"Quadruple-checked," Olivia replied, her lips curving into a half-smile. The meticulous dance of measuring, sifting, and whisking continued, each movement a testament to Olivia's unwavering dedication to her craft. Every ingredient was measured with care, each recipe step followed with precision, all for the love of creating something wonderful that would bring joy to others.

"Ah, but did you account for the barometric pressure and the gravitational pull?" Sam joked, waggling his eyebrows.

"Only after consulting the almanac and aligning the stars," Olivia shot back, her eyes twinkling with amusement even as she remained absorbed in her work.

The flour, sugar, and eggs transformed under her skillful touch, promising to emerge from the heat of the oven as golden-brown delights, their glossy peaks of meringue standing tall and proud like sentinels of flavor. This was more than baking; this was Olivia's way of weaving herself into the fabric of Bayside Cove's history, one delicious slice at a time.

A shaft of sunlight spilled onto the floor of the bakery, where Basil, Olivia's rotund tabby cat, had claimed his territory. He lounged there, a king in his sun-drenched domain, one paw draped casually over the edge of his cushion. Every so often, he'd open an eye to survey the scene or offer a supportive "meow" that seemed to cheer on Olivia's efforts.

"Basil approves," Sam announced with a grin, as he caught the cat's eye and received a languid blink in return. "Looks like you've got a feline quality control manager."

"Good thing, too," Olivia responded, brushing a stray lock of hair from her forehead with the back of her flour-dusted hand. "He's the only one who can keep you in line."

"Ha! As if anyone could." Sam chuckled and reached for the rolling pin. "But speaking of keeping things straight, your pie crusts are looking almost as good as mine these days."

"Almost?" Olivia feigned indignation. "I'll have you know my crusts have been flaky and perfect since I was knee-high to that mixing bowl. Yours, on the other hand, still need a prayer and a miracle."

"Ouch, Liv! You wound me with your words!" He clutched at his chest dramatically before breaking into laughter. The light-hearted jest filled the room, mingling with the scent of lemon zest and vanilla.

"Seriously though, Sam," Olivia said, a playful glint in her eye as she expertly trimmed excess dough from a pie shell. "Keep this up, and I might just promote you from sous-chef to master of the oven mitts."

The Frosted Felony

"Promote away, but remember who taught you the secret of the perfect meringue." Sam wagged a finger at her. "It's all in the wrist flick."

"Sure, sure, as long as that 'wrist flick' doesn't send our meringue to the moon," Olivia quipped, her laughter echoing his.

They fell into a companionable silence, punctuated by the soft thud of rolling pins and the occasional contented purr from Basil. The bakery hummed with energy, a testament to their friendship—a blend of sweet and savory, just like the treats that filled the display case.

Olivia dusted her hands, sending a cloud of flour into the air, which caught the golden light streaming through the bakery's windows. "I can't wait to see everyone's faces when they taste our new ginger-spice cookies at the Winter Festival," she said, placing a tray of shaped dough into the oven.

"Especially Mrs. Henderson," Sam added with a chuckle. "She's been dropping hints about those cookies since last year's festival." He glanced at Olivia, his blue eyes twinkling in amusement.

"Who would have thought ginger-spice would be such a hit?" Olivia mused, tucking a stray lock of hair behind her ear. "We'll need to double the batch just to keep up with demand."

"Triple," Sam corrected her, waving a spatula like a conductor's baton. "Never underestimate the power of a well-spiced cookie."

Laughter bubbled up from Olivia's throat as she watched Sam's mock-serious expression. Yet, as their laughter faded, snippets of conversation from the front of the shop drifted back to them, carrying a different weight.

"Mayor Bennett's got big plans for Bayside Cove... entire blocks might change if he gets his way..."

"Imagine that, our little town turning into some sort of tourist trap..."

"Shh, not so loud. You know how much Olivia loves this place."

Olivia's brow furrowed, and she shared a glance with Sam. Her hands, momentarily still, now resumed their work with a hint of tension. "Sam, do you think the Mayor's development plans will change things too much? I mean, we've always had that small-town charm."

"Hey, Liv," Sam said, leaning closer, his tone softening. "We've weathered plenty of storms together, right? No fancy development is going to wash away the heart of Bayside Cove. Not on our watch."

"Right." A determined spark lit Olivia's eyes. "This bakery is more than just a shop; it's a piece of home for everyone who walks through that door. We'll keep the heart beating strong."

"Exactly." Sam nodded, his freckled face earnest. "Besides, we've got the Winter Festival to focus on. Let's give them a celebration they'll never forget."

"Agreed." Olivia smiled, the warmth returning to her gaze as she reached for another tray. "Now, help me get these pies ready. The festival isn't going to wait for us, and neither will Mrs. Henderson's sweet tooth."

As the scent of baking spices filled the air, the duo returned to their dance of rolling pins and measuring spoons, each movement a silent pledge to preserve the spirit of Bayside Cove—one pastry at a time.

Olivia sprinkled a pinch of cinnamon over the apple tart, her deft fingers creating a swirl that was as much art as it was baking. She set the tray aside and wiped her hands on her apron, turning to Sam with a resolve that matched the firm set of her jaw.

"Sam, we need to do something," she said, her voice low but firm. "The Mayor's plans could turn Bayside Cove into something unrecognizable. We can't just stand by."

"Like a silent protest?" Sam suggested, half-joking as he piped frosting onto cupcakes with practiced ease. "Or maybe a bake sale for awareness?" His tone might have been light, but his eyes were serious, reflecting his shared concern.

"Actually, a petition might work," Olivia mused, tapping a finger against her chin thoughtfully. "Get enough signatures, and we could at least get a town meeting going. People need to understand what's at stake."

"Count me in," Sam replied, giving her an encouraging nod. "You know I'm all about preserving our secret ingredient—community spirit."

As they spoke, a shadow fell across the counter where rows of pastries basked in the afternoon sun. Olivia glanced up, distracted by the silhouette of a man peering through the shop window. His features were obscured by the reflection of late-autumn trees on the glass, but there was something undeniably striking about him. He had the kind of rugged appeal that belonged more to windswept cliffs and wild oceans than the quaintness of Bayside Cove.

"Who's that?" Olivia murmured, her curiosity piqued as she leaned ever so slightly closer to the window.

The Frosted Felony

"New in town, maybe?" Sam offered, craning his neck to catch a glimpse. "He certainly doesn't look like he's from around here."

"Maybe he's lost," Olivia speculated, her gaze lingering on the stranger. The contours of his face were strong—chiseled jawline, prominent cheekbones, and eyes that seemed to hold a secret or two. A lock of dark hair fell carelessly over his brow, adding to the mysterious allure that radiated from him.

"Or maybe he's found exactly what he's looking for," Sam quipped, nudging her gently with his elbow.

"Maybe," Olivia echoed, feeling an inexplicable warmth blossom within her. She shook her head, laughing softly at herself. "Focus, Olivia. You've got a petition to start and pies to finish."

"Right you are," Sam agreed, grinning as he returned to his cupcakes.

Together, they dove back into the rhythm of their work, Olivia's thoughts occasionally drifting to the intriguing stranger outside their window. As the aroma of freshly baked goods filled the bakery, she couldn't shake the sense that this Winter Festival would bring with it winds of change. And perhaps, just perhaps, a dash of unexpected romance.

The bell above the bakery door chimed, pulling Olivia's attention away from the lemon zest she was grating. As she looked up, she noticed that the stranger had slipped inside amidst a cluster of chattering customers. She met Sam's eyes across the crowded room, and they exchanged a silent conversation made up of raised eyebrows and shrugs.

"Who do you reckon he is?" Sam whispered as he slid a tray of pastries into the display case.

"Could be anyone," Olivia replied, wiping her hands on her apron. "But he definitely has that out-of-town vibe."

"Maybe he's a food critic," Sam suggested with a playful glint in his eye. "He heard about your pies and couldn't resist."

"Or maybe he's just looking for a warm place to sit and a cup of coffee," she countered, though her intuition told her there was more to this man than met the eye.

Their musings were cut short as the man began weaving through the tables with an air of intention. He wasn't here for the baked goods; it was clear in the way his eyes scanned the room methodically, seemingly uninterested in the array of treats laid out before him. It was almost as if —

"Detective James Holbrook," the man introduced himself abruptly, extending a hand to Olivia who stood closest to him. His grip was firm, his voice steady as he locked eyes with her. "I'm new to Bayside Cove. I've heard great things about this place."

"Olivia Pierce," she said, returning the handshake and feeling a flutter of surprise at the contact. "And this is Sam Turner."

"Nice to meet you, Detective," Sam chimed in, his easy smile not quite masking the curiosity in his tone. "What brings you to our little corner of the world?"

"Work, mostly," Holbrook answered vaguely, his gaze sweeping the bakery once more. "But I'm also looking forward to trying some of these famous pastries I keep hearing about."

"Then you're in luck," Olivia said, motioning towards the counter laden with sweets. "We've got plenty to choose from."

"Indeed," Detective Holbrook murmured, but it seemed his mind was only half on the culinary delights. There was a sharpness in his gaze, a sense of purpose that hinted at deeper layers beneath the cordial exchange.

As he finally turned away to survey the menu board, Olivia and Sam shared another look, their earlier levity replaced by a tingle of intrigue. Who was this Detective Holbrook, and what exactly was he searching for in Bayside Cove?

Olivia's eyes lingered on the detective as he perused the menu, her mind a whirl of questions. "Detective Holbrook, huh?" she mused aloud, brushing a stray lock of hair from her forehead with the back of her flour-dusted hand. "Never thought we'd see one of those in Bayside Cove."

"Especially one who looks like he's stepped out of a crime noir film, trench coat and all," Sam added with a grin, leaning against the counter.

"Maybe he's here to solve the Mystery of the Missing Scones," Olivia jested, her attempt at humor masking the flutter of excitement in her stomach. This was new, different—a break from the comforting routine of kneading dough and frosting cupcakes.

"Or perhaps he's after the Secret of the Perfect Pie Crust," Sam retorted, winking. But his playful smirk faded as he caught Olivia's thoughtful gaze fixed on the detective.

The Frosted Felony

"Something tells me that Detective Holbrook's story runs a bit deeper than our bakery's secrets," Olivia said, her voice dropping to a whisper. The intrigue surrounding this newcomer seemed to fill the room with a new energy, sparking a curiosity in her that she hadn't felt in a long time.

"Speaking of secrets," Sam quipped, breaking the momentary silence, "we've got a festival to prepare for, remember? Those lemon meringue pies won't bake themselves!"

"Right you are, Chef Turner," Olivia replied, a smile returning to her lips as she turned back to the stainless steel bowl before her. With skilled hands, she resumed measuring out ingredients, the scent of fresh citrus filling the air as she zested lemons with practiced ease.

"Best not keep the townsfolk waiting," Sam agreed, tying on a clean apron and scooping up a handful of flour, which he playfully sprinkled in Olivia's direction. She laughed, the sound mingling with the soft hum of ovens and the gentle clatter of bakeware.

As they worked in tandem, the rhythm of their movements synchronized like the ticking of a well-oiled clock, Olivia couldn't help but glance occasionally towards the front of the store where Detective Holbrook stood, now chatting softly with Mrs. Henderson about her weekly order of rye bread.

"Who knows what sort of tales he might unravel in our quiet little town," Olivia whispered to herself, a twinge of anticipation sending a shiver down her spine.

"Focus, Olivia," Sam chided gently, nudging her with his elbow. "Those pies aren't going to be famous by themselves."

"Right," she said, shaking off the distraction and smiling at her friend's nudge. "Let's give them something truly unforgettable this year."

And with that, their laughter and banter resumed, filling the cozy bakery with warmth and the promise of sweet delights. They were a team, a pair woven into the fabric of Bayside Cove through shared memories and unspoken bonds. Yet, as they returned to their craft, neither could shake the sense that the arrival of Detective James Holbrook heralded a change—what kind, only time would tell.

Chapter 2

A Bitter Taste of Murder

Olivia Pierce's hands moved with practiced ease, dusting a final sprinkle of powdered sugar over a freshly baked batch of raspberry linzer cookies. The Winter Festival had transformed Bayside Cove into a wonderland of twinkling lights and festive cheer, and Olivia's booth was a beacon of warmth in the crisp winter air. Laughter bubbled around her as she served customer after customer, her booth a symphony of clinking coins and rustling paper as pastries exchanged hands.

"Olivia, these cinnamon rolls are to die for," Mrs. Henderson exclaimed, her voice carrying over the hum of contented festival-goers.

"Only the best for you, Mrs. H," Olivia replied with a wink, wrapping up another roll with deft fingers. "Gotta keep you coming back for more."

The scents of buttery crusts and spiced fillings mingled amidst the pines and cold breeze, ensnaring the senses of all who passed by. Olivia's passion for baking was evident in every flaky layer of pastry, each dollop of cream precisely piped. She stood back for a moment, admiring the array of mouthwatering delights that adorned her booth: from the deep, rich chocolate tarts to the delicate, lemon-kissed Madeleines.

"Looks like the whole town can't resist your magic touch, Olivia," chuckled a familiar voice, smooth as the silk scarf draped around his neck.

Olivia turned to find Mayor Jonathan Bennett, the silver streaks in his hair catching the soft glow of the fairy lights strung above. His blue eyes sparkled with a mirth that matched the season's spirit.

The Frosted Felony

"Mayor Bennett," she greeted, her voice a melody of surprise and delight. "What brings you to my humble corner of the festival?"

"I couldn't resist the siren call of your legendary lemon meringue pie," he confessed, gesturing towards the golden peaks of perfectly torched meringue. "Your booth is the talk of the town, Olivia. I dare say it outshines even the Christmas tree at the square."

Olivia felt a blush warm her cheeks, as much from the compliment as from the biting wind. "You're too kind, Mayor. Here, let me cut you a slice. On the house, of course."

As she sliced through the crisp crust, she could feel the mayor's keen gaze on her, assessing, always calculating. But today, his usual political sharpness seemed softened by genuine admiration for her craft.

"Your dedication to perfection is truly remarkable," he said, accepting the plate she offered. "It's artisans like you who make Bayside Cove such a special place."

"Thank you," Olivia replied, her gratitude genuine. "I just hope to add a little sweetness to everyone's day."

"Mission accomplished," Mayor Bennett affirmed, taking a bite and closing his eyes in momentary bliss. "This pie could very well be the key to world peace."

Olivia laughed, the sound mingling with the jingle of bells and joyful exclamations around them. "Now that's an ambition I wouldn't mind aspiring to."

"Keep baking like this, and you'll get there," he assured her before excelling himself into the crowd with a nod of thanks.

Watching him go, Olivia's smile lingered. The festival buzzed around her, alive with the spirit of community, and she knew she was right where she belonged.

The crisp air was suddenly split by a piercing shriek that spiraled up from the direction of the town hall, slicing through the merry chatter like a cold knife. Olivia's head snapped up, her hand pausing mid-air with a dusting of flour poised to settle on a fresh batch of raspberry tarts. She wasn't the only one; the entire festival seemed to freeze for a heartbeat before erupting into chaos.

"Did you hear that?" someone gasped.

"What's happening over there?" another voice trembled, tinged with alarm.

In an instant, the warm bubble of laughter and holiday spirit burst, giving way to a tide of confusion that swept through the crowd. People clutched their knitted scarves and woolen hats closer as they surged towards the source of the commotion, abandoning half-eaten pastries and mulled cider in their wake. The scent of cinnamon and pine was quickly overpowered by the sharp tang of anxiety.

Olivia felt her heart thump against her chest, each beat quickening with a mix of fear and determination. She couldn't just stand there; something serious had happened, and every instinct told her she needed to be part of whatever was unfolding. With a quick "Excuse me" to the patrons at her booth, she vaulted over the display table, her hands still wearing their powdery gloves of flour.

"Olivia, where are you going?" called out a concerned regular, but she barely heard them over the din.

"Sorry, I need to check this out!" she replied, her usually calm demeanor giving way to urgency.

She shouldered her way through the throng, her sensible boots slipping slightly on the cobblestone path slick with winter's frost. The closer she got to the town hall, the thicker the crowd became, and the shriller the voices grew, laced now with hints of hysteria.

"Make way, please!" she implored, ducking under a raised elbow here, sidestepping a stroller there. Her pulse raced, echoing the hurried steps of her fellow townsfolk as they all converged on the scene.

"Is everyone okay?" she managed to ask a flustered woman who looked as though she might faint.

"I don't know, dear," the woman responded, her face pale. "Something terrible must've happened."

As Olivia finally broke through the last barrier of bodies, she stood on tiptoes, trying to catch a glimpse of the cause of all this mayhem. Her breath caught in her throat, her baker's hands now clenched at her sides. Whatever lay ahead, it was clear that the Winter Festival—and possibly her life in Bayside Cove—would never be the same again.

Olivia's breath condensed in the frosty air as she edged closer to the town hall, her gaze locked on the scene unfurling before her. People were circling something, or rather someone, on the ground. The sweet scent of citrus that she knew all too well cut through the crisp winter chill, and her heart plummeted. There, sprawled ungracefully with one arm flung wide, was Mayor Bennett, face-down in the golden crusted glory of her lemon meringue pie.

"Good heavens," Olivia murmured, her voice a mere whisper amidst the buzzing crowd. Her shock was palpable; it was as if the world had tilted, skewing her reality. This was more than an accident; it was a spectacle with her pastry playing an unfortunate starring role.

"Stand back, give him some space!" A firm yet composed voice broke through the clamor. Detective James Holbrook made his way through the mass of people, a small notebook already in hand. His piercing blue eyes scanned the scene methodically until they met Olivia's. In that brief moment of eye contact, a silent acknowledgment passed between them—an understanding that this was no ordinary incident.

"Miss Pierce, I presume?" James asked, approaching after he had assessed Mayor Bennett with a professional detachment.

"Y-Yes, that's me," Olivia replied, trying to recover from the initial jolt of disbelief. "That's...that was my pie."

"Unfortunate place for dessert," James noted, a hint of dry humor softening the gravity of the situation. "Seems we'll need to ask you a few questions, understandably."

"Of course," Olivia said, her composure slowly knitting itself back together. She instinctively brushed off her apron, leaving white streaks of flour on the fabric—a baker's involuntary reflex.

James gave a nod, the corners of his mouth twitching ever so slightly as if to say there was more to this than met the eye. They both knew it; the festival's cheery atmosphere had been tainted, and for Olivia, clearing her name was now as important as solving the mystery at hand.

Olivia's mind raced as she stared down at the chaotic swirl of raspberry reduction and meringue where Mayor Bennett's face had come to rest. The once-pristine pie, a testament to her culinary prowess, now bore the macabre imprint of tragedy. With each murmur in the crowd, she felt the weight of suspicion casting a shadow over her bakery, Sweet Temptations. She knew the whispers would start soon—if they hadn't already—speculating about the role her confections might have played in the mayor's untimely demise.

"Miss Pierce," Detective Holbrook began, snapping Olivia from her internal turmoil. "I'll need to gather some information from you later. For now, tell me, did anyone else have access to your booth before the incident?"

"Only my assistant, but she left early with a migraine," Olivia replied, her voice steadier now. She was acutely aware that every detail mattered. "Nobody else should have been behind there."

"Good to know." James scribbled something in his notebook, then looked up, his gaze locking with hers again. "You understand how important it is to keep the integrity of the scene until we've gathered all necessary evidence."

"Of course," she said, nodding. Despite the frosty air, warmth spread through her at the thought of collaborating with James—even under such dire circumstances. "Is there anything I can do to help? I know everyone here; maybe I could..."

"Actually," he paused, considering her offer. "An insider's perspective could be useful. But I can't have you interfering with official police work."

"Understood," Olivia agreed quickly, relief washing over her. "I just want to clear my name and ensure my customers trust my baking again."

James closed his notebook and tucked it into his coat pocket. "We share a common goal, then—to find the truth. Keep your eyes open, Miss Pierce. And your ears. Sometimes the smallest detail speaks volumes."

"Will do, Detective Holbrook," Olivia said, a determined glint in her eye. The scent of sugar and spice lingered in the air, intermingled with the sharp tang of fear and uncertainty. But beneath it all, Olivia felt a growing sense of purpose. This was her town, her community, and she'd do everything in her power to protect it—and her reputation along with it.

Whispers swirled like the bitter winter wind through Bayside Cove's Winter Festival, each one prickling Olivia's skin with unease. The cheerful chimes of laughter that had once filled the air were now replaced by hushed tones and wide-eyed looks of horror. A ripple of panic seemed to spread from the town hall, washing over the festivalgoers in waves.

"Did you hear about Mayor Bennett?" a woman gasped, clutching her companion's arm.

"Face-down in a pie," another muttered, shaking his head in disbelief.

Olivia's heart clenched as she caught snippets of conversation, each word a weighty stone added to the burden she already carried. Her hands, still dusted with flour, clenched into fists at her sides. She had to find out what happened, not just for her bakery's sake, but for the community that was now trembling on the edge of fear.

"Mayor Bennett was such a kind man," an elderly customer said to Olivia, her voice quivering like the last leaf clinging to a barren tree. "Who could do such a thing?"

Olivia offered a gentle smile, though it felt more like a grimace. "I'm sure the police will figure it out, Mrs. Halloway."

As much as she wanted to comfort her fellow townsfolk, Olivia's own fears gnawed at her insides. What if people started to believe her pastries were to blame? Her reputation was on the line, but more importantly, so was the trust she'd painstakingly built within her community.

She watched Detective Holbrook cordon off the area around the town hall, his movements precise and authoritative. The crowd parted for him like the sea for a ship, their eyes tracing his every step. Olivia knew he was their beacon of order amidst the chaos, and she couldn't help but feel a pull towards him—a desire to be part of the solution.

But doubts clouded her mind, casting long shadows over her resolve. How much could she really contribute? She was a baker, not a detective. And yet, the thought of sitting idly by while suspicion blossomed around her was unbearable.

"Olivia? Are you alright?" a familiar voice asked, breaking through her tumultuous thoughts.

She turned to see her assistant, concern etching her young face. Olivia mustered a reassuring smile, though it took more effort than kneading the stiffest dough.

"Of course, Jenna. Just worried about... everything." She let out a breath she hadn't realized she'd been holding. "I need to do something. I can't let this... incident destroy all I've worked for."

"Then you'll figure it out," Jenna said with unwavering confidence. "You're the most determined person I know."

Determination was one thing; trusting herself to step into the unknown was another. Olivia's history of misplaced trust—in friends, in lovers—had left a tapestry of scars that made the very idea of opening up, of relying on others, a daunting prospect. But standing on the sidelines wasn't an option, not with stakes this high.

With a deep inhale, Olivia let the scent of sugar and cinnamon ground her. This was her element, her sanctuary. Yet, outside this booth lay a mystery that threatened to unravel the peace she cherished. She would have to step out of her comfort zone, navigate the murky waters of trust once again, and hope that this time she wouldn't drown.

"Jenna, hold down the fort," Olivia instructed, her voice steadier than she felt. "I have some detective work to do."

"Go get 'em, boss," Jenna cheered, offering a thumbs-up that bolstered Olivia's courage.

As Olivia moved toward the scene, each step felt like wading through molasses—slow and uncertain. But her determination burned bright, fueled by the love for her town and the unyielding desire to clear her name. It was time to rise to the occasion, to prove that even the warm-hearted baker could confront the shadows cast upon Bayside Cove.

The frosty air nipped at Olivia's cheeks as she briskly walked away from the comforting glow of her booth, the once-festive Winter Festival now a blur of police tape and hushed whispers. With each step, the thrumming in her chest escalated, a metronome ticking off the seconds she couldn't afford to lose.

"Detective Holbrook," she called out, her breath forming clouds in the chill. He turned, his piercing blue eyes locking onto hers with an intensity that both unsettled and reassured her.

"Miss Pierce, I need to ask that you..." he began, but she cut him off, urgency lacing her words.

"Time isn't on my side, Detective. My bakery, my reputation—it's all hanging by a thread. I have to help find out who did this."

Holbrook's gaze softened, and he took a moment before nodding slightly. "I can't condone civilian involvement in police matters, but I'm not blind to what's at stake for you. If you happen to come across anything... unusual, let me know."

"Unusual is my middle name these days," Olivia quipped, trying to mask her nerves with a smile that didn't quite reach her eyes.

Her mind was already racing, piecing together a plan amidst the chaos. She would need to revisit every conversation, recall every face at the festival. Someone must have seen something, some clue that could lead to the truth. She'd start with her regulars; they were always keen observers, especially when it came to town gossip.

"Thank you, Detective. I'll be careful," she assured him, her resolve hardening like the sugar crust on her famous crème brûlée.

The Frosted Felony

"Please do. And call me James," he said, the corner of his mouth twitching upward in a fleeting half-smile that hinted at camaraderie.

"James," she nodded, feeling the weight of the task ahead. Olivia drew in a deep breath, the cold sharpening her senses as if to prepare her for the journey ahead. With one last glance at her beloved booth—now under the watchful eye of Jenna—Olivia set off toward the heart of the festival.

She moved with purpose, weaving through the crowd, her ears tuned to the murmurs and snippets of conversation that floated on the air. The sweet aroma of hot chocolate mingled with the tang of pine needles, a stark contrast to the bitter undercurrent of suspicion that had seeped into the festival's atmosphere.

"Olivia, what are you going to do?" a familiar voice called out.

"Find the truth," she replied without breaking stride, her tone firmer than she expected.

"Be safe!" another added, concern etched in their voice.

"Always am," Olivia threw back over her shoulder, though her pulse danced at the lie.

As the chapter closed, Olivia's first steps into the investigation were cautious yet determined, her mind buzzing with possibilities. She was no detective, but she knew her town, her people, and most importantly, she knew her pastries never lied. Bayside Cove might look serene on the outside, but Olivia was ready to sift through the sugar-coated surface to reveal the secrets beneath.

And so, under the twinkling lights that adorned the town hall, with the echo of the mayor's untimely demise in the air, Olivia Pierce, the warm-hearted baker with a newfound taste for sleuthing, embarked on a quest that would test her mettle and tug at the very fabric of her world.

Chapter 3

Whisking Up Clues

Olivia's steps echoed through Sweet Sensations, each footfall a sharp punctuation in the quiet of the early morning. Her bakery, usually a haven of sweet aromas and cheerful chatter, felt oppressively silent as she paced. Sunlight streamed through the front windows, casting long shadows over the display case stocked with her finest creations. Though the scent of freshly baked croissants and raspberry tarts lingered in the air, it did little to soothe her frayed nerves.

Her hands clenched and unclenched at her sides, a telltale sign of her inner turmoil. The furrow on her brow deepened as she replayed the accusations in her mind, her warm-hearted nature now besieged by the cold sting of suspicion from the townsfolk she had served for years.

"Hey, Liv, you're going to wear a trench in the floor at this rate," Sam's voice broke through her troubled thoughts as he stepped into the bakery, his blue eyes laced with concern. He leaned against the counter, a towel slung over his shoulder, the corners of his mouth tipping down in an empathetic frown.

"Sorry, I just can't stand still when my whole life is being turned upside down," Olivia replied, forcing a weak smile that didn't quite reach her expressive eyes. She looked at Sam, her childhood friend who knew her better than anyone else. "I have to do something, Sam."

"Of course, we will," Sam said with a reassuring nod. He sauntered over to the table where they often brainstormed new recipes, his movements easy and familiar in the space they both loved. "We'll start by making a list of potential suspects. It's like figuring out the secret ingredient in a complex dish – process of elimination."

The Frosted Felony

"Right," Olivia sighed, her agitation giving way to the determination he always admired in her. She joined him at the table, her posture straightening as if readying herself for battle. "But where do we even begin?"

"Whoever started this rumor has their own agenda," he mused aloud, tapping a finger against his lips. "It's like trying to guess who snuck in and ate the last chocolate éclair. Not an easy mystery to solve, but not impossible either."

"Hardly the same stakes, though," Olivia quipped, a touch of her usual humor returning. "Last I checked, no one's reputation was ruined over a missing pastry."

"True, but we've got this," Sam encouraged, flashing her a grin that could make even the sourest sourdough rise. "Let's sit down, brew some of that coffee that can knock socks off, and get to work."

Together, they settled in, surrounded by the comforting smells and sounds of the bakery. With each sip of strong coffee and scratch of pen on paper, Olivia felt a sliver of hope. If anyone could help her sift through this mess, it was Sam, with his unwavering support and his knack for seeing the sweetness amidst the bitter.

Olivia's fingertips trailed over the stacks of papers as she settled into the worn chair at the back of Sweet Sensations, the aroma of cinnamon and vanilla wrapping around her like a comforting shawl. Across from her, Sam was a picture of concentration, his sandy hair catching the soft glow of the overhead lights, his bright blue eyes scanning their makeshift war room.

"Okay," Sam said, uncapping a marker with a decisive pop. "First up on our list is Victor Wellington. The guy has more interest in concrete than a sidewalk."

"Ha, very funny," Olivia replied, the corners of her mouth tilting upward despite the gravity of the situation. She leaned forward, resting her elbows on the table. "But you're not wrong. He's been trying to turn Bayside Cove into his personal Monopoly board for years."

"Right?" Sam drew a large V on the whiteboard and scribbled 'Wellington' underneath. "The mayor's been blocking his high-rise project for months. If anyone had a grudge potent enough to stir up trouble, it's Victor."

"True." Olivia nodded, her gaze fixed on the letters as if they were pieces of a puzzle waiting to be solved. "I saw them once at a town meeting; Victor's stare could have curdled the cream in my éclairs. He's not the type to take no for an answer."

"Would he go this far, though?" Sam asked, tapping the whiteboard. "From sky-scraping egos to ruining reputations—it's a big leap."

"Desperate times," Olivia murmured, "call for desperate measures. And Victor's ambition is taller than any building he wants to erect."

"Point taken." Sam made a few more notes, then glanced at Olivia with a raised eyebrow. "Ready for suspect number two?"

"Hit me," Olivia said, bracing herself.

"Evelyn Grant," Sam announced, writing her name in green—fitting for the eco-warrior whose love for nature was as fierce as her temper. "She's been like a thorn in the mayor's side, especially with the new industrial park on the table."

"More like a whole rosebush," Olivia corrected, a wry smile flickering across her face. "She doesn't just have arguments; she has crusades."

"Exactly." Sam underlined Evelyn's name for emphasis. "Her commitment to the environment is... intense. If she felt the mayor was threatening Bayside Cove's green spaces, who knows what lengths she'd go to protect them."

"Still, Evelyn seems more likely to chain herself to a tree than resort to sabotage," Olivia considered, her fingers drumming a soft rhythm on the table. "Passion can fuel both creation and destruction, though."

"Let's not forget," Sam added, "the mayor's pro-development agenda was the antithesis of everything she stands for. That's motive enough for some."

"True." Olivia let out a deep breath, her warm eyes reflecting the bakery's golden light but also the worry that lingered within. "We've got our work cut out for us, don't we?"

"Nothing we can't handle." Sam flashed her a reassuring smile. "After all, we're talking about the dynamic duo who once turned a baking disaster into the most sought-after 'Mystery Muffins' this side of the bay."

"Only because you convinced everyone burnt edges were a delicacy," Olivia chuckled, shaking her head. The tension eased from her shoulders, if only for a moment.

The Frosted Felony

"Perception is everything," Sam winked, standing up to stretch his arms above his head. "Shall we take a little break? I think there are some of those 'delicacies' left in the case."

"Lead the way, Chef," Olivia said, rising to follow him. As they stepped away from the table, the papers rustling in their wake, she felt a flicker of hope. With Sam by her side, perhaps the truth wasn't so out of reach.

Olivia returned to the table, a half-eaten 'Mystery Muffin' in hand. The crumbs scattered on the whiteboard didn't bother her; it was a canvas of chaos as they mapped out the twisted web of Bayside Cove's secrets.

"Okay," she said, brushing off her hands, "what about Councilman Richard Cornwall? He's been at odds with the mayor for years."

"Richard Cornwall..." Sam echoed, his voice trailing off as he pictured the councilman. "Tailored suits, hair never out of place, and those piercing eyes that make you feel like he's looking right through you."

"Exactly." Olivia grabbed a marker and wrote 'Cornwall' in bold letters under the list of suspects. "He's ambitious, power-hungry. The kind of man who believes the ends always justify the means."

"Right." Sam nodded, leaning closer to study the board. "If anyone would go to extremes to get the mayor out of his way, it'd be him."

"Plus, he's always had this... intensity," Olivia added, remembering how the councilman's gaze felt like a physical force. "Like he's playing chess while everyone else is playing checkers."

"Chess with people's lives," Sam murmured, his face grim. They both knew Cornwall's reputation for strategic maneuvers, the kind that could easily tip into something darker if provoked.

"Let's not forget about Margaret Foster either," Olivia said, shifting gears as she scribbled another name on the board. The owner of 'Flour Power' had been a thorn in her side since day one.

"Margaret..." Sam hummed thoughtfully. "She has a knack for making every word sound like she's doing you a favor when really she's twisting the knife."

"Her bakery hasn't been doing as well since Sweet Sensations opened. She blames me for stealing her customers." Olivia sighed, feeling the weight of suspicion and rivalry heavy in the air of her own bakery.

"Jealousy is a powerful motive," Sam agreed. "But we need more than just motive. We need proof, or at least a lead."

"True." Olivia tapped the marker against her chin. "We'll have to dig deeper into both of them. For now, they're on the list."

"Anyone else we should consider?" Sam asked, his gaze scanning the papers strewn across the table.

"Let's stick with these for now," Olivia said decisively. "One step at a time."

"Sounds like a plan." Sam stood up, stretching his back with a groan. "This detective work is harder than kneading bread dough."

"Only because we can't punch it when we're frustrated," Olivia quipped, a small smile tugging at her lips despite the gravity of their situation.

"Come on, Sherlock Holmes," Sam chuckled, offering her a mock salute. "Let's clean this up and call it a night. Tomorrow's another day, and we'll crack this case yet."

"Elementary, my dear Watson," Olivia played along as they began gathering the papers, her determination simmering beneath her light-hearted banter. She wouldn't rest until the truth was uncovered, no matter what shadows lingered in Bayside Cove's quaint streets.

The chime of the bakery door jangled through the air, a familiar melody that usually heralded the arrival of late-night sweet seekers or early risers in search of their first pastry fix. But this time, it cut through the silence with the precision of a secret unveiled. Olivia's head snapped up from the papers, her eyes widening as an all-too-familiar face crossed the threshold of Sweet Sensations.

"Em?" Olivia's voice wavered between disbelief and caution, a cocktail of emotions swirling in her gut as Emily Pierce, her estranged sister, stepped into the warm glow of the bakery. The scent of sugar and spice hung heavy around them, a stark contrast to the sudden tension.

"Hey, Liv." Emily's greeting held a casual lilt, but her eyes were scanning, taking in the scene like pages of a book she hadn't read in years.

"Emily." Olivia straightened, dusting her hands on her apron, leaving white floury prints like ghostly reminders of her restless day. "What are you doing here?" Her words were edged with a guarded curiosity, the way one might approach a curious artifact in a museum—close enough to see, but too cautious to touch.

"Can't a girl visit her hometown without an interrogation?" Emily quipped, but there was a softness behind her jest, a bridge tentatively extended.

"Normally, yes. But you don't just visit, Em. You appear, like a plot twist nobody saw coming." Olivia's lips twitched upward despite the uncertainty that pinched at her heart. She leaned back against a worktable, arms crossed, the posture of a woman bracing for whatever storm her sister might bring.

"Guess I've always had a flair for the dramatic," Emily admitted, her gaze flickering to the stacks of paper and the whiteboard etched with names and notes. "Looks like I'm not the only one."

"Things have been… complicated," Olivia said, the word feeling like an understatement as vast as the ocean lapping at Bayside Cove's shores.

"Complicated how?" Emily moved closer, the question hanging between them like a dare.

"Someone's trying to frame me for something I didn't do." Olivia watched Emily carefully, searching for any sign of insincerity or hidden agendas in those green eyes that mirrored her own.

"Frame you?" Emily's eyebrows knitted together in concern, her stance shifting from aloof to alert. "That's serious, Liv. Why would anyone want to do that?"

"Good question," Olivia replied, her tone a blend of frustration and fatigue. "One I intend to answer."

"Mind if I help?" Emily offered, a note of earnestness creeping into her voice. It wasn't lost on Olivia, the vulnerability that tinged the edges of Emily's confident exterior.

"Help? You?" Doubt laced Olivia's words, though part of her yearned for the solidarity of family, for the reassurance that came with shared blood and history.

"Surprising, I know," Emily said, a wry smile tugging at her lips. "But I believe in your innocence. Besides, two Pierces are better than one, right?"

"Maybe," Olivia conceded, her skepticism a stubborn shadow that refused to completely recede. "But I need to be careful about who I trust."

"Understood." Emily nodded, the understanding between them fragile yet binding. "Just know I'm here, Liv. No matter what."

"Thanks, Em." Olivia let out a breath she hadn't realized she'd been holding, the bakery's comforting scents wrapping around her like a promise. A promise that, no matter how unpredictable the recipe for truth might be, she wouldn't have to face the oven's heat alone.

Sam cleared his throat, the sound cutting through the thick tension that had settled over Sweet Sensations like a heavy frosting. "Okay, so we've got a bit of a family reunion here," he said, flashing a grin that failed to reach his eyes. "But let's remember why we're all in this kitchen, right? We've got a mystery to solve, and Olivia, your name isn't going to clear itself."

Olivia paused, her arms folded as she appraised her sister. Despite her reservations, the aroma of freshly baked croissants served as a gentle reminder of the bakery's role as a place of comfort and unity, not just for her customers but also, perhaps, for her fractured family.

"Sam's right," Olivia admitted, her voice softer now. The warmth from the ovens seemed to seep into her words, melting the frost from her earlier tone. "Emily, you've always been... perceptive. Maybe you can see something we've missed."

Emily's eyes lit up, and she straightened her posture, accepting the olive branch with a nod. "I'll do what I can. Two heads—or should I say, three—are better than one, especially when they're Pierce heads."

"Alright, team Pierce it is," Sam chimed in, pulling a chair out for Emily with a flourish. "Now, let's get back to the matter at hand. First on the list, Victor Wellington. He's had his eye on modernizing Bayside Cove, and the mayor was a thorn in his side."

"Thorn might be putting it mildly," Olivia mused, her brow furrowed as she considered the developer's well-known temper. "He's not exactly the type to settle for a bake-off when he wants a piece of the pie."

"True, but would he risk his high-rising ambitions for a slice of revenge?" Emily pondered aloud, tapping a finger against her chin thoughtfully.

"Then there's Evelyn Grant," Sam said, redirecting their focus as he scribbled on the whiteboard. "Her environmental crusade clashed pretty hard with the mayor's plans."

"Clashed? They were like oil and vinegar—never quite mixing," Olivia added, recalling the heated debates that had spilled out from town meetings onto the streets. "She's passionate, that's for sure. Could passion have turned into action?"

"Passion can curdle under pressure," Emily remarked, her eyes narrowing slightly. "Speaking of which, Richard Cornwall isn't exactly a beacon of tranquility either."

"Ah, the councilman with mayoral aspirations," Sam said, drawing a circle around Cornwall's name. "If ambition were a cake, he'd want the biggest slice."

"And don't forget Margaret Foster," Olivia interjected, her hands kneading an imaginary dough as if working through her thoughts. "Her bakery might be called 'Flour Power,' but I wouldn't put it past her to sprinkle a little sabotage into the mix."

"Margaret has motive, but we need more proof before we start icing accusations," Sam cautioned, a hint of seriousness beneath his playful metaphor.

"Right," Olivia agreed, taking a deep breath that filled her lungs with the comforting scent of cinnamon and sugar. She looked between Sam and Emily, feeling a renewed sense of purpose. "Let's keep digging, follow the crumbs, and see where they lead us."

"Sounds like a plan," Emily said, a spark of determination flickering in her green eyes. "Lead the way, sister."

"Okay, Team Pierce," Olivia smiled, the weight of suspicion lifting ever so slightly. "Let's get to the bottom of this, one suspect at a time."

Olivia's fingers danced across the whiteboard, her hand steady as she listed the names and motives next to each suspect. The fluorescent lights hummed overhead, casting a glow that seemed to ignite the determination etched on her face. She stepped back, assessing their work with a critical eye.

"Victor Wellington is ambitious enough to have done something drastic," Olivia mused aloud, tapping the marker against her chin. "But ambition doesn't always equate to murder."

"True," Sam agreed, scribbling additional notes onto a pad. "And Evelyn's passion for the environment is fierce, but I can't picture her harming anyone."

"Me neither," Olivia sighed, the furrowed brow softening as she scanned the room filled with the comforting aroma of baked goods and the warmth of ovens working overtime. "But we can't rule out anything or anyone. Not when my name is on the line."

"Your name will be cleared," Sam asserted, offering a reassuring smile. "We just need to keep peeling back the layers, like onions in a stew."

"Or apples in a pie," Olivia quipped, a hint of humor lighting up her eyes momentarily.

"Exactly," Sam chuckled. "And we'll find the core of the truth, no matter how many layers there are."

"Speaking of truth," Olivia said, her tone shifting back to solemnity as she glanced at the door where Emily had exited moments ago. "I can't shake off the feeling that Emily knows more than she's letting on."

"Then we'll add it to the list," Sam said, jotting down another note. "Every detail matters."

"Right," Olivia nodded, taking the marker once more and making a decisive check next to Cornwall's name. "Councilman Cornwall has been too quiet lately. That silence speaks volumes."

"Volumes of what, though?" Sam pondered, leaning back in his chair. "Intrigue? Fear? Guilt?"

"Only time will tell," Olivia replied, the resolve in her voice unwavering. "But we'll uncover it. This town is small; secrets don't stay buried for long."

"Especially not with you on the case," Sam teased gently, his admiration for her tenacity clear in his gaze.

"Someone has to protect Sweet Sensations' reputation—and our livelihood," Olivia stated firmly, her hands now planted firmly on the table.

"Speaking of which," Sam began, only to be interrupted by the shrill ring of the phone that shattered the evening's calm. It was a sound that usually signaled a late order or an inquiry about the next day's specials.

However, this time, as Olivia reached for the receiver, her heart hammered with the intensity of someone who knew that this call could be the turning point they desperately needed.

"Sweet Sensations, Olivia speaking," she answered, her voice steady despite the pounding in her chest.

Sam watched her closely, reading each subtle change in her expression as she listened to the caller. Her eyes widened, and the color drained from her cheeks, replaced by a ghostly pallor.

"Understood. Yes, I'll be there first thing in the morning," Olivia whispered into the phone before hanging up. She stood frozen, the receiver slipping slightly from her grasp.

"Olivia?" Sam asked tentatively, his brow creasing with concern. "What is it? What did they say?"

Olivia turned to him, her voice barely above a whisper, yet carrying the weight of the world. "That was Detective Harris. They found another body—by the cove. And it's someone we know."

The room, still scented with the sweetness of confectionery, now felt suffocating as the implications of her words hung heavily in the air. The chapter closed with a heavy sense of foreboding, leaving both Olivia and Sam on the precipice of a discovery that could change everything.

Chapter 4

A Dash of Expertise

Olivia Pierce pushed open the heavy oak door of the Bayside Cove Library, and a familiar wave of tranquility washed over her. The soft creak of the hinges was a quaint welcome as she stepped into the realm of whispered stories and hushed secrets. Her pulse quickened, not from fear, but from the thrill that always accompanied the start of an investigation.

The library's ambiance embraced her like a well-worn sweater. A labyrinth of bookshelves stood like silent guardians of wisdom, their spines offering a rainbow of faded colors. Sunlight filtered through lace curtains, casting a golden hue on the polished wood floors, while the scent of aged paper and leather bindings filled the air, a perfume that spoke of time and memory.

"Ah, the bouquet of bygone eras," Olivia murmured to herself, her voice barely above the sound of her own footsteps. Each breath she took seemed to stir the dust of stories untold, the very essence of the library's charm.

Ahead, Martha Caldwell, the gatekeeper of knowledge, sat ensconced behind the circulation desk. The librarian's silver hair glinted in the quiet light, each strand meticulously wound into a bun that claimed as much respect as the leather-bound volumes that surrounded her. She was so engrossed in her reading that not even the whisper of turning pages disturbed her focus.

Olivia approached, her fingers absently tracing the smooth grain of a nearby bookshelf. She could always count on Martha for guidance, even if it meant interrupting her literary communion. Taking a deep breath, Olivia paused, gathering the courage to bridge the silence between them. She cleared her throat, a subtle herald to announce her presence.

The Frosted Felony

"Martha?" she ventured, her tone laced with both respect and a hint of urgency. "I'm sorry to disturb you, but I could use your help."

Martha's gaze lifted from the ancient pages, immediately piercing through Olivia's practiced composure with eyes that seemed to have done this dance of silent inquiry countless times before. "What troubles you today, dear?" Martha asked, her voice a comforting blend of curiosity and concern.

"Actually, I'm hoping you might shed some light on Bayside Cove's less savory moments," Olivia began, feeling the weight of the investigation resting heavily on her shoulders. The librarian's eyes narrowed slightly, not in judgment, but as if she were peering into the depths of history itself.

"Scandals, my dear? Our little town has seen its fair share," Martha replied, her hands clasping together atop the book, as though it was a vault of secrets only she could unlock.

"Specifically," Olivia hesitated, "I'm looking into the relationships among the founding families. There might be something there that could give us a lead on the murder." She felt odd, standing there amidst the quiet stacks, talking of such grim matters.

Martha leaned back in her chair, a creak echoing softly in the hush of the library. She studied Olivia for a moment, her discerning eyes tracing the earnest lines of worry etched upon the baker's face. Then, as if making a decision, she nodded slowly.

"Old ties bind tightly, and sometimes they strangle," Martha mused, her voice taking on the rhythm of a well-read passage. "The founding families... yes, indeed. Their roots run deep, and not all that grows from them is wholesome."

"Whispers of feuds turned bitter, fortunes gained by dubious means, and loyalties tested in the dark." She paused, allowing the gravity of her words to settle like dust motes in a beam of sunlight. "But beware, Olivia. Some secrets are like pandora's box; once opened, they can't be closed again."

Olivia absorbed every word, her resolve strengthening like dough beneath her kneading fingers. She knew Martha was right; she had to tread carefully. Each piece of the past could be a vital ingredient to solving this mystery or an unnecessary addition that would spoil the entire recipe. "I understand the risks," she assured Martha. "And I'm ready to face them."

"Then you'll need more than just my old tales," Martha said, standing up from her desk with a grace that belied her age. She walked over to a towering bookcase and ran her fingers along the spines of books that looked older than the town itself. "Let's see if we can't find you a breadcrumb trail to follow."

"Thank you, Martha. Really," Olivia breathed out, her heart racing with excitement, nerves, and an unmistakable dash of gratitude. She watched the librarian work, thinking how much the woman reminded her of a guardian of lore, each movement deliberate, holding the key to unlocking the stories that shaped their shared home.

"Let's start with the legend of the lighthouse keeper's treasure," Martha suggested, pulling out a tome that sent a puff of musty air swirling into the room. "It's not just idle talk for tourists, you know."

"Treasure?" Olivia echoed, a smile tugging at the corner of her lips despite the seriousness of her quest. "Now you're speaking my language."

"Ah, but which language is that? The dialect of gold and silver, or the tongue of truth and justice?" Martha teased, offering Olivia a knowing wink.

"Both, if I have anything to say about it," Olivia quipped back, the warmth in her chest blooming like the first hints of yeast in warm water. She was ready to dive into the annals of history, with Martha as her guide, and uncover what lay hidden beneath the quaint, cobblestone surface of Bayside Cove.

The musty scent of aged paper and the soft creak of leather-bound spines filled the air as Olivia leaned forward, a crease forming between her brows. Martha's tales had woven a complex tapestry of Bayside Cove's history, one that seemed to ensnare the present mystery with invisible threads.

"Martha, you've been an absolute trove of information," Olivia said, her voice low and earnest. "But I can't shake the feeling there's more —hidden layers to this story. Are there any archives, something beyond what's on these shelves, that might shine a light on things?"

Martha paused, her fingers tracing the edge of the book she'd just closed. A sly smile played at her lips before she replied, "Well now, Olivia, some say the most intriguing chapters of history are those seldom read."

Her eyes gleamed with a spark of mischief, like sunlight glinting off the sea at dawn. She leaned back in her chair, the old wood groaning softly under her weight. "There may be such a place, where records and memories gather more dust than attention. But such places ask for a seeker who's willing to look beyond the surface... and keep a secret or two."

"Secrets?" Olivia's pulse quickened. The word danced in her mind, conjuring images of shadowed corners and forgotten wisdom waiting to be rediscovered. She met Martha's gaze squarely, determination etched in her features. "I'm no stranger to secrets. You know I'll respect whatever trust you place in me."

"Ah, but respecting trust is only half the journey," Martha mused, her tone airy yet laced with gravity. "Finding the path is quite another."

Olivia watched the librarian, sensing the unspoken challenge in her words. Martha was a gatekeeper, one who held the power to grant access to hidden truths—or withhold them. Olivia's heart thrummed with anticipation, knowing that each clue could bring her closer to unveiling the darkness that lurked beneath the picturesque charm of Bayside Cove.

The air shifted in the library, carrying with it a new charge that prickled against Olivia's skin. She parted her lips to ask another question when the heavy wooden door swung open with an authoritative creak. Detective James Holbrook stepped inside, his tall frame momentarily eclipsing the sunlight that spilled through the entrance. Olivia's heart performed an unexpected somersault, and for a split second, she forgot all about the elusive archives.

"Detective," she greeted, her voice steady despite the flutter in her chest.

"Ms. Pierce." His nod was curt, professional, yet there was a glint in his eye that suggested something more lay beneath his composed exterior.

"Can I help you with something?" Olivia asked, folding her hands atop the desk as if they were errant children needing to be kept in place.

"Actually, yes." Holbrook's voice was a low rumble that seemed out of place amongst the whispers of turning pages. "I have some questions about your findings at the crime scene."

"Of course," Olivia replied, swallowing the nerves that threatened to lace her words. Her mind whirred, ready to sift through every detail she had meticulously stored away. "What do you need to know?"

Martha observed from behind her desk, her eyes narrowing slightly, not missing a beat of the exchange. The corners of her mouth hinted at a smile, yet she remained silent, a sphinx enjoying the unfolding riddle.

"Your account mentioned fresh footprints leading away from the bakery. Did you notice anything peculiar about them?" Holbrook inquired, his gaze never wavering from Olivia's face.

"Only that they seemed... deliberate," Olivia said, her brow furrowing as she recalled the scene. "As if the person was being careful, but not careful enough to avoid leaving a trail."

"Interesting." Holbrook's eyebrow lifted ever so slightly. "And your intuition? What does it tell you?"

"Intuition?" A small laugh escaped her, tinged with both self-consciousness and amusement. "Well, if my gut had its say, we're looking for someone who knows their way around a kitchen—or at least around my kitchen."

"Thank you, Ms. Pierce." There was a warmth in Holbrook's voice now, appreciative of her input. "That's helpful."

"Happy to assist, Detective," Olivia replied, allowing herself a brief moment of pride. She might just be a baker, but here she was, contributing to a real murder investigation.

Holbrook nodded, his stance softening as if he'd found what he came for. He turned to leave, but not before casting a lingering glance back at Olivia. Their silent communication spoke volumes, bridging the gap between professional courtesy and mutual respect.

"Take care, Olivia," he said, his use of her first name a subtle indication of the rapport they'd begun to build.

"You too, Detective," she responded, her heart skipping once more as he disappeared through the door.

Olivia exhaled slowly, her thoughts returning to the task at hand. With Martha's cryptic clues and Holbrook's vote of confidence, she felt an invigorating rush of purpose. She was ready to unravel the secrets of Bayside Cove, come what may.

"Detective Holbrook, I must say, your timing is uncannily perfect—or perfectly inconvenient." Olivia's words emerged with a playful edge as she regarded the detective standing before her. The corners of her mouth tugged upward in a half-smile, despite the gravity of the subject at hand.

"Is it?" James raised an eyebrow, his voice carrying a note of mock surprise. "Perhaps it's just good detective work. Or maybe...I was simply hoping to cross paths with Bayside Cove's most talented baker."

Her cheeks warmed slightly at the veiled compliment. "Flattery will get you everywhere—or at least get you a fresh batch of scones. But let's stick to the case for now, shall we?" Olivia deflected smoothly.

"Of course," he agreed, though the twinkle in his eye betrayed his delight in their repartee.

The library around them hummed with the quiet energy of whispered conversations and rustling pages, a stark contrast to the current of electricity that seemed to pulse between Olivia and Detective Holbrook. She could almost taste the dust motes dancing in the slants of sunlight filtering through the leaded windows, time hanging suspended like the old grandfather clock ticking in the corner.

"Your gut feeling about the kitchen could be key," James continued, leaning against the book-laden table with casual ease. "Although, I have to wonder if there's more intuition where that came from."

"Maybe," Olivia conceded, her gaze lingering on him a moment longer than necessary. "But intuition isn't always enough, is it? We need evidence, hard facts."

"True," he said, his gaze intense yet softening around the edges. "But never underestimate the power of a hunch, especially when it comes from someone who knows the town—and its people—as well as you do."

Olivia swallowed, feeling the weight of his words and the responsibility they carried. She was torn between the fluttering sensation in her stomach and the stern voice in her head reminding her of the task at hand. Here she was, standing close to a man whose presence managed to both unsettle and intrigue her, all while she was supposed to be focusing on solving a murder.

"James," she began, wading through her whirlwind of thoughts. "I appreciate your confidence in me. And your...presence here." Her voice faltered for a split second before she caught herself. "But I can't afford distractions. There's too much at stake."

"Understood," he responded softly, his expression unreadable for a moment before he offered her a small, reassuring smile. "And for the record, working with you is anything but a distraction."

Their eyes held a silent conversation, one filled with the promise of unspoken possibilities and the acknowledgment of shared goals. Olivia felt the air around them grow thick with tension and possibility, challenging her to maintain her focus. She needed to keep her feelings at bay, at least until the mystery that enshrouded Bayside Cove was solved.

"Thank you, Detective," Olivia said finally, her voice steady once again. "Let's catch a killer."

"Agreed," James replied, his tone echoing her resolve. They shared a brief nod, an unspoken pact between them before stepping away to follow their respective paths—one leading towards justice, the other towards the unraveling of a heart.

Olivia Pierce felt the weight of Martha Caldwell's gaze as she and Detective James Holbrook stood amidst the towering bookshelves. The silver-haired librarian had paused in her task of reshelving a worn copy of "Wuthering Heights" to observe their exchange, her lips curving into a knowing smile that reached her sharp blue eyes. It was as if Martha could see through the layers of professional veneer to the tender undercurrents swirling between them.

"Something tells me you've seen this sort of thing before," Olivia said, addressing Martha with a light chuckle, trying to break the spell of the moment.

"More times than I can count, dear," Martha replied, her voice carrying the warmth of late summer. "The heart has a way of making itself heard, no matter how much the head protests." Her eyes twinkled merrily, reflecting a lifetime of watching narratives unfold within and beyond the pages of her cherished tomes.

"Thank you for everything today, Martha," Olivia said earnestly, her gratitude mingling with the scents of leather and parchment that filled the air. "Your insights have been invaluable. If I stumble upon anything else, may I come back?"

"Of course, Olivia," Martha nodded, her expression softening with encouragement. "This library is a beacon for seekers of truth. You're always welcome here."

"Then I'll hold you to that," Olivia replied with a playful wink. She glanced around the quiet sanctuary of the library, feeling a sense of solace in its timeless embrace. The rows of books stood like silent sentinels, guarding the stories and secrets of Bayside Cove—a comforting thought as she prepared to navigate the murky waters of the investigation ahead.

"Until next time," Olivia murmured, offering a small wave as she turned to leave, her steps echoing softly against the polished wooden floor. She carried with her not only Martha's wisdom but the librarian's subtle blessing on whatever might bloom between her and the enigmatic detective.

Olivia lingered for a moment, her gaze locked with Detective Holbrook's. A silent conversation passed between them, an acknowledgment of the day's revelations and the uncertain path ahead. The air hummed with tension, the kind that hinted at possibilities too fragile to voice. She took a deep breath, feeling the weight of his stare like a physical touch, stirring something deep within her.

"Be careful," James said, the timbre of his voice low and laced with concern. His eyes held hers, the blue depths seeming to search for something more than just professional courtesy.

"I always am," Olivia replied with a half-smile that didn't quite reach her eyes. It was their little dance of words, tiptoeing around the edges of what was left unsaid.

"Good." He nodded, the corners of his mouth lifting in a subtle smile that suggested he knew better. "Because this town... it has its secrets. And they don't always play nice."

"Neither do I," she quipped, a spark of defiant humor lighting up her features.

With that, they parted ways, each carrying the weight of their unspoken connection. Olivia felt it still, lingering like the echo of a whispered promise, as she turned and pushed through the heavy wooden doors of the library.

The moment she stepped outside, the quaint charm of Main Street enveloped her. The gentle afternoon sun cast dappled shadows on the cobblestone walkway, and the familiar jingle of the bakery's doorbell in the distance tugged at her heartstrings. But there was no time for nostalgia; she had work to do.

Her mind spun with the threads of the story Martha had unraveled, each one weaving a tapestry of intrigue that begged to be explored. This was more than just about finding a murderer; it was about peeling back the layers of a town that thrived on secrets and her own place within it.

"Time to get to the bottom of this," Olivia murmured to herself, determination settling in her chest. With every step, she felt her resolve harden, the pieces of the puzzle beckoning her to fit them together. As she walked, she couldn't help but glance back once more at the library, its windows reflecting the golden light.

"Watch out, Bayside Cove," she chuckled under her breath, "your secrets won't stay hidden for long." With a bounce in her step, Olivia set off down Main Street, ready to unravel the mysteries that lay tangled in the heart of her beloved town.

Olivia's footsteps echoed on the cobblestone street, a rhythmic counterpoint to the thrumming of her heart. She felt every gaze from the storefronts as she passed, each step a beat in a dance of determination and uncertainty. The late afternoon breeze carried with it the salty tang of the sea mixed with the sweet allure of cinnamon and sugar from Mrs. Henley's pie shop.

"Revelations indeed," she thought, her lips curving into a half-smile at the prospect of uncovering Bayside Cove's secrets. It was a challenge that stirred something deep within her—a yearning not only to bring justice but also to understand the intricate quilt of human connections that made up her town.

She paused for a moment, taking in the sights and sounds; the gentle clink of a spoon against a coffee cup at the outdoor cafe, the soft murmur of conversations that wove through the air like delicate threads. With each breath, Olivia drew in the comfort of her surroundings, the comforting familiarity that grounded her even as she ventured into the unknown.

"Who knew amateur sleuthing could work up such an appetite?" she said to no one in particular, chuckling softly at her own jest. There was something about the promise of mystery that made the mundane sparkle with new intrigue. Every passerby could be a witness, every whisper a clue.

The sun dipped lower, casting a warm glow that seemed to wrap around her like a supportive embrace. She tilted her face towards the sky for a moment, closing her eyes and letting the sunlight kiss her cheeks. In this place, where past and present intertwined, Olivia found the courage to face the shadows.

With a deep breath, she opened her eyes, the golden hue reflecting in the windowpanes, turning the world into a canvas painted with hope.

The Frosted Felony

She nodded to herself, affirming her readiness to peel back the layers of Bayside Cove's history, to challenge the silence that shrouded its scandals.

"Time to turn the page on this chapter of Bayside Cove," she whispered, her voice a blend of resolve and wonder. Olivia's journey was more than a quest for truth—it was a path to personal discovery, one that promised to test her limits and perhaps even heal old wounds.

And so, with the scent of freshly baked treats lingering in the air like an invitation to tomorrow, Olivia Pierce moved forward, her spirit buoyed by the knowledge that each step took her closer to revelations that would change her life forever.

Chapter 5

Folding in Allies

Olivia glanced at the door as the bell chimed, signaling Emily's return. Her sister strode into the bakery with a confidence that seemed to fill the quaint space, her green eyes scanning the room before settling on Olivia.

"Em," Olivia started, wiping flour from her hands onto her apron, "I'm not sure this is such a good idea."

"Come on, Liv," Emily said, leaning against the counter with ease. "We both know you're dying to figure out what happened. And I can help. Besides, we're family."

"Family who didn't speak for years," Olivia reminded her, though her lips twitched, betraying a hint of amusement in the midst of her skepticism.

"Let's chalk it up to... extended personal growth time." Emily's smile was wry and unapologetic. "We've got bigger fish to fry now. And hey, I missed your cupcakes."

"Flattery will get you nowhere," Olivia retorted, but she felt the resistance within her begin to crumble like the flaky crust of her signature apple tarts.

"Look, I know our past is as complicated as one of your recipes," Emily continued, her tone softening. "But I wouldn't be here if I didn't think it was important."

"Important enough for a surprise visit to Bayside Cove?" Olivia questioned, arching an eyebrow even as her curiosity piqued.

Emily hesitated, the flicker of something unreadable in her gaze. "There are things I need to settle," she admitted, and there was a weight to her words that hinted at more than just familial reconciliation. "Secrets that tie back to this place—and to us."

"Us?" The single word hung between them, charged with the potential of untold stories.

"Let's just say the past has a way of resurfacing when you least expect it," Emily said cryptically, pushing off from the counter. "I promise you'll get the full scoop, but right now, we have a mystery to unravel."

"Fine," Olivia conceded, though her mind raced with questions. "But if we're doing this, we do it my way. Low-key and careful. I have a business and a reputation to maintain."

"Wouldn't dream of doing it any other way," Emily replied, the corner of her mouth lifting. "Partners?"

"Reluctantly so," Olivia said, extending her hand across the counter. As their fingers clasped, she couldn't help but feel the stirrings of an old bond, intertwined with the thrill of the unknown.

"Reluctantly is better than not at all," Emily said with a wink, sealing their unconventional pact.

The chime of the polished brass bell announced Olivia and Emily's arrival as they stepped into the hushed expanse of Victor Wellington's office. They were immediately enveloped by a cool blast of air conditioning, a stark contrast to the warm coastal breeze that had tousled their hair moments before.

"Olivia Pierce and Emily Pierce to see Mr. Wellington," Olivia informed the receptionist with a practiced smile that belied her inner turmoil.

"Ah, yes, the catering discussion," the receptionist said, returning the smile. "Mr. Wellington is expecting you. Please, right this way."

They were led down a corridor, the plush carpet muffling their steps. The walls were adorned with black-and-white photographs of Bayside Cove's shoreline, each perfectly lit and framed, capturing the essence of the town yet somehow stripping it of its warmth.

Victor's office was a testament to his meticulous nature. Expansive windows offered a commanding view of the cove, but the room itself was devoid of any personal touch. A model of the latest development project took pride of place on a mahogany desk that could easily double as a boardroom table. The lighting was subtle, casting a soft glow that did little to dispel the overarching austerity.

"Olivia, Emily, a pleasure," Victor greeted them, rising from his leather chair. His handshake was firm, almost too studied, as if each movement was choreographed for effect.

"Mr. Wellington, thank you for seeing us," Emily said, matching his formality. Her voice carried an undercurrent of confidence that made Olivia glance at her sister with a newfound respect.

"Please, call me Victor. I gather this is about your delightful pastries gracing one of my events?" he inquired, gesturing toward the seating area with a sweep of his hand.

"Exactly," Olivia chimed in. "We thought something local would add a nice touch to the grand opening of the new marina."

"Local charm does have its appeal," Victor mused, the corners of his lips curving into a semblance of a smile. Yet, his eyes remained sharp, the blue irises dissecting their every word.

"Indeed," Emily interjected, crossing her legs as she settled onto the sofa. "Bayside Cove has always prided itself on community spirit."

"Ah, but progress often requires a broader vision," Victor countered, the words smooth like the scotch he poured from a crystal decanter. "One must look beyond quaint traditions to truly realize potential."

"Of course," Olivia agreed, though the taste of the word was bitter on her tongue. She accepted the scotch, noting the way Victor watched her over the rim of his glass, calculating, always calculating.

"Shall we discuss menu options?" Emily suggested, steering the conversation back to safer waters.

"By all means," Victor said, leaning back and steepling his fingers as if granting permission for them to proceed.

As they spoke of flaky croissants and delicate éclairs, Olivia couldn't shake the feeling that Victor's mind was elsewhere, perhaps tallying assets or plotting his next move in the chess game he called business. Despite the friendly banter, the room seemed to close in around her, the air charged with unspoken agendas.

"Thank you for your time, Victor. We'll send over some samples," Olivia concluded, rising with a grace she didn't feel.

"Looking forward to it," Victor replied, his tone suggesting interest, but his gaze never quite meeting theirs as they took their leave.

"Something's off," Olivia murmured to Emily once they were out of earshot.

"Agreed," Emily said, her eyes narrowing in thought. "But let's not jump to conclusions. We have more digging to do."

The Frosted Felony

Stepping back into the sunlight, the sisters exchanged a look that conveyed their shared suspicion. The investigation was only just beginning, and already the waters of Bayside Cove seemed murkier than ever.

Olivia fiddled with the edge of her notepad, the one she'd pretended to jot menu details on while Emily led their conversation with Victor. She couldn't help but scan the room for anything out of place—an unusual book title, a hastily closed drawer, even the way Victor's eyes darted to a painting on the wall as he mentioned the night of the murder.

"Victor, I must say, your choice in art is... intriguing," Olivia ventured, nodding toward the painting.

"Ah, yes, a little piece I picked up at an auction recently," Victor replied nonchalantly, but his fingers twitched, betraying a momentary lapse in composure.

"Is that so?" Emily chimed in, leaning forward with feigned interest. "I've always found art to be quite revealing about its owner."

"Indeed," Victor said, a sly smile creeping onto his lips. "But let's not get sidetracked. I'm more interested in the delightful pastries you're known for, Miss Pierce."

"Of course," Olivia said, quickly shifting gears. "Our raspberry tarts are quite popular."

As they wrapped up their meeting, the sisters' eyes met, both catching the faint glimmer of something unsaid hanging between them and Victor.

Stepping out into the fresh air, they made their way to The Seaside Bean, a local café whose windows fogged up from the warmth within. The aroma of freshly ground coffee beans enveloped them as they pushed open the door, the cozy clink of cups and subdued chatter grounding them back into normalcy.

"Emily, look who's here," Olivia whispered, motioning toward the corner where Evelyn Grant sat surrounded by stacks of environmental campaign pamphlets.

"Let's go say hi," Emily suggested, her tone casual but eyes sharp with intent.

"Hey, Evelyn," Olivia greeted, sliding into the chair across from her. "These new flyers look amazing."

"Thanks, Olivia," Evelyn responded, her gaze fervent. "We've got a rally coming up to protect the bay. It's crucial we get the word out."

"Sounds like important work," Emily remarked, stirring her coffee. "And demanding, too. You must have been busy planning on the day of..."

"Absolutely swamped," Evelyn cut in, her ponytail swinging as she nodded emphatically. "That whole week was a blur of meetings and phone calls."

"Must be tough balancing it all," Olivia said sympathetically, watching Evelyn's face for any telltale signs.

"Someone has to do it," Evelyn countered, the determination in her voice matching the conviction in her eyes.

"Speaking of which," Emily interjected, "do you know if the Wellingtons support your cause?"

"Victor? Ha! He only cares about lining his pockets," Evelyn scoffed, rolling her eyes.

"Right," Olivia said, exchanging a glance with Emily. "Well, thanks for chatting with us, Evelyn. We should let you get back to your mission."

"Thanks, girls," Evelyn smiled, returning her focus to the flyers as the sisters stood up.

"Keep fighting the good fight," Emily called over her shoulder, leaving Evelyn with a wave.

"Always do," came the resolute reply.

Once outside, Olivia and Emily walked in thoughtful silence, the weight of their investigation pressing down on them amidst the quaint streets of Bayside Cove.

Olivia leaned against the counter, the worn wood familiar beneath her palms as she observed Evelyn's fervor. The eco-warrior's hands moved animatedly, each gesture underscoring her dedication to the cause.

"Every signature is a step towards saving our coastline," Evelyn proclaimed, her eyes alight with passion. "Without our intervention, there won't be much left for future generations."

"That's admirable," Olivia said, genuinely impressed. "You're really making a difference."

"Thank you," Evelyn replied, her smile genuine but fleeting. "Though it's not without its challenges."

"Speaking of challenges," Emily chimed in, her tone casual, "you must have been tied up on the day of the murder. I can't imagine you had any time to spare."

The Frosted Felony

"Murder?" Evelyn quirked an eyebrow, pausing mid-sentence. "Yes, well, my days are packed with groundwork. I was out on the field that entire week."

"Out in the field?" Olivia echoed, her curiosity piqued. "All day?"

"From dawn till dusk," Evelyn confirmed, her posture rigid with the weight of her convictions. "The natural world doesn't operate on a nine-to-five schedule, and neither do I."

"Of course," Emily said, nodding. "It's a 24/7 commitment."

"Exactly," Evelyn agreed, locking eyes with Emily. "If we don't stand up for the environment, who will?"

"True," Olivia mused, picking up on the unmistakable steel in Evelyn's voice. "And I suppose someone like Victor Wellington isn't exactly on your list of allies?"

"Hardly," Evelyn snorted. "That man wouldn't know the importance of a wetland if it was his own backyard."

"Interesting," Emily murmured, sharing a fleeting look with Olivia.

"Anyway," Evelyn concluded, gathering her flyers with purpose, "I should get back to work."

"Good luck," Olivia offered, her admiration for Evelyn's tenacity genuine despite the questions swirling in her mind.

"Thanks," Evelyn said, shouldering her bag with ease. "Remember, every action counts."

"Indeed it does," Emily replied, watching Evelyn stride away with a mix of respect and suspicion.

"Quite the force of nature," Olivia commented once they were alone again.

"Absolutely," Emily agreed, her gaze lingering in the direction Evelyn had gone. "But we still need more pieces to this puzzle."

"Let's keep looking then," Olivia decided, her determination matching that of the woman they'd just interviewed.

Olivia pushed open the door to Seaside Café, the cozy little nook they had chosen for a brief respite. The aroma of freshly brewed coffee immediately enveloped them, mingling with the scent of cinnamon rolls and the faintest hint of sea salt carried on the breeze from the bay. It was the kind of place that made you want to curl up in one of the overstuffed armchairs with a good book and forget the world outside.

"Smells like heaven if heaven were a bakery," Emily noted, her voice light as she pulled out a chair by the window.

"Or a coffee shop," Olivia corrected with a small smile, taking the seat across from her. They both knew Olivia's heart belonged to the sweet alchemy of flour and sugar back at her own establishment.

The café buzzed with the gentle murmur of conversation, the clink of porcelain on wood, and the soft hiss of the espresso machine crafting another masterpiece. Warmth radiated from the fireplace in the corner, casting a golden glow over the patrons who seemed more like characters in a storybook than mere townsfolk.

"Feels nice to sit down without an agenda for once," Olivia sighed, allowing herself to enjoy the momentary calm. "Even if it's just for a few minutes."

"Agreed," Emily said, flagging down a waitress to order two lattes. As they waited, their discussion meandered from trivial town gossip to the complexities of their current investigation, careful not to let the gravity of their situation dampen the café's cheerful atmosphere.

The sun dipped lower in the sky, painting the horizon in hues of orange and pink. Olivia glanced at the clock on the wall, noting the hour. "We should head back soon," she said reluctantly, the weight of their task seeping back into her thoughts.

"Right," Emily acknowledged, but there was a reluctance in her eyes too, a shared understanding that their brief respite was coming to an end.

As they stepped out onto the cobblestone street, the air had taken on the crisp chill of evening. Olivia locked the café door behind them, the click echoing slightly louder than she expected. That was when she felt it —a prickle along the back of her neck, a sense that something was not quite right.

"Basil?" Olivia called out softly, searching for her intuitive tabby who had a knack for appearing whenever trouble was afoot. The cat emerged from the shadows near the bakery, his amber eyes fixed intently on a darkened alleyway beside the building.

"Is he always this cryptic, or does he save it just for us?" Emily joked, though her gaze followed Basil' line of sight.

"Only when he's trying to tell us something important," Olivia murmured, stepping closer to the feline. Basil let out a low growl, his tail flicking with unease.

The Frosted Felony

Olivia's heart quickened as she peered into the gloom, straining to see. There, barely distinguishable against the dark brick, a shadowy figure loomed, still as the grave. Whoever it was seemed to be watching the bakery, their intentions unreadable.

"Who do you think..." Emily began, but Olivia shushed her with a raised hand, her friendly demeanor replaced by the protective instincts of a woman who knew her sanctuary was being threatened.

"Let's get inside," Olivia whispered, a surge of adrenaline tinged with fear urging her forward. She could feel the eyes of the mysterious voyeur boring into her back as they hurried to the safety of the bakery.

"Tomorrow," Olivia vowed silently, "we'll figure out what you're up to." With Basil flanking her side, she closed the door on the chilling scene, the warmth of the oven offering little comfort against the cold dread that settled in her bones.

The click of the lock echoed in the quiet bakery as Olivia and Emily exchanged a glance, a silent conversation passing between them. They stood motionless for a moment, listening to the muffled noises of Bayside Cove's nightlife outside the reinforced windows.

"Did you see anything? Any details?" Emily asked, her voice low and tense.

"Nothing clear," Olivia admitted, her brows knitting together as she leaned closer to the glass, trying to pierce the darkness with her determined gaze. "But there was something... off about that silhouette. Too still, too deliberate."

"Like it knew we were watching," Emily added, crossing her arms. The dim light from the streetlamps outside cast shadows over her face, deepening the lines of concern around her eyes.

"Exactly." Olivia's pulse thrummed in her ears. Her fingers traced the outline of a rolling pin left on the counter, a familiar weight and potential weapon if needed. She was accustomed to the sweet scent of sugar and flour that lingered in the air, but now a tang of metallic fear tainted her senses.

"Could be someone casing the place," Emily suggested, moving toward the back door to double-check the locks.

"Or someone who knows we're getting too close to something they want hidden," Olivia murmured. Basil, sensing the tension, let out a soft meow and rubbed against Olivia's leg, his green eyes bright and alert.

"Then we need to be careful," Emily said, coming back to stand beside her sister. "We can't afford any rash moves."

"Agreed. We'll start fresh in the morning, go over everything we've learned so far," Olivia said, her voice steady despite the turmoil inside her.

"Right, because nothing says 'good morning' like a hot cup of coffee and a side of conspiracy," Emily quipped, but the humor didn't quite reach her eyes.

Olivia managed a wry smile. "I'll bake some scones. Murder investigations are always better with pastries."

They moved away from the window, retreating to the relative safety of the heart of the bakery. The ovens had cooled, and the comforting warmth was fading, leaving a chill that seemed to seep into their very bones. But it wasn't just the temperature; it was the creeping realization that their little investigation had stirred waters much murkier than either of them had anticipated.

"Tomorrow, Em," Olivia said, pausing at the foot of the stairs leading to her apartment above the bakery. "We'll find out what's really going on. And we'll do it together."

"Got your back, Liv," Emily affirmed, her hand resting briefly on Olivia's shoulder before they parted ways for the night.

As Olivia ascended the stairs, her thoughts raced. There was no mistaking it: danger lurked in the shadowy corners of Bayside Cove. And as she reached the top step, she resolved that come sunrise, she would be ready to face whatever—or whoever—was hiding in the dark.

Chapter 6

A Pinch of Paranormal

The heavy wooden door creaked open as Olivia, with flour still dusting the hem of her apron, stepped into the dimly lit archives of the Bayside Cove Historical Society. A gust of air, redolent with the scent of aging paper and leather, enveloped her and Emily. Olivia inhaled deeply, the musty aroma triggering a cascade of memories from bygone days spent thumbing through forgotten recipes in her grandmother's attic.

"Smells like history," Emily quipped, her eyes scanning the labyrinth of dusty shelves that loomed like silent sentinels guarding their secrets.

"Or just old moisture and mothballs," Olivia replied, her voice echoing slightly in the hushed expanse of the room. She glanced at her sister, whose posture spoke of an unspoken anticipation, a shared awareness that these archives might hold more than just benign records of the past.

"Ah, you've arrived!" came a voice, soft yet clear, cutting through the quiet. Martha Caldwell, the librarian whose reputation for wisdom was as established as the archives themselves, materialized from behind a stack of ancient tomes. Her silver hair and the earth-toned cardigan she wore seemed to blend seamlessly with the surroundings, as if she were an extension of the archive's soul itself.

"Martha," Olivia greeted, her expression brightening at the sight of the familiar face. "We could use your help."

"Help often comes in unexpected forms," Martha said, her blue eyes twinkling with a knowing light. "Sometimes it is not what we find, but what we seek that truly matters."

"Sounds like you're preparing us for a treasure hunt," Emily remarked, her tone laced with both amusement and curiosity.

"Perhaps I am," Martha conceded, a mysterious smile playing upon her lips. "Look beyond the bindings of the books, delve into the heart of their stories, and there you may uncover what you desire."

"Is that a hint or just good library advice?" Olivia asked, her wit surfacing despite the gravity of their search.

"Both," Martha replied succinctly, before turning to glide away between the rows of shelving, leaving the faintest trace of lavender in her wake.

"Guess we start digging," Olivia said, rolling up her sleeves metaphorically, though they were already quite literally rolled up and specked with the day's work.

"Let's hope we don't need to interpret her Dewey Decimal system too," Emily added, stepping towards the nearest shelf with resolve.

Together, the sisters began their quest through the archives, guided by cryptic counsel and a determination to unearth the town's veiled past.

The quiet expanse of the archive room seemed to close in on Olivia and Emily as they moved deeper into the heart of the labyrinthine shelves, their footsteps a soft murmur against the creaking wooden floor. Rows upon rows of leather-bound spines cast long shadows in the dim light, creating an atmosphere that was both reverent and eerie.

"Em, check this out," Olivia whispered, her voice barely rising above a hush as she traced her fingers over an embossed title, leaving a faint trail on the dusty cover. Emily leaned in, her green eyes scanning the faded gold lettering.

Just then, a heavy thud echoed through the archives as a book tumbled off a shelf several feet away, landing with a puff of dust on the floor. They jumped, their gazes snapping toward the disturbance. Another book followed, then another, as if an invisible hand were rifling through the volumes with urgent discontent.

"Okay, that's not normal," Olivia murmured, trying to keep the edge from her voice as she eyed the cascading books.

"Definitely beyond the ordinary," Emily replied, the playful spark in her tone now replaced by a note of apprehension.

As they cautiously approached the fallen tomes, Emily's breath caught in her throat. A chill swept through the room, sudden and inexplicable, wrapping around her like a cold embrace. She rubbed her arms vigorously, trying to dispel the goosebumps that had erupted across her skin.

"Olivia, do you feel that?" Emily asked, her voice barely a whisper.

"Feel what? The draft?" Olivia scanned the room for any open windows but found none. "This place could do with some weatherproofing."

But it wasn't just the temperature that unsettled Emily. Faint whispers seemed to weave through the air, murmurs too soft to discern but insistent enough to make her heart race. Emily swiveled her head, searching for the source, but the shifting shadows offered no clues.

"Can you hear that? It's like—"

"Like someone left their phone on with a podcast playing?" Olivia suggested, though a part of her wondered if there was more to it. She refused to let the strangeness of the situation dampen her focus. "Come on, let's see what these books are about. Maybe they'll give us a clue."

Emily nodded, but as she bent down to gather the scattered pages, her hands trembled slightly. This was not just the wind or an unstable shelf. Something was stirring in the archives, something that reached out from the silent depths of history with a whisper and a shiver.

Olivia chuckled lightly, brushing a thin film of dust from an ancient leather-bound volume. "Em, you've got to admit, the idea of a ghost librarian is pretty far-fetched. This shelf here—" She gave it a nudge, and it wobbled precariously, "—looks like it hasn't seen a good tightening since the place was built."

Emily remained unconvinced, her eyes darting to the corners of the room where shadows seemed to play tricks on her vision. "I'm telling you, Liv, there's something off about this place."

"Off or not, we're here for answers, not ghost stories." Olivia's practical nature wouldn't allow her to be deterred by a drafty room and old building quirks. Her fingers trailed along the spines of books until she found a section with records so old the ink had faded to a ghostly gray.

"Look at this," Olivia said, her voice tinged with excitement as she carefully extracted a thick ledger from its resting place. The pages creaked in protest, echoing through the silence of the archives.

"Town records," Emily noted, leaning in close. They both watched as Olivia flipped through the crackling pages, their faces illuminated by the soft glow of the overhead lamp.

"Here," Olivia pointed. "It says something about a pact...a binding agreement between the founding families." Her eyebrows knitted together as she tried to make out the archaic handwriting.

"Does it mention a curse?" Emily's voice was hushed, almost reverent.

"Sort of." Olivia squinted at the text. "'Upon this ground, they did condemn, lest all their fortunes meet their end.'" She looked up at Emily, her skepticism giving way to intrigue. "That sounds pretty curselike, doesn't it?"

"Definitely not your everyday town charter." Emily's earlier apprehension morphed into the kind of fervor that often came with the thrill of the hunt. "What else does it say?"

"Something about darkness and light, debts unpaid..." Olivia trailed off. "But it's all so vague and cryptic. We need something concrete."

"Maybe there's more," Emily suggested, her eyes scanning the shelf. "If it's hidden, it has to be important, right?"

"Or just forgotten," Olivia countered, but the glimmer in her eye betrayed her growing curiosity. She stood resolute amid the whispers of the past, her warm-hearted tenacity shining like a beacon as they delved deeper into the mysteries of Bayside Cove.

Olivia's finger traced the delicate, yellowed script that twined like ivy across the parchment. "The Bennetts and the Wellingtons," she read aloud, her voice a soft murmur in the stillness of the archives. "Bound by blood and shadow to the fate of Bayside Cove."

"Shadow, huh?" Emily quipped, though her quick smile didn't quite reach her eyes. She leaned closer, peering at the record. "Sounds more like a gothic novel than town history."

"Could be both," Olivia suggested with a half-hearted chuckle, trying to maintain the lightness that usually marked their banter. But the mustiness of the room seemed to press in on her, and the words before her felt too weighty to be taken lightly.

"Listen to this," Olivia continued, her curiosity piquing as she deciphered more of the text. "'In the year of our Lord, a pact was struck amidst a tempest's rage, sealing the prosperity of these families at a terrible cost.'"

The Frosted Felony

"Terrible cost," Emily repeated, her tone sober. The air around them grew inexplicably colder, prompting both women to wrap their arms around themselves.

"Did you feel that?" Emily asked, her breath forming a faint cloud in front of her.

"Drafty old building," Olivia replied automatically, though her rational explanation sounded hollow even to her own ears.

"Right, because buildings always get drafty when you mention curses and terrible costs." Emily's wry observation was punctuated by another book slipping from its place on the shelf and thumping to the floor with a cloud of dust.

"Coincidence," Olivia insisted, bending down to pick up the book, but her hands were shaking just slightly—a fact she hoped Emily didn't notice.

"Of course," Emily said, though her gaze lingered on the displaced tome as if it might hold answers.

They moved through the aisles of towering shelves, the silence broken only by the soft shuffling of papers and the occasional eerie creak of wood. Suddenly, Olivia stopped short, her heart skipping a beat. A frigid gust brushed past her, leaving goosebumps on her skin and a whisper of unease in her mind.

"Olivia?" Emily's voice was tinged with concern.

"Another cold spot." Olivia forced a laugh. "This place could really use some better insulation."

"Or an exorcist," Emily muttered under her breath, pulling her cardigan tighter around her shoulders.

"Let's keep looking," Olivia said, her determination steeling her against the chill. "There has to be something else here—something that can tell us more about the curse and what happened between the Bennetts and Wellingtons."

"Agreed," Emily nodded, her expression set with a resilience that matched her sister's. "We'll figure this out, one chilly mystery at a time."

As they turned back to the records, the air seemed to hum with secrets yet to be unveiled, the past clinging to the present with a tenacity that whispered of things not easily forgotten.

Olivia brushed a cobweb away with the back of her hand, squinting at the faded ink on the parchment. "Emily, look at this." Her finger traced the lines of a family tree that sprawled across the page like ancient ivy. The names Bennett and Wellington interwove through generations until they met at a point that made Olivia's breath hitch.

"Is that...?" Emily leaned closer, her green eyes wide with realization.

"Victor Wellington and Jonathan Bennett," Olivia murmured. "They're related."

"Half-brothers?" Emily's voice held a note of disbelief. "That can't be right."

"Given Victor's penchant for secrecy, who knows what skeletons are in his impeccably tailored closets?" Olivia mused, her skepticism fading as the puzzle pieces began to fit together in a way she couldn't ignore.

"Secrets upon secrets." Emily shook her head, but there was a spark of excitement in her gaze. "This changes everything."

"Indeed, it does." Olivia closed the book with care, feeling the weight of history in her hands. "We need to find out more."

A sudden clatter from the corner of the room drew their attention. Basil, the sleek black cat with a penchant for appearing at the most opportune times, pawed at a loose floorboard near the archives' entrance.

"Basil, what have you found now?" Olivia asked, bemused by the cat's antics.

"Knowing him, it could be anything from a dead mouse to the crown jewels." Emily chuckled as they approached the feline investigator.

"Let's hope for something less... perishable," Olivia replied, crouching beside Basil as he continued to scratch insistently at the wooden panel.

"Good boy, Basil," Emily coaxed, her fingers finding the edge of the floorboard. With a gentle tug, it came away, revealing a dark hollow beneath.

"An actual hidden compartment in our own bakery," Olivia said, astonishment coloring her tone. "You'd think we would've noticed it by now."

"Maybe we weren't meant to find it until today," Emily suggested, peering into the shadows.

"Or maybe we've just been too busy baking pies and dodging ghosts," Olivia added with a wry grin.

"Both are equally plausible in Bayside Cove," Emily agreed, her smile reflecting the warmth of shared sisterhood even amid the strangeness enveloping them.

Together, they reached into the darkness, the air tingling with anticipation, ready to unearth whatever secrets lay waiting to be discovered.

Olivia's fingers grazed something cool and metallic nestled within the velvet darkness of the hidden compartment. A gasp escaped her as she drew out a locket, its surface etched with elaborate filigree that danced in the dim light like shadows playing at dusk. It felt heavier than it looked, as if weighed down by the history it carried.

"Would you look at this?" Olivia held it up, the locket swinging gently from its chain. "This isn't just any old trinket, Em."

Emily leaned closer, her eyes tracing the intricate patterns on the locket's face. "It's beautiful," she murmured, "and it looks ancient. This might be what we've been searching for."

"Or it might just be a very fancy way to hold pictures of your cats," Olivia quipped, though her heart wasn't really in the jest. The locket seemed to pulse with an energy that resonated against her palm—a silent echo of times long past.

"Let's see if there's a picture inside," Emily suggested, her voice laced with the thrill of discovery.

Olivia nodded and attempted to pry open the locket, but it resisted her efforts. "Seems like it doesn't want to give up its secrets so easily," she said, frustration creeping into her tone.

"Like everything else in Bayside Cove," Emily added, a wry smile touching her lips. "Secrets upon secrets."

"Maybe it's cursed," Olivia half-joked, but her laughter didn't quite mask the tremor of unease that had settled over her.

"Or maybe it's the key to breaking the curse." Emily's eyes gleamed with determination, her posture straightening with resolve. "We need to find out more."

Olivia met her sister's gaze, the weight of the locket in her hand anchoring her to the moment. "This could change everything," she agreed, a sense of urgency winding tight in her chest. The locket was more than just a piece of jewelry; it was a link to the town's veiled history, to the whispered curse that twined through the generations like a dark vine.

"Tomorrow," Olivia decided, "we'll start fresh. Research, questions, digging into every nook and cranny of history this town has to offer."

"Until then," Emily said, reaching out to touch the locket's cold surface, "we keep this close. This is our lead, Liv. Our very own mystery wrapped in silver—or is it gold?"

"Only time will tell," Olivia replied, a newfound excitement kindling within her. They stood together in silent camaraderie, two sisters bound by blood and the enigmatic allure of the locket between them, each keenly aware that the path ahead would be fraught with challenges.

And as the chapter closed, they remained there in the bakery, the musty scent of old books still clinging to the air, staring at the locket with piqued curiosity and a shared resolve to unravel the secrets it held and its connection to the tangled history of Bayside Cove.

Chapter 7

Kneading Out the Truth

The Winter Festival of Bayside Cove was in full swing, the air sweet with the scent of mulled wine and roasting chestnuts. Olivia Pierce navigated the bustling crowd with ease, her heart light despite the chill in the air. The town square was aglow with twinkling lights, casting a festive sheen over the snow-dusted stalls. But the merriment came to an abrupt halt as Margaret Foster stepped into Olivia's path, her eyes sharp as icicles.

"Olivia Pierce," Margaret declared, voice loud enough to slice through the jovial hum of the festival. "This town should know the truth! You're not just a baker; you're a murderer!"

A collective gasp rose from the onlookers as they turned their attention to the spectacle. Olivia felt her pulse hammering in her ears, her cheeks flaring with heat despite the cold. "Murderer? Margaret, what madness is this?"

"Your poisoned pie claimed the life of our dear Mayor Thompson!" Margaret thrust a gloved finger towards Olivia, accusation written in every line of her body.

"Poisoned?" Olivia sputtered, disbelief clouding her expressive eyes. "That's preposterous! My pies are made with love, not lethal substances."

But Margaret was relentless, her words spewing like venom. "And yet, the mayor dined at your bakery before his untimely demise. Coincidence? I think not!"

As murmurs rippled through the crowd, Detective James Holbrook watched from a short distance, his rugged features etched with conflict. He knew he had to step in but hesitated for a breath—one that drew out too long as he caught Olivia's bewildered gaze. His role as a detective warred with the burgeoning affection he harbored for the warm-hearted baker who now stood accused.

"Alright, that's enough," James finally said, voice calm but firm as he moved closer, parting the throng of onlookers with his broad shoulders. "Ms. Foster, Ms. Pierce, let's settle this matter without causing a scene."

Margaret folded her arms, her lips pursed in silent protest, while Olivia clutched her hands together, flour clinging stubbornly to her apron—a testament to her dedication and perhaps her innocence.

"Detective Holbrook," Olivia began, her tone pleading, "you don't believe these outrageous claims, do you?"

"Let's discuss this at the station," James replied, his blue eyes revealing a storm of emotions beneath his composed exterior. "I have to bring you in for questioning, Olivia. It's procedure."

Olivia's heart sank as she nodded, the warmth that usually encompassed her turning to frost. She knew James was right, but it didn't dull the sting of betrayal that pricked at her skin. The weight of suspicion was a heavy cloak that threatened to suffocate her spirit, and the strain between them—a bond still in its tender stages—grew taut like the string of a violin.

"Of course, I understand," she whispered, though her voice held a tremor that belied her composure.

As James escorted her away from the festival, past the gingerbread houses and candy cane stalls, Olivia couldn't help but feel as if she were leaving behind more than just her beloved bakery. She was stepping into the unknown, her fate intertwined with a man who was both her protector and, in this chilling moment, her captor.

The flickering fluorescent light above cast an unforgiving glow over the small interrogation room, where Olivia Pierce sat across from Detective James Holbrook. She held herself with a poise that seemed almost out of place amidst the stark surroundings, her hands folded neatly on the table. The air was thick with tension, as if it had materialized into a dense fog that threatened to choke the truth before it could be spoken.

"Detective," Olivia said, breaking the silence that loomed between them. Her voice was steady, though it carried the weight of the accusation that hung over her head like a dark cloud. "I assure you, I would never harm anyone, let alone with one of my pastries."

The Frosted Felony

James met her gaze, his expression unreadable. "Olivia, we found traces of poison in the pie you served at the festival. That's not something I can just overlook." His words were measured, cloaked in the professionalism his job demanded, but there was a hint of something else—a reluctance that tugged at the corners of his mouth.

"Of course not," she replied, her eyes unflinching. "But consider this: my bakery is my life. Why would I jeopardize everything I've built on a whim? Besides, I tasted that pie myself this morning."

"And yet, here we are," he pointed out, the hint of skepticism in his voice betraying the conflict inherent in his role as both investigator and admirer.

"Someone is trying to frame me," Olivia stated, her composure unshaken despite the gravity of her situation. "You've been to my bakery, James. You've seen the care I put into every batch of cookies, every loaf of bread. Does that strike you as the work of a murderer?"

He leaned back in his chair, arms crossing over his chest—an involuntary shield against the pull of her earnestness. "It's not about what I believe personally, Olivia. It's about evidence."

"Then let's talk evidence," she countered, leaning in, her gaze sharp and focused. "Let's talk about how I have no motive, no reason whatsoever to hurt the mayor. Let's talk about the countless customers who can vouch for my character."

"Olivia," James began, but she cut him off with a gentle raise of her hand, an oddly charming gesture in such dire circumstances.

"Or perhaps we should discuss the possibility that someone with access to my kitchen tampered with the pie after I finished baking it." Her words hung in the air, a challenge wrapped in a question, her eyes searching his for any sign of doubt.

James sighed, the sound heavy with the burden of his duty. "We will investigate all angles, Olivia. That's a promise." There was warmth there, a softening around his eyes that betrayed his concern for her beyond the scope of his professional obligations.

For a moment, they simply looked at each other, the unspoken understanding between them as palpable as the chill that seeped in from outside the interrogation room walls. Then Olivia straightened, her resolve as firm as the crust on her famous apple pies.

"Good," she said, a smile flirting at the edges of her lips despite the seriousness of her predicament. "Because clearing my name is just the appetizer. Finding the real culprit—that'll be the main course."

The warm scent of cinnamon and freshly baked bread wafted through Olivia's bakery, a stark contrast to the cold that gripped Bayside Cove outside. Sam Turner, with his tousled sandy hair and an apron dusted with flour, sat huddled with Emily Pierce in a cozy corner. The tables around them were laden with ledgers, receipts, and printouts, the evidence of their diligent search into Margaret Foster's murky financial history.

"Look at this," Sam said, tapping on a column of numbers with a vigor that sent his freckles dancing. "Margaret's been making regular payments to some offshore account. It's like she's funding a small country or a secret pie-tasting society."

Emily leaned in, her striking green eyes scanning the figures with laser focus. "Or hush money," she countered, her tone carrying the weight of experience from beyond the cove. "We need to trace where this money is going—if it ties back to Victor Wellington, we could have our missing link."

Sam nodded, but his optimism was as hard to dampen as a soufflé in a well-timed oven. "Exactly! We're like detectives with spatulas—serving justice one crumb trail at a time."

Their camaraderie was palpable, each feeding off the other's energy. Sam's quick wit and Emily's measured approach interlacing like the lattice atop one of Olivia's famous pies.

But as the hours ticked by, the trail they had followed turned to crumbs leading nowhere. They hit a dead end, and frustration simmered between them like a pot left too long on the stove.

"Maybe we're kneading this dough too much," Sam suggested, trying to lighten the mood with his culinary puns. "Could be we should let it proof for a bit, let the answers rise on their own."

"Or maybe," Emily replied, her brows knitting together, "we're not looking in the right places. We can't afford to wait for things to 'rise.' Time isn't a luxury Olivia has right now."

"Right, but running around like chickens with our heads cut off won't help either." Sam's cheeky smile waned a touch, his blue eyes reflecting concern. "We need a plan, Em."

"Then let's think outside the box," Emily urged, her voice firm yet not unkind. "If the direct trail has gone cold, we need to circle around, look at connections we might have missed."

"Like the kind of connections you'd find hidden in a secret recipe?" Sam quipped, though the edge of worry in his voice betrayed his usual jovial tone.

"Exactly," Emily affirmed, her posture relaxing as she recognized Sam's attempt to keep spirits high. "Let's revisit what we know, work our way backward, and see if something new pops up."

"Backward it is," Sam agreed, reaching for another stack of papers. "I just hope this recipe yields more than just a batch of unanswered questions."

As they settled back into their investigation, the warmth of the bakery enveloped them, a gentle reminder of the friend they were fighting to protect. Their methods might differ, but their goal was the same: to clear Olivia's name and to serve up justice, no matter how elusive the ingredients might seem.

The air in the interrogation room was thick with tension, the only sound the faint hum of a flickering fluorescent light. Detective Holbrook leaned forward, his elbows resting on the cold metal table that separated him from Olivia. His eyes, usually a comforting shade of chestnut, now held a stormy seriousness that belied his concern.

"Olivia," he began, his voice a blend of duty and regret, "I need to ask about your relationship with the mayor. Did you have any disagreements, any reason that might give you a motive?"

Olivia's hands clenched beneath the table, her knuckles white. "No, detective," she replied, a slight quiver betraying her calm exterior. "The mayor was more than just a patron; he was a friend. He believed in my bakery, in me. I would never harm him."

"Can you think of anyone who would want to?" Holbrook asked, searching her face for any hint of falsehood.

"Absolutely not," Olivia said, shaking her head vehemently, her expressive eyes wide with sincerity. "He was loved by everyone. This whole thing is a nightmare."

"Okay, Olivia." Holbrook sighed, running a hand through his hair, his professional façade cracking just enough to reveal a glimpse of empathy. "I believe you, but we have to cover all our bases."

"Of course," she nodded, her posture stiff yet resolved. She understood the necessity, even as it pained her.

Meanwhile, across town in the cozy confines of Olivia's bakery, Sam and Emily hunched over a labyrinth of financial documents spread out like a treasure map on the sturdy oak table. Sam's sandy hair fell into his eyes as he leaned closer, his finger tracing a line of numbers that seemed to jump off the page.

"Emily, look at this," Sam exclaimed, his voice barely above a whisper but laden with discovery. "Margaret's name here, tied to a series of payments to Victor Wellington. That can't be a coincidence."

Emily peered over, her green eyes narrowing as she absorbed the information. "You're right," she breathed out, the corners of her mouth lifting in cautious excitement. "This... this could be the breakthrough we've been looking for!"

"Exactly!" Sam's habitual culinary metaphors bubbled to the surface as his enthusiasm grew. "We've found the missing ingredient in this half-baked mystery."

"Half-baked indeed," Emily chuckled despite the gravity of their find. Her tone shifted to one of resolve. "Now we just need to figure out what they were cooking up together."

"Looks like Margaret's pie isn't the only thing with a secret recipe," Sam quipped, though the implication of deceit left a bitter taste.

"Let's dig deeper," Emily said, the warmth of her determination matching the oven's glow from the kitchen. "We owe it to Olivia to uncover the full story."

Sam nodded, his apprehension replaced by the thrill of the chase. "To the bottom of the mixing bowl, then."

As they delved back into the sea of numbers and names, a sense of purpose united them. The scent of freshly baked bread wafted through the air, reminding them of the innocence they sought to defend and the justice they were determined to serve. Together, they were one step closer to unraveling the truth behind the mayor's untimely demise.

The room felt colder than the festival outside, the tension between Detective Holbrook and Olivia Pierce thick enough to rival the winter's frost. She sat across from him, her hands clasped tightly under the table, every muscle taut with frustration.

The Frosted Felony

"Olivia," James started, his voice carrying a blend of professional detachment and underlying concern, "where were you on the night of the mayor's murder?"

She met his gaze steadily, though inside her thoughts churned like the batter for her infamous chocolate torte. "I was at home, James. Alone," she said, each word deliberate, hoping to convey the truth she felt so deeply.

"No one who can verify that?" he pressed, not unkindly.

Her lips thinned. "No, I'm afraid not. You know how it is after a long day of baking—the quiet is a welcome reprieve."

He nodded, scribbling a note. Olivia's mind raced. No alibi. Just her word against a town swirling with rumors and fear. 'I have to find something, anything, to clear my name,' she thought, her determination rising like dough in a warm kitchen.

The interrogation paused when an officer handed James a slip of paper. He glanced at it and then slid it across the table to Olivia. "This just came for you."

Curious, she unfolded the paper with trembling fingers. The message, written in jagged, anonymous print, cut through her like a knife through chilled butter: "Stop digging into the past or you'll be buried alongside your secrets."

A gasp escaped her as she dropped the note, her eyes wide with shock. The warmth that usually radiated from her seemed to vanish, replaced by a cold current of fear. The scent of antiseptic in the room became overpowering, the walls inching closer.

"Who sent this?" she whispered, her voice a brittle shell of its usual rich timbre.

"We don't know yet," James replied, his blue eyes sharpening with concern. "But we'll find out."

Swallowing her fear, Olivia straightened her posture. Whoever wanted to scare her was sorely mistaken. With a resolute spark igniting in her expressive eyes, she mentally rolled up her sleeves. Threats be damned; she'd peel back the layers of this mystery until the truth was laid bare, as surely as the center of a well-baked pie.

"Good luck with that," she said, her voice steady despite the tremor she felt. "Because I'm not stopping until I clear my name. And when I do, whoever wrote this will be the one needing to watch their back."

James studied her for a moment, the unspoken promise in his gaze acknowledging the courage behind her words. Outside, the festival carried on, oblivious to the drama unfolding within the stark confines of the police station. But inside, Olivia Pierce had just lit the fuse on a determination that would either lead to her exoneration or ignite an even deeper peril.

The silence in the interrogation room stretched out, an invisible thread pulling taut between Olivia and Detective Holbrook. Olivia's fingers drummed a nervous rhythm on the cold metal table, her thoughts racing like wild horses. She could feel James's gaze upon her, heavy with something more than just professional concern.

"Olivia," James began, his voice softening as he leaned forward, elbows resting on the table before him. "I know this is hard, and it might not mean much, but I believe you didn't do this."

His words hung in the air, sincere and unexpectedly gentle. Olivia's heart skipped, her breath catching in her throat. His eyes, usually so piercing, now held a warmth that made her own defenses waver for a moment.

"Thank you," she managed to say, the tremble in her voice betraying her steel facade. "But it seems the whole town has already pronounced me guilty."

"Let them talk," James said, his hand tentatively reaching out, then retreating. "They don't know you like I've come to. We'll sort through the facts and clear your name. I promise."

Their eyes locked, and Olivia recognized the depths of his conviction. It was a lifeline thrown into the choppy seas of her fear, and she clung to it with newfound resolve.

"Okay," she whispered, allowing herself the comfort of his assurance. "Okay."

"Alright, let's get you out of here," James said, standing up. He moved to the door, holding it open for her as if she were leaving a bakery instead of a bleak interrogation room.

Stepping out into the corridor, Olivia felt the weight of suspicion lift ever so slightly from her shoulders. As they walked toward the exit, murmurs and sideways glances from the other officers trailed after them like shadows at dusk.

"James," Olivia paused, her voice steady despite the storm inside her. "Whoever is behind this... they won't stop until they've destroyed everything I've built."

"Then we won't stop until we find them," James replied, the determination in his tone matching her own.

The station doors closed behind them with a definitive click, sealing away the sterile scent and harsh lighting. Olivia breathed in the crisp evening air, its chill whispering promises of secrets yet untold.

As she watched James retreat back into the lion's den of law and order, a shiver ran down her spine that wasn't just from the cold. Her bakery, once a haven of sweet scents and happier times, now loomed in her mind, a battleground where the next phase of her fight would begin.

"Be careful, Olivia Pierce," she muttered to herself, her steps quickening towards home. "This is far from over."

And indeed, as the moon climbed higher, casting ghostly shadows across Bayside Cove, Olivia knew that somewhere out there, a piece of the puzzle was waiting to be found. Or perhaps, more chillingly, it was waiting to find her.

Chapter 8

A Sprinkle of Romance

Olivia leaned back against the cushioned chair, her gaze fixed on James as he sifted through the papers strewn across the table. They had claimed a quiet corner in Sweet Sensations, the bakery she nurtured into a local haven. The mid-morning sun streamed through the lace curtains, casting dappled light on their work.

"Looks like we've got our work cut out for us," James said, his voice a low murmur that blended with the soft hum of conversation around them.

"Indeed," Olivia replied, her attention momentarily drawn away by the delicate chime of the door as another customer entered. "But I have a hunch about the Henderson angle."

The air was rich with the aroma of freshly brewed coffee, a scent that felt both comforting and invigorating. It mingled with the sweet fragrance of cinnamon and vanilla wafting from the kitchen, where a batch of Olivia's favorite pastries, the apple-cranberry tarts, were cooling on the rack. She could almost taste the tangy fruit filling complemented by the buttery flakiness of the pastry, a recipe that had taken her months to perfect.

"Your hunches tend to pan out," James acknowledged with a nod, offering a smile that softened the analytical sharpness of his features.

"It's all in the details," Olivia said, a playful glint in her eye. She loved the challenge of piecing together clues, much like she enjoyed creating complex flavors in her baking. "Speaking of which, what do you make of this?" She slid a photograph across the table towards him.

The Frosted Felony

James studied the image, his brow furrowing slightly before he set it down. "Interesting," he murmured, reaching for his coffee cup. "This might just be the piece we're missing."

The cozy ambiance of the bakery enveloped them, the gentle clinking of cups and the occasional whirr of the espresso machine providing a soothing backdrop. Olivia always found solace in the rhythm of her establishment; it was a place where worries seemed to melt away like sugar in hot tea.

"By the way," Olivia ventured, seizing an opportune lull in their discussion, "have you tried the tarts yet? They're today's special."

"Can't say I have," James admitted, looking intrigued. "But I'm willing to be persuaded."

"Consider this a personal recommendation then," Olivia said, signaling one of her staff to bring over a plate of the tarts. As she watched James savor the first bite, his eyes closing briefly in appreciation, a tiny flutter of satisfaction tickled her chest. Sharing her culinary creations was akin to sharing a piece of her heart—a heart that carefully measured whom to trust, but was generous nonetheless.

Olivia felt the warmth of James' presence as much as she did the heat emanating from her freshly brewed coffee. She reached across the table, ostensibly for her cup, but as her fingers grazed his hand, she allowed herself the luxury of a fleeting touch. It was an innocent brush, yet it sent a ripple of anticipation shivering through her.

"Sorry," she murmured with a smile that didn't quite reach her eyes, betraying her nervousness.

"Nothing to apologize for," James replied, his voice a low hum that resonated within her. There was a softness in his eyes that she hadn't noticed before, and it made him seem less like the enigmatic detective and more like... someone she could really get to know.

The bakery's cozy interior, with its exposed brick walls adorned with local artwork and shelves lined with homemade preserves and jams, seemed to shrink around them, creating an intimate sphere where confidences were easily traded over the remnants of pastry flakes.

"Actually, Olivia," James said, leaning back in his chair and fixing her with a thoughtful gaze, "this place reminds me of a case I once worked on back in the city."

"Really?" Olivia leaned forward, intrigued. Her interest wasn't solely professional; she found herself wanting to peel back the layers of this man who had breezed into her quiet life like a gust of autumn wind, unpredictable and refreshing.

"Yep," he continued, a shadow flickering across his face as he recalled the memory. "It was a bakery, not unlike Sweet Sensations. Family-owned for generations. They'd been receiving threats, and I was assigned to find out who was behind it."

"And did you?" she asked, savoring the richness of the coffee as it complemented the sweetness of her favorite pastry.

"I did." James nodded, his gaze momentarily distant as if he were seeing the events play out before him. "But it took its toll. The family was torn apart by suspicion and fear. It was a stark reminder that even the warmest places can harbor dark secrets."

Olivia watched him, noticing the subtle crease between his brows, a testament to the burden he carried from his past experiences. The detective had layers, and each one seemed to draw her in further.

"Sounds like it was tough," she said softly, her own heart aching for the pain hidden behind his stoic facade.

"It was," he admitted. "But it also taught me a lot. About resilience. About hope."

Their eyes locked, and in that moment, Olivia understood him a little better. James wasn't just a detective; he was someone who fought against shadows, hoping to bring light. And perhaps that's what drew her to him—the promise of warmth amidst the chill of unsolved mysteries.

"Thank you for sharing that with me, James," she said sincerely, her hand inching closer to his across the tablecloth.

"Thank you for listening," he replied with a small, genuine smile that reached his eyes, making them crinkle at the corners.

In the comforting cocoon of her bakery, surrounded by the scent of cinnamon and sugar, Olivia felt a connection to James that went beyond their shared goal of solving the case. It was as though their souls recognized something kindred in each other, and she found herself quietly hopeful about what might blossom from this unexpected partnership.

James leaned back in his chair, the contented murmur of customers blending with the gentle clinking of cups and saucers. He looked around Sweet Sensations, taking in the quaint charm of the bakery that so perfectly encapsulated the essence of Bayside Cove.

The Frosted Felony

"Something about this place," James began, his gaze returning to Olivia's, "it's like stepping into another world—a slower, more deliberate pace of life. I guess that's why I chose to come here."

"From the hustle of the city to the tranquility of Bayside Cove," Olivia said with a smile, tucking a stray lock of hair behind her ear. "Quite the change."

"Indeed," he replied, the corners of his mouth twitching upward. "The roar of sirens every hour, the relentless chase—it takes its toll. Here, I thought I could find some peace... Maybe even a fresh start."

"Sounds idyllic," she mused, her fingers tracing the rim of her coffee cup. "I hope it's everything you wanted."

"It's getting there," he said, his eyes holding a hint of the warmth that had been absent when they first met. "Especially now with—"

His words cut off as the sharp trill of his cell phone sliced through the cozy atmosphere, the ringtone startling a nearby patron into spilling a bit of tea. With an apologetic glance at Olivia, James reached into his coat pocket and answered the call.

"Detective Holbrook speaking," he said, his voice shifting back into professional mode. Olivia watched him carefully, noting the subtle shift in his demeanor as he listened to the caller.

"I see," he murmured after a moment. There was a significant pause, and then, "Yes, I'll be right there."

He snapped the phone shut and stood abruptly, his chair scraping against the wood floor. "I'm sorry, I have to go. New evidence has come to light."

"Is everything okay?" Olivia asked, concern knitting her brow as she rose to her feet.

"Hopefully, it's a breakthrough," James said, reaching for his coat with a sense of urgency that seemed out of place amidst the lingering sweetness of pastries. "Thank you for the coffee—and the company."

"Of course," she replied, trying to quell the sudden unease that settled in the pit of her stomach. "Good luck."

"Thanks, Olivia," he said, offering her one last brief, yet intense look before heading towards the door, his detective's stride purposeful as he disappeared into the crisp air outside.

Olivia stood there for a moment, watching the door swing gently closed, the bell above jingling softly. The bakery suddenly felt much too large, and the whispers of steam rising from her forgotten cup of coffee did little to warm the sudden chill of his absence.

Olivia sank back into her chair, the cushion accepting her weight as if nothing had changed. But the space James had occupied was now just an echo of his presence. She wrapped her hands around her coffee cup, seeking comfort in its familiar warmth, but even that couldn't dispel the twist of disappointment in her chest.

"Men," she muttered to herself, a wry smile tugging at her lips despite the heaviness settling over her. "They always leave at the most inconvenient times."

"Especially when they're dashing detectives with important cases," a voice chimed in, light and teasing.

Olivia glanced up to see her sister, Emily, sliding into the seat James had vacated. Emily's green eyes sparkled with knowing amusement as she reached across the table, plucking a stray flake of pastry from Olivia's plate and popping it into her mouth.

"Detectives or not, I hate being left behind," Olivia confessed, fiddling with the edge of the napkin. Her gaze lingered on the door, half-expecting James to reappear.

"Let me guess, he got a call about the case?" Emily asked, leaning back in her chair, her posture relaxed but her attention entirely on Olivia.

"Exactly." Olivia sighed, then allowed herself a small, rueful laugh. "You'd think I'd be used to sudden departures, growing up with you."

"Ouch, sis," Emily said, feigning a wounded heart. "But since I'm here, spill. What's this I hear about you and tall, dark, and mysterious?"

A blush crept over Olivia's cheeks, the heat competing with the steam still drifting lazily from her mug. "It's... complicated," she admitted, tracing the rim of her cup. "I like him, Em. More than I expected to."

"Complicated is just another word for interesting," Emily pointed out with a smirk. "So, are you worried about getting your heart broken by Detective Heartthrob?"

"Maybe." Olivia's expression grew serious, her usual confidence wobbling like a poorly set jelly. "What if I let my guard down and he leaves? Like everyone else seems to."

"Olivia Pierce, queen of confections and conqueror of hearts," Emily declared, reaching out to lay a reassuring hand over Olivia's.

"You've always been braver than you give yourself credit for. Besides, what's life without a little risk?"

"Full of intact hearts?" Olivia offered weakly, earning a chuckle from Emily.

"Also full of missed chances," Emily countered gently. "Look, we Pierces are made of sterner stuff. You can handle a detective with baggage."

"Baggage I can manage," Olivia mused. "It's the unknown that scares me."

"Isn't that the best part?" Emily's eyes danced with mischief. "The mystery, the discovery—the thrill of finding out whether he takes his eggs scrambled or poached."

"Scrambled," Olivia replied automatically, before realizing Emily's ploy. "Oh, you're good."

"Years of practice," Emily said with a grin. "Now come on, tell me everything. And spare no detail—especially not the swoon-worthy ones."

As Olivia launched into the tale of her and James's encounters, the aroma of coffee and the cozy ambiance of the bakery wrapped around them like a warm embrace. With each word, she felt the weight of uncertainty lift bit by bit, replaced by the comforting presence of family and the gentle pull of hope—perhaps for something more than just pastries and coffee shared at a quaint table in Sweet Sensations.

Emily took a sip of her herbal tea, the steam curling around her face like a delicate veil. She set the cup down with a thoughtful clink against the saucer, her gaze meeting Olivia's across the table.

"James isn't the first to upend my expectations, you know," Emily began, tucking a loose strand of auburn hair behind her ear. "There was a time when I thought love was only found in grand gestures and epic moments."

Olivia leaned forward, her elbows resting on the table, her curiosity piqued by this rare glimpse into Emily's guarded heart. The warm glow from the overhead lights cast a soft halo around them, creating an intimate space amidst the bustle of the bakery.

"Turns out, it's the small things that matter. Like someone remembering how you take your coffee, or just being there when you've had one of those days." Emily's smile was tinged with nostalgia, and perhaps a hint of regret.

"Sounds... nice," Olivia murmured, her mind drifting to the way James had noticed her penchant for cinnamon in her latte without her having to say a word.

"It is. But it's also terrifying," Emily admitted, locking eyes with Olivia. "Because when you start caring about those little things, it means you're all in. And sometimes, life has other plans."

"Is that why you left?" Olivia asked gently, reaching for her own cup but finding it cold.

"Partly," Emily conceded, her green eyes reflecting a depth of emotion she rarely showed. "I loved someone once, fiercely. But we wanted different things—I craved adventure, he sought stability. In the end, our hearts couldn't build a bridge between those two worlds."

A bell over the door jingled as a couple entered the bakery, seeking refuge from the coastal chill. They laughed, shaking off the crisp autumn air, wrapping themselves in the comforting scent of baked goods and the promise of caffeine.

"Sometimes I wonder if I made the right choice," Emily continued, her voice barely above a whisper. "But then I see you here, building something beautiful, and I'm reminded that there are many ways to find happiness."

"Even with someone like James?" Olivia asked, hope lacing her words.

"Especially with someone like James." Emily reached across the table, squeezing Olivia's hand. "He sees you, Liv. Really sees you. And that kind of connection? It's worth exploring."

"Easy for you to say," Olivia said with a half-hearted laugh. "You're the brave one."

"Bravery isn't the absence of fear," Emily replied, a mischievous spark lighting up her eyes. "It's deciding something else is more important. Besides, since when do Pierces back down from a challenge?"

"Since never," Olivia answered, a smile breaking through her uncertainty. Emily's confidence was infectious, and in that moment, Olivia felt a surge of courage.

"Exactly," Emily said with a nod. "So, what are you going to do about Detective Charming and his scrambled eggs?"

Olivia glanced at the empty seat across from her, where James had sat just moments ago, and felt a warmth spread through her chest—a mixture of anticipation and resolve.

The Frosted Felony

"I'm going to take a chance," she declared, her determination solidifying with every word. "I'm going to trust my heart."

"And your head?" Emily teased, raising an eyebrow.

"Both," Olivia replied, her voice steady. "Together, they make a pretty good team."

"Then go get him, sister," Emily said, pride evident in her tone. "And remember, I've got your back, no matter what."

"Thanks, Em," Olivia said, standing up with newfound purpose. "I think I'm going to need it."

As Olivia walked away from the table, a trail of laughter followed her, the bond of sisterhood a reassuring anchor in the unpredictable waters of romance.

Olivia's fingertips traced the delicate contours of the locket that hung from her neck, a habit she'd formed whenever thoughts clouded her mind. The bakery was quiet in the hour before closing, the soft hum of the refrigerators like a lullaby for the day's end. As she wiped down the counter, her movements were automatic, freeing her mind to wander through the maze of emotions left in James's wake.

The locket, a vintage piece that complemented her simple yet elegant style, had been a gift from her grandmother—an heirloom passed down with whispers of mystery and old family legends. Olivia had always found comfort in its weight against her chest, a tangible connection to her lineage. But tonight, the metal felt cooler, almost urging her to look closer.

"Olivia?" called out Emily, but her voice seemed distant, muffled by the cacophony of Olivia's racing heart. She didn't respond, captivated by the sudden discovery that a part of the locket seemed movable, a section near the hinge that had never budged before.

With gentle pressure, Olivia slid the piece, and a previously unseen compartment revealed itself, holding a thin strip of parchment, aged and delicate. Her breath hitched in her throat as she carefully extracted the paper with the precision that came from years of handling fragile pastry decorations.

The writing on it was unlike anything she had seen: looping characters interspersed with symbols that tugged at her memory, resonating with a depth that defied explanation. It was ancient script, she was sure of it, but from what language or time, she couldn't even begin to guess.

"Em, look at this," Olivia finally managed, her voice a mix of wonder and disbelief. Emily leaned over, her eyes widening as she took in the sight of the cryptic message.

"Is that... is that from grandma's locket?" Emily asked, her curiosity piqued as she peered closer.

"Apparently, there's more to this heirloom than sentimental value," Olivia replied, the warmth of mystery igniting a spark in her gaze.

"Can you read it?" Emily questioned, her tone laced with the excitement of shared secrets between sisters.

"Not even a word," Olivia admitted, a playful frown knitting her brows. "But I bet it's something grand. A treasure map, maybe, or a secret recipe for the world's best chocolate cake."

"Or maybe it's just grandma's grocery list in really fancy lettering," Emily quipped, eliciting a chuckle from Olivia.

"Either way," Olivia said, determination lacing her words, "I need to find out what it says."

Her sister nodded in agreement, the thrill of adventure evident in her eyes. "We'll figure it out. And hey, if it's a centuries-old shopping list, we can at least say our family had taste."

"Quite literally," Olivia added, the corners of her lips twitching into a smile.

As they stood there, surrounded by the familiar scents of vanilla and sugar, the day's fatigue gave way to an electric anticipation. The locket's message, whatever it held, promised a journey neither of them expected, but one Olivia knew they were meant to take.

The locket lay open in Olivia's palm, its delicate chain cascading over her fingers like a stream of liquid silver. The symbols etched into the metal were as mysterious as they were alluring, whispering secrets from the past that only the initiated could understand. She was no linguist of ancient scripts, but the weight of the message's significance pressed upon her with an undeniable gravity.

"Olivia, are you alright? You look like you've seen a ghost," Emily observed, her voice pulling Olivia back from the precipice of her thoughts.

"Sorry, I just..." Olivia hesitated, the gears in her mind turning. James. She needed to tell James. His detective's mind and his connections could unearth the meaning hidden within the locket's cryptic markings. "I

The Frosted Felony

think this might be important—more than just a family heirloom. It could be a clue, something significant to the case."

"James," Emily said, her tone shifting to one of understanding. "You're thinking of taking this to him?"

"Exactly." Olivia's heart skipped a beat at the mention of his name. She felt a connection to James that transcended the professional; it was as though their paths had intertwined for a reason beyond solving cases and chasing down leads.

"Then you should go," Emily encouraged, her eyes reflecting the resolve that Olivia felt burgeoning within her own chest. "Who knows what doors this could open?"

"You're right." Olivia took a deep breath, her decision made. She carefully closed the locket, feeling the cool metal against her skin. Standing up, she brushed off her apron, sending a puff of flour into the air like a soft cloud. "I'll go first thing in the morning."

"Good," Emily smiled, reaching out to give Olivia's hand a reassuring squeeze. "And Olivia, whatever happens, remember this is your journey too. Trust yourself as much as you trust that detective's instincts."

"Thanks, Em." Olivia returned the smile, warmth spreading through her at her sister's words. Her gaze drifted back to the locket, which now seemed less like a simple piece of jewelry and more like a key—one that could unlock the answers to questions she hadn't even thought to ask.

With purpose fueling her steps, Olivia stored the locket in her pocket, already envisioning the conversation with James. The message would be a new thread in the tapestry of their growing partnership, one that promised to draw them closer in the shared quest for truth.

As she turned off the lights of Sweet Sensations, the comforting scent of baked goods lingered in the air, a silent witness to the chapter that had just closed. And with the promise of dawn came the anticipation of what the following day would bring—a day that would see Olivia and James delving deeper not only into the mystery at hand but also into the connection that was steadily forming between them.

Olivia had always been an early riser, but the morning after her conversation with Emily found her especially eager to greet the dawn. The first light of day spilled through the windows of Sweet Sensations, casting a warm, golden hue over the bakery's familiar

Chapter 7

Kneading Out the Truth

The Winter Festival of Bayside Cove was in full swing, the air sweet with the scent of mulled wine and roasting chestnuts. Olivia Pierce navigated the bustling crowd with ease, her heart light despite the chill in the air. The town square was aglow with twinkling lights, casting a festive sheen over the snow-dusted stalls. But the merriment came to an abrupt halt as Margaret Foster stepped into Olivia's path, her eyes sharp as icicles.

"Olivia Pierce," Margaret declared, voice loud enough to slice through the jovial hum of the festival. "This town should know the truth! You're not just a baker; you're a murderer!"

A collective gasp rose from the onlookers as they turned their attention to the spectacle. Olivia felt her pulse hammering in her ears, her cheeks flaring with heat despite the cold. "Murderer? Margaret, what madness is this?"

"Your poisoned pie claimed the life of our dear Mayor Thompson!" Margaret thrust a gloved finger towards Olivia, accusation written in every line of her body.

"Poisoned?" Olivia sputtered, disbelief clouding her expressive eyes. "That's preposterous! My pies are made with love, not lethal substances."

But Margaret was relentless, her words spewing like venom. "And yet, the mayor dined at your bakery before his untimely demise. Coincidence? I think not!"

As murmurs rippled through the crowd, Detective James Holbrook watched from a short distance, his rugged features etched with conflict. He knew he had to step in but hesitated for a breath—one that drew out too long as he caught Olivia's bewildered gaze. His role as a detective warred with the burgeoning affection he harbored for the warm-hearted baker who now stood accused.

"Alright, that's enough," James finally said, voice calm but firm as he moved closer, parting the throng of onlookers with his broad shoulders. "Ms. Foster, Ms. Pierce, let's settle this matter without causing a scene."

Margaret folded her arms, her lips pursed in silent protest, while Olivia clutched her hands together, flour clinging stubbornly to her apron—a testament to her dedication and perhaps her innocence.

"Detective Holbrook," Olivia began, her tone pleading, "you don't believe these outrageous claims, do you?"

"Let's discuss this at the station," James replied, his blue eyes revealing a storm of emotions beneath his composed exterior. "I have to bring you in for questioning, Olivia. It's procedure."

Olivia's heart sank as she nodded, the warmth that usually encompassed her turning to frost. She knew James was right, but it didn't dull the sting of betrayal that pricked at her skin. The weight of suspicion was a heavy cloak that threatened to suffocate her spirit, and the strain between them—a bond still in its tender stages—grew taut like the string of a violin.

"Of course, I understand," she whispered, though her voice held a tremor that belied her composure.

As James escorted her away from the festival, past the gingerbread houses and candy cane stalls, Olivia couldn't help but feel as if she were leaving behind more than just her beloved bakery. She was stepping into the unknown, her fate intertwined with a man who was both her protector and, in this chilling moment, her captor.

The flickering fluorescent light above cast an unforgiving glow over the small interrogation room, where Olivia Pierce sat across from Detective James Holbrook. She held herself with a poise that seemed almost out of place amidst the stark surroundings, her hands folded neatly on the table. The air was thick with tension, as if it had materialized into a dense fog that threatened to choke the truth before it could be spoken.

"Detective," Olivia said, breaking the silence that loomed between them. Her voice was steady, though it carried the weight of the accusation that hung over her head like a dark cloud. "I assure you, I would never harm anyone, let alone with one of my pastries."

James met her gaze, his expression unreadable. "Olivia, we found traces of poison in the pie you served at the festival. That's not something

I can just overlook." His words were measured, cloaked in the professionalism his job demanded, but there was a hint of something else—a reluctance that tugged at the corners of his mouth.

"Of course not," she replied, her eyes unflinching. "But consider this: my bakery is my life. Why would I jeopardize everything I've built on a whim? Besides, I tasted that pie myself this morning."

"And yet, here we are," he pointed out, the hint of skepticism in his voice betraying the conflict inherent in his role as both investigator and admirer.

"Someone is trying to frame me," Olivia stated, her composure unshaken despite the gravity of her situation. "You've been to my bakery, James. You've seen the care I put into every batch of cookies, every loaf of bread. Does that strike you as the work of a murderer?"

He leaned back in his chair, arms crossing over his chest—an involuntary shield against the pull of her earnestness. "It's not about what I believe personally, Olivia. It's about evidence."

"Then let's talk evidence," she countered, leaning in, her gaze sharp and focused. "Let's talk about how I have no motive, no reason whatsoever to hurt the mayor. Let's talk about the countless customers who can vouch for my character."

"Olivia," James began, but she cut him off with a gentle raise of her hand, an oddly charming gesture in such dire circumstances.

"Or perhaps we should discuss the possibility that someone with access to my kitchen tampered with the pie after I finished baking it." Her words hung in the air, a challenge wrapped in a question, her eyes searching his for any sign of doubt.

James sighed, the sound heavy with the burden of his duty. "We will investigate all angles, Olivia. That's a promise." There was warmth there, a softening around his eyes that betrayed his concern for her beyond the scope of his professional obligations.

For a moment, they simply looked at each other, the unspoken understanding between them as palpable as the chill that seeped in from outside the interrogation room walls. Then Olivia straightened, her resolve as firm as the crust on her famous apple pies.

"Good," she said, a smile flirting at the edges of her lips despite the seriousness of her predicament. "Because clearing my name is just the appetizer. Finding the real culprit—that'll be the main course."

The Frosted Felony

The warm scent of cinnamon and freshly baked bread wafted through Olivia's bakery, a stark contrast to the cold that gripped Bayside Cove outside. Sam Turner, with his tousled sandy hair and an apron dusted with flour, sat huddled with Emily Pierce in a cozy corner. The tables around them were laden with ledgers, receipts, and printouts, the evidence of their diligent search into Margaret Foster's murky financial history.

"Look at this," Sam said, tapping on a column of numbers with a vigor that sent his freckles dancing. "Margaret's been making regular payments to some offshore account. It's like she's funding a small country or a secret pie-tasting society."

Emily leaned in, her striking green eyes scanning the figures with laser focus. "Or hush money," she countered, her tone carrying the weight of experience from beyond the cove. "We need to trace where this money is going—if it ties back to Victor Wellington, we could have our missing link."

Sam nodded, but his optimism was as hard to dampen as a soufflé in a well-timed oven. "Exactly! We're like detectives with spatulas—serving justice one crumb trail at a time."

Their camaraderie was palpable, each feeding off the other's energy. Sam's quick wit and Emily's measured approach interlacing like the lattice atop one of Olivia's famous pies.

But as the hours ticked by, the trail they had followed turned to crumbs leading nowhere. They hit a dead end, and frustration simmered between them like a pot left too long on the stove.

"Maybe we're kneading this dough too much," Sam suggested, trying to lighten the mood with his culinary puns. "Could be we should let it proof for a bit, let the answers rise on their own."

"Or maybe," Emily replied, her brows knitting together, "we're not looking in the right places. We can't afford to wait for things to 'rise.' Time isn't a luxury Olivia has right now."

"Right, but running around like chickens with our heads cut off won't help either." Sam's cheeky smile waned a touch, his blue eyes reflecting concern. "We need a plan, Em."

"Then let's think outside the box," Emily urged, her voice firm yet not unkind. "If the direct trail has gone cold, we need to circle around, look at connections we might have missed."

"Like the kind of connections you'd find hidden in a secret recipe?" Sam quipped, though the edge of worry in his voice betrayed his usual jovial tone.

"Exactly," Emily affirmed, her posture relaxing as she recognized Sam's attempt to keep spirits high. "Let's revisit what we know, work our way backward, and see if something new pops up."

"Backward it is," Sam agreed, reaching for another stack of papers. "I just hope this recipe yields more than just a batch of unanswered questions."

As they settled back into their investigation, the warmth of the bakery enveloped them, a gentle reminder of the friend they were fighting to protect. Their methods might differ, but their goal was the same: to clear Olivia's name and to serve up justice, no matter how elusive the ingredients might seem.

The air in the interrogation room was thick with tension, the only sound the faint hum of a flickering fluorescent light. Detective Holbrook leaned forward, his elbows resting on the cold metal table that separated him from Olivia. His eyes, usually a comforting shade of chestnut, now held a stormy seriousness that belied his concern.

"Olivia," he began, his voice a blend of duty and regret, "I need to ask about your relationship with the mayor. Did you have any disagreements, any reason that might give you a motive?"

Olivia's hands clenched beneath the table, her knuckles white. "No, detective," she replied, a slight quiver betraying her calm exterior. "The mayor was more than just a patron; he was a friend. He believed in my bakery, in me. I would never harm him."

"Can you think of anyone who would want to?" Holbrook asked, searching her face for any hint of falsehood.

"Absolutely not," Olivia said, shaking her head vehemently, her expressive eyes wide with sincerity. "He was loved by everyone. This whole thing is a nightmare."

"Okay, Olivia." Holbrook sighed, running a hand through his hair, his professional façade cracking just enough to reveal a glimpse of empathy. "I believe you, but we have to cover all our bases."

"Of course," she nodded, her posture stiff yet resolved. She understood the necessity, even as it pained her.

Meanwhile, across town in the cozy confines of Olivia's bakery, Sam and Emily hunched over a labyrinth of financial documents spread

The Frosted Felony

out like a treasure map on the sturdy oak table. Sam's sandy hair fell into his eyes as he leaned closer, his finger tracing a line of numbers that seemed to jump off the page.

"Emily, look at this," Sam exclaimed, his voice barely above a whisper but laden with discovery. "Margaret's name here, tied to a series of payments to Victor Wellington. That can't be a coincidence."

Emily peered over, her green eyes narrowing as she absorbed the information. "You're right," she breathed out, the corners of her mouth lifting in cautious excitement. "This... this could be the breakthrough we've been looking for!"

"Exactly!" Sam's habitual culinary metaphors bubbled to the surface as his enthusiasm grew. "We've found the missing ingredient in this half-baked mystery."

"Half-baked indeed," Emily chuckled despite the gravity of their find. Her tone shifted to one of resolve. "Now we just need to figure out what they were cooking up together."

"Looks like Margaret's pie isn't the only thing with a secret recipe," Sam quipped, though the implication of deceit left a bitter taste.

"Let's dig deeper," Emily said, the warmth of her determination matching the oven's glow from the kitchen. "We owe it to Olivia to uncover the full story."

Sam nodded, his apprehension replaced by the thrill of the chase. "To the bottom of the mixing bowl, then."

As they delved back into the sea of numbers and names, a sense of purpose united them. The scent of freshly baked bread wafted through the air, reminding them of the innocence they sought to defend and the justice they were determined to serve. Together, they were one step closer to unraveling the truth

The room felt colder than the festival outside, the tension between Detective Holbrook and Olivia Pierce thick enough to rival the winter's frost. She sat across from him, her hands clasped tightly under the table, every muscle taut with frustration.

"Olivia," James started, his voice carrying a blend of professional detachment and underlying concern, "where were you on the night of the mayor's murder?"

She met his gaze steadily, though inside her thoughts churned like the batter for her infamous chocolate torte. "I was at home, James.

Alone," she said, each word deliberate, hoping to convey the truth she felt so deeply.

"No one who can verify that?" he pressed, not unkindly.

Her lips thinned. "No, I'm afraid not. You know how it is after a long day of baking—the quiet is a welcome reprieve."

He nodded, scribbling a note. Olivia's mind raced. No alibi. Just her word against a town swirling with rumors and fear. 'I have to find something, anything, to clear my name,' she thought, her determination rising like dough in a warm kitchen.

The interrogation paused when an officer handed James a slip of paper. He glanced at it and then slid it across the table to Olivia. "This just came for you."

Curious, she unfolded the paper with trembling fingers. The message, written in jagged, anonymous print, cut through her like a knife through chilled butter: "Stop digging into the past or you'll be buried alongside your secrets."

A gasp escaped her as she dropped the note, her eyes wide with shock. The warmth that usually radiated from her seemed to vanish, replaced by a cold current of fear. The scent of antiseptic in the room became overpowering, the walls inching closer.

"Who sent this?" she whispered, her voice a brittle shell of its usual rich timbre.

"We don't know yet," James replied, his blue eyes sharpening with concern. "But we'll find out."

Swallowing her fear, Olivia straightened her posture. Whoever wanted to scare her was sorely mistaken. With a resolute spark igniting in her expressive eyes, she mentally rolled up her sleeves. Threats be damned; she'd peel back the layers of this mystery until the truth was laid bare, as surely as the center of a well-baked pie.

"Good luck with that," she said, her voice steady despite the tremor she felt. "Because I'm not stopping until I clear my name. And when I do, whoever wrote this will be the one needing to watch their back."

James studied her for a moment, the unspoken promise in his gaze acknowledging the courage behind her words. Outside, the festival carried on, oblivious to the drama unfolding within the stark confines of the police station. But inside, Olivia Pierce had just lit the fuse on a determination that would either lead to her exoneration or ignite an even deeper peril.

The silence in the interrogation room stretched out, an invisible thread pulling taut between Olivia and Detective Holbrook. Olivia's fingers drummed a nervous rhythm on the cold metal table, her thoughts racing like wild horses. She could feel James's gaze upon her, heavy with something more than just professional concern.

"Olivia," James began, his voice softening as he leaned forward, elbows resting on the table before him. "I know this is hard, and it might not mean much, but I believe you didn't do this."

His words hung in the air, sincere and unexpectedly gentle. Olivia's heart skipped, her breath catching in her throat. His eyes, usually so piercing, now held a warmth that made her own defenses waver for a moment.

"Thank you," she managed to say, the tremble in her voice betraying her steel facade. "But it seems the whole town has already pronounced me guilty."

"Let them talk," James said, his hand tentatively reaching out, then retreating. "They don't know you like I've come to. We'll sort through the facts and clear your name. I promise."

Their eyes locked, and Olivia recognized the depths of his conviction. It was a lifeline thrown into the choppy seas of her fear, and she clung to it with newfound resolve.

"Okay," she whispered, allowing herself the comfort of his assurance. "Okay."

"Alright, let's get you out of here," James said, standing up. He moved to the door, holding it open for her as if she were leaving a bakery instead of a bleak interrogation room.

Stepping out into the corridor, Olivia felt the weight of suspicion lift ever so slightly from her shoulders. As they walked toward the exit, murmurs and sideways glances from the other officers trailed after them like shadows at dusk.

"James," Olivia paused, her voice steady despite the storm inside her. "Whoever is behind this... they won't stop until they've destroyed everything I've built."

"Then we won't stop until we find them," James replied, the determination in his tone matching her own.

The station doors closed behind them with a definitive click, sealing away the sterile scent and harsh lighting. Olivia breathed in the crisp evening air, its chill whispering promises of secrets yet untold.

As she watched James retreat back into the lion's den of law and order, a shiver ran down her spine that wasn't just from the cold. Her bakery, once a haven of sweet scents and happier times, now loomed in her mind, a battleground where the next phase of her fight would begin.

"Be careful, Olivia Pierce," she muttered to herself, her steps quickening towards home. "This is far from over."

And indeed, as the moon climbed higher, casting ghostly shadows across Bayside Cove, Olivia knew that somewhere out there, a piece of the puzzle was waiting to be found. Or perhaps, more chillingly, it was waiting to find her.

Chapter 8

A Sprinkle of Romance

Olivia leaned back against the cushioned chair, her gaze fixed on James as he sifted through the papers strewn across the table. They had claimed a quiet corner in Sweet Sensations, the bakery she nurtured into a local haven. The mid-morning sun streamed through the lace curtains, casting dappled light on their work.

"Looks like we've got our work cut out for us," James said, his voice a low murmur that blended with the soft hum of conversation around them.

"Indeed," Olivia replied, her attention momentarily drawn away by the delicate chime of the door as another customer entered. "But I have a hunch about the Henderson angle."

The air was rich with the aroma of freshly brewed coffee, a scent that felt both comforting and invigorating. It mingled with the sweet fragrance of cinnamon and vanilla wafting from the kitchen, where a batch of Olivia's favorite pastries, the apple-cranberry tarts, were cooling on the rack. She could almost taste the tangy fruit filling complemented by the buttery flakiness of the pastry, a recipe that had taken her months to perfect.

"Your hunches tend to pan out," James acknowledged with a nod, offering a smile that softened the analytical sharpness of his features.

"It's all in the details," Olivia said, a playful glint in her eye. She loved the challenge of piecing together clues, much like she enjoyed creating complex flavors in her baking. "Speaking of which, what do you make of this?" She slid a photograph across the table towards him.

James studied the image, his brow furrowing slightly before he set it down. "Interesting," he murmured, reaching for his coffee cup. "This might just be the piece we're missing."

The cozy ambiance of the bakery enveloped them, the gentle clinking of cups and the occasional whirr of the espresso machine providing a soothing backdrop. Olivia always found solace in the rhythm of her establishment; it was a place where worries seemed to melt away like sugar in hot tea.

"By the way," Olivia ventured, seizing an opportune lull in their discussion, "have you tried the tarts yet? They're today's special."

"Can't say I have," James admitted, looking intrigued. "But I'm willing to be persuaded."

"Consider this a personal recommendation then," Olivia said, signaling one of her staff to bring over a plate of the tarts. As she watched James savor the first bite, his eyes closing briefly in appreciation, a tiny flutter of satisfaction tickled her chest. Sharing her culinary creations was akin to sharing a piece of her heart—a heart that carefully measured whom to trust, but was generous nonetheless.

Olivia felt the warmth of James' presence as much as she did the heat emanating from her freshly brewed coffee. She reached across the table, ostensibly for her cup, but as her fingers grazed his hand, she allowed herself the luxury of a fleeting touch. It was an innocent brush, yet it sent a ripple of anticipation shivering through her.

"Sorry," she murmured with a smile that didn't quite reach her eyes, betraying her nervousness.

"Nothing to apologize for," James replied, his voice a low hum that resonated within her. There was a softness in his eyes that she hadn't noticed before, and it made him seem less like the enigmatic detective and more like... someone she could really get to know.

The bakery's cozy interior, with its exposed brick walls adorned with local artwork and shelves lined with homemade preserves and jams, seemed to shrink around them, creating an intimate sphere where confidences were easily traded over the remnants of pastry flakes.

"Actually, Olivia," James said, leaning back in his chair and fixing her with a thoughtful gaze, "this place reminds me of a case I once worked on back in the city."

"Really?" Olivia leaned forward, intrigued. Her interest wasn't solely professional; she found herself wanting to peel back the layers of this man who had breezed into her quiet life like a gust of autumn wind, unpredictable and refreshing.

"Yep," he continued, a shadow flickering across his face as he recalled the memory. "It was a bakery, not unlike Sweet Sensations. Family-owned for generations. They'd been receiving threats, and I was assigned to find out who was behind it."

"And did you?" she asked, savoring the richness of the coffee as it complemented the sweetness of her favorite pastry.

"I did." James nodded, his gaze momentarily distant as if he were seeing the events play out before him. "But it took its toll. The family was torn apart by suspicion and fear. It was a stark reminder that even the warmest places can harbor dark secrets."

Olivia watched him, noticing the subtle crease between his brows, a testament to the burden he carried from his past experiences. The detective had layers, and each one seemed to draw her in further.

"Sounds like it was tough," she said softly, her own heart aching for the pain hidden behind his stoic facade.

"It was," he admitted. "But it also taught me a lot. About resilience. About hope."

Their eyes locked, and in that moment, Olivia understood him a little better. James wasn't just a detective; he was someone who fought against shadows, hoping to bring light. And perhaps that's what drew her to him—the promise of warmth amidst the chill of unsolved mysteries.

"Thank you for sharing that with me, James," she said sincerely, her hand inching closer to his across the tablecloth.

"Thank you for listening," he replied with a small, genuine smile that reached his eyes, making them crinkle at the corners.

In the comforting cocoon of her bakery, surrounded by the scent of cinnamon and sugar, Olivia felt a connection to James that went beyond their shared goal of solving the case. It was as though their souls recognized something kindred in each other, and she found herself quietly hopeful about what might blossom from this unexpected partnership.

James leaned back in his chair, the contented murmur of customers blending with the gentle clinking of cups and saucers. He looked around Sweet Sensations, taking in the quaint charm of the bakery that so perfectly encapsulated the essence of Bayside Cove.

"Something about this place," James began, his gaze returning to Olivia's, "it's like stepping into another world—a slower, more deliberate pace of life. I guess that's why I chose to come here."

"From the hustle of the city to the tranquility of Bayside Cove," Olivia said with a smile, tucking a stray lock of hair behind her ear. "Quite the change."

"Indeed," he replied, the corners of his mouth twitching upward. "The roar of sirens every hour, the relentless chase—it takes its toll. Here, I thought I could find some peace... Maybe even a fresh start."

"Sounds idyllic," she mused, her fingers tracing the rim of her coffee cup. "I hope it's everything you wanted."

"It's getting there," he said, his eyes holding a hint of the warmth that had been absent when they first met. "Especially now with—"

His words cut off as the sharp trill of his cell phone sliced through the cozy atmosphere, the ringtone startling a nearby patron into spilling a bit of tea. With an apologetic glance at Olivia, James reached into his coat pocket and answered the call.

"Detective Holbrook speaking," he said, his voice shifting back into professional mode. Olivia watched him carefully, noting the subtle shift in his demeanor as he listened to the caller.

"I see," he murmured after a moment. There was a significant pause, and then, "Yes, I'll be right there."

He snapped the phone shut and stood abruptly, his chair scraping against the wood floor. "I'm sorry, I have to go. New evidence has come to light."

"Is everything okay?" Olivia asked, concern knitting her brow as she rose to her feet.

"Hopefully, it's a breakthrough," James said, reaching for his coat with a sense of urgency that seemed out of place amidst the lingering sweetness of pastries. "Thank you for the coffee—and the company."

"Of course," she replied, trying to quell the sudden unease that settled in the pit of her stomach. "Good luck."

"Thanks, Olivia," he said, offering her one last brief, yet intense look before heading towards the door, his detective's stride purposeful as he disappeared into the crisp air outside.

Olivia stood there for a moment, watching the door swing gently closed, the bell above jingling softly. The bakery suddenly felt much too large, and the whispers of steam rising from her forgotten cup of coffee did little to warm the sudden chill of his absence.

Olivia sank back into her chair, the cushion accepting her weight as if nothing had changed. But the space James had occupied was now just an echo of his presence. She wrapped her hands around her coffee cup, seeking comfort in its familiar warmth, but even that couldn't dispel the twist of disappointment in her chest.

"Men," she muttered to herself, a wry smile tugging at her lips despite the heaviness settling over her. "They always leave at the most inconvenient times."

"Especially when they're dashing detectives with important cases," a voice chimed in, light and teasing.

Olivia glanced up to see her sister, Emily, sliding into the seat James had vacated. Emily's green eyes sparkled with knowing amusement as she reached across the table, plucking a stray flake of pastry from Olivia's plate and popping it into her mouth.

"Detectives or not, I hate being left behind," Olivia confessed, fiddling with the edge of the napkin. Her gaze lingered on the door, half-expecting James to reappear.

"Let me guess, he got a call about the case?" Emily asked, leaning back in her chair, her posture relaxed but her attention entirely on Olivia.

"Exactly." Olivia sighed, then allowed herself a small, rueful laugh. "You'd think I'd be used to sudden departures, growing up with you."

"Ouch, sis," Emily said, feigning a wounded heart. "But since I'm here, spill. What's this I hear about you and tall, dark, and mysterious?"

A blush crept over Olivia's cheeks, the heat competing with the steam still drifting lazily from her mug. "It's... complicated," she admitted, tracing the rim of her cup. "I like him, Em. More than I expected to."

"Complicated is just another word for interesting," Emily pointed out with a smirk. "So, are you worried about getting your heart broken by Detective Heartthrob?"

"Maybe." Olivia's expression grew serious, her usual confidence wobbling like a poorly set jelly. "What if I let my guard down and he leaves? Like everyone else seems to."

"Olivia Pierce, queen of confections and conqueror of hearts," Emily declared, reaching out to lay a reassuring hand over Olivia's.

"You've always been braver than you give yourself credit for. Besides, what's life without a little risk?"

"Full of intact hearts?" Olivia offered weakly, earning a chuckle from Emily.

"Also full of missed chances," Emily countered gently. "Look, we Pierces are made of sterner stuff. You can handle a detective with baggage."

"Baggage I can manage," Olivia mused. "It's the unknown that scares me."

"Isn't that the best part?" Emily's eyes danced with mischief. "The mystery, the discovery—the thrill of finding out whether he takes his eggs scrambled or poached."

"Scrambled," Olivia replied automatically, before realizing Emily's ploy. "Oh, you're good."

"Years of practice," Emily said with a grin. "Now come on, tell me everything. And spare no detail—especially not the swoon-worthy ones."

As Olivia launched into the tale of her and James's encounters, the aroma of coffee and the cozy ambiance of the bakery wrapped around them like a warm embrace. With each word, she felt the weight of uncertainty lift bit by bit, replaced by the comforting presence of family and the gentle pull of hope—perhaps for something more than just pastries and coffee shared at a quaint table in Sweet Sensations.

Emily took a sip of her herbal tea, the steam curling around her face like a delicate veil. She set the cup down with a thoughtful clink against the saucer, her gaze meeting Olivia's across the table.

"James isn't the first to upend my expectations, you know," Emily began, tucking a loose strand of auburn hair behind her ear. "There was a time when I thought love was only found in grand gestures and epic moments."

Olivia leaned forward, her elbows resting on the table, her curiosity piqued by this rare glimpse into Emily's guarded heart. The warm glow from the overhead lights cast a soft halo around them, creating an intimate space amidst the bustle of the bakery.

"Turns out, it's the small things that matter. Like someone remembering how you take your coffee, or just being there when you've had one of those days." Emily's smile was tinged with nostalgia, and perhaps a hint of regret.

The Frosted Felony

"Sounds... nice," Olivia murmured, her mind drifting to the way James had noticed her penchant for cinnamon in her latte without her having to say a word.

"It is. But it's also terrifying," Emily admitted, locking eyes with Olivia. "Because when you start caring about those little things, it means you're all in. And sometimes, life has other plans."

"Is that why you left?" Olivia asked gently, reaching for her own cup but finding it cold.

"Partly," Emily conceded, her green eyes reflecting a depth of emotion she rarely showed. "I loved someone once, fiercely. But we wanted different things—I craved adventure, he sought stability. In the end, our hearts couldn't build a bridge between those two worlds."

A bell over the door jingled as a couple entered the bakery, seeking refuge from the coastal chill. They laughed, shaking off the crisp autumn air, wrapping themselves in the comforting scent of baked goods and the promise of caffeine.

"Sometimes I wonder if I made the right choice," Emily continued, her voice barely above a whisper. "But then I see you here, building something beautiful, and I'm reminded that there are many ways to find happiness."

"Even with someone like James?" Olivia asked, hope lacing her words.

"Especially with someone like James." Emily reached across the table, squeezing Olivia's hand. "He sees you, Liv. Really sees you. And that kind of connection? It's worth exploring."

"Easy for you to say," Olivia said with a half-hearted laugh. "You're the brave one."

"Bravery isn't the absence of fear," Emily replied, a mischievous spark lighting up her eyes. "It's deciding something else is more important. Besides, since when do Pierces back down from a challenge?"

"Since never," Olivia answered, a smile breaking through her uncertainty. Emily's confidence was infectious, and in that moment, Olivia felt a surge of courage.

"Exactly," Emily said with a nod. "So, what are you going to do about Detective Charming and his scrambled eggs?"

Olivia glanced at the empty seat across from her, where James had sat just moments ago, and felt a warmth spread through her chest—a mixture of anticipation and resolve.

"I'm going to take a chance," she declared, her determination solidifying with every word. "I'm going to trust my heart."

"And your head?" Emily teased, raising an eyebrow.

"Both," Olivia replied, her voice steady. "Together, they make a pretty good team."

"Then go get him, sister," Emily said, pride evident in her tone. "And remember, I've got your back, no matter what."

"Thanks, Em," Olivia said, standing up with newfound purpose. "I think I'm going to need it."

As Olivia walked away from the table, a trail of laughter followed her, the bond of sisterhood a reassuring anchor in the unpredictable waters of romance.

Olivia's fingertips traced the delicate contours of the locket that hung from her neck, a habit she'd formed whenever thoughts clouded her mind. The bakery was quiet in the hour before closing, the soft hum of the refrigerators like a lullaby for the day's end. As she wiped down the counter, her movements were automatic, freeing her mind to wander through the maze of emotions left in James's wake.

The locket, a vintage piece that complemented her simple yet elegant style, had been a gift from her grandmother—an heirloom passed down with whispers of mystery and old family legends. Olivia had always found comfort in its weight against her chest, a tangible connection to her lineage. But tonight, the metal felt cooler, almost urging her to look closer.

"Olivia?" called out Emily, but her voice seemed distant, muffled by the cacophony of Olivia's racing heart. She didn't respond, captivated by the sudden discovery that a part of the locket seemed movable, a section near the hinge that had never budged before.

With gentle pressure, Olivia slid the piece, and a previously unseen compartment revealed itself, holding a thin strip of parchment, aged and delicate. Her breath hitched in her throat as she carefully extracted the paper with the precision that came from years of handling fragile pastry decorations.

The writing on it was unlike anything she had seen: looping characters interspersed with symbols that tugged at her memory, resonating with a depth that defied explanation. It was ancient script, she was sure of it, but from what language or time, she couldn't even begin to guess.

The Frosted Felony

"Em, look at this," Olivia finally managed, her voice a mix of wonder and disbelief. Emily leaned over, her eyes widening as she took in the sight of the cryptic message.

"Is that... is that from grandma's locket?" Emily asked, her curiosity piqued as she peered closer.

"Apparently, there's more to this heirloom than sentimental value," Olivia replied, the warmth of mystery igniting a spark in her gaze.

"Can you read it?" Emily questioned, her tone laced with the excitement of shared secrets between sisters.

"Not even a word," Olivia admitted, a playful frown knitting her brows. "But I bet it's something grand. A treasure map, maybe, or a secret recipe for the world's best chocolate cake."

"Or maybe it's just grandma's grocery list in really fancy lettering," Emily quipped, eliciting a chuckle from Olivia.

"Either way," Olivia said, determination lacing her words, "I need to find out what it says."

Her sister nodded in agreement, the thrill of adventure evident in her eyes. "We'll figure it out. And hey, if it's a centuries-old shopping list, we can at least say our family had taste."

"Quite literally," Olivia added, the corners of her lips twitching into a smile.

As they stood there, surrounded by the familiar scents of vanilla and sugar, the day's fatigue gave way to an electric anticipation. The locket's message, whatever it held, promised a journey neither of them expected, but one Olivia knew they were meant to take.

The locket lay open in Olivia's palm, its delicate chain cascading over her fingers like a stream of liquid silver. The symbols etched into the metal were as mysterious as they were alluring, whispering secrets from the past that only the initiated could understand. She was no linguist of ancient scripts, but the weight of the message's significance pressed upon her with an undeniable gravity.

"Olivia, are you alright? You look like you've seen a ghost," Emily observed, her voice pulling Olivia back from the precipice of her thoughts.

"Sorry, I just..." Olivia hesitated, the gears in her mind turning. James. She needed to tell James. His detective's mind and his connections could unearth the meaning hidden within the locket's cryptic markings. "I think this might be important—more than just a family heirloom. It could be a clue, something significant to the case."

"James," Emily said, her tone shifting to one of understanding. "You're thinking of taking this to him?"

"Exactly." Olivia's heart skipped a beat at the mention of his name. She felt a connection to James that transcended the professional; it was as though their paths had intertwined for a reason beyond solving cases and chasing down leads.

"Then you should go," Emily encouraged, her eyes reflecting the resolve that Olivia felt burgeoning within her own chest. "Who knows what doors this could open?"

"You're right." Olivia took a deep breath, her decision made. She carefully closed the locket, feeling the cool metal against her skin. Standing up, she brushed off her apron, sending a puff of flour into the air like a soft cloud. "I'll go first thing in the morning."

"Good," Emily smiled, reaching out to give Olivia's hand a reassuring squeeze. "And Olivia, whatever happens, remember this is your journey too. Trust yourself as much as you trust that detective's instincts."

"Thanks, Em." Olivia returned the smile, warmth spreading through her at her sister's words. Her gaze drifted back to the locket, which now seemed less like a simple piece of jewelry and more like a key—one that could unlock the answers to questions she hadn't even thought to ask.

With purpose fueling her steps, Olivia stored the locket in her pocket, already envisioning the conversation with James. The message would be a new thread in the tapestry of their growing partnership, one that promised to draw them closer in the shared quest for truth.

As she turned off the lights of Sweet Sensations, the comforting scent of baked goods lingered in the air, a silent witness to the chapter that had just closed. And with the promise of dawn came the anticipation of what the following day would bring—a day that would see Olivia and James delving deeper not only into the mystery at hand but also into the connection that was steadily forming between them.

Olivia had always been an early riser, but the morning after her conversation with Emily found her especially eager to greet the dawn. The first light of day spilled through the windows of Sweet Sensations, casting a warm, golden hue over the bakery's familiar

The Frosted Felony

"Lost in thought?" Sam's voice sliced through her reverie like a knife through one of his perfectly risen soufflés. He leaned against the counter, blue eyes twinkling with a mix of curiosity and mischief.

"Always," Olivia replied, tucking the locket beneath her apron and offering him a lopsided grin. "But this time, it's important. I found something in my locket. Something... ancient."

"Sounds like the start of a great adventure—or a fabulous dessert." Sam's playful tone was as comforting as the scent of vanilla that lingered in the air. "Either way, I'm in."

"Thanks, Sam." The corner of Olivia's mouth quirked up, though she couldn't quite shake the nervous flutter in her stomach. She watched as Sam returned to his dance around the kitchen, singing off-key to a tune only he could hear, his movements precise yet whimsical.

The bell over the door jingled, heralding Emily's arrival. Her confident stride brought her directly to Olivia's table. "So, what's this I hear about you and the dashing Detective Holbrook?" Emily teased, eyebrows arching in mock scandal.

"James? It's not like that," Olivia protested, but even she heard the note of hopefulness in her voice.

"Yet," Emily added with a knowing look. She reached across the table, her hand briefly squeezing Olivia's. "Whatever it is, or isn't, just be careful with your heart."

"Speaking from experience?" Olivia asked gently, sensing the layers of untold stories lurking behind Emily's green eyes.

"Maybe." Emily shrugged, the ghost of a smile playing on her lips. "Just remember, some things—and people—are worth taking a risk for."

"Like deciphering an enigmatic message with someone who might just see through my floury facade?" Olivia half-joked, her expression softening.

"Exactly like that." Emily stood, brushing a crumb from her sleeve. "And Olivia? Whatever happens, you've got us. You're not alone."

As Emily departed, leaving a trail of quiet strength in her wake, Basil, the tabby cat, sauntered over, weaving between Olivia's legs. His green gaze seemed to pierce right through her, as if urging her on.

"Okay, Basil," Olivia murmured, bending to scratch behind his ears. "You're right. It's time to take a leap."

Standing with newfound resolve, Olivia tidied her station with brisk movements. The familiar comfort of Sweet Sensations surrounded her—the hum of conversation, the clinking of coffee cups, and the golden glow of the setting sun filtering through the windowpanes.

"Sam," she called out, slipping the locket into her pocket, "I'm stepping out for a bit. Hold down the fort?"

"Got it, boss!" Sam flashed her a thumbs-up, his sandy hair glowing like a halo in the bakery's warmth.

With a deep breath to steady her racing heart, Olivia stepped out into the cool evening air of Bayside Cove. The cobbled streets whispered secrets of their own, urging her towards James and the next chapter of their intertwined fates.

Chapter 9

Turning Up the Heat

The warm scent of freshly baked croissants mingled with the tangy zest of lemon tarts as Olivia Pierce wiped a smudge of flour from her brow. Her bakery was a sanctuary of sugar and spice, where the clink of coffee cups punctuated the murmurs of loyal patrons. But today, after hours, it transformed into an impromptu headquarters for an investigation that had the entire town of Bayside Cove tangled in its web.

"Alright, team," Olivia said, her voice carrying over the hum of the industrial oven cooling down in the background. "Let's lay it all out on the table—figuratively speaking, of course. We need some fresh leads."

Around the polished wooden table typically reserved for decorating delicate pastries, her makeshift crew of amateur sleuths nodded in agreement, their faces serious but hopeful. Olivia leaned in, her expressive eyes scanning the documents and photos spread before them like a strange recipe they had yet to master.

"Any thoughts on this?" she asked, tapping a finger on a blurry photograph that had seen better days.

"Could be nothing, or it could be our missing link," one ally mused, stroking his chin thoughtfully.

"Or it could be a thumbprint smudge," another quipped, earning a collective chuckle.

The group's laughter was a fleeting reprieve from the weight of unsolved mysteries. Yet, beneath Olivia's warm-hearted banter lay a sharp, calculating mind, piecing together fragments of evidence with the same precision she used to craft her renowned pastries.

"Okay, back to business," Olivia said, her tone shifting as she slid away from the table and approached the mayor's computer, which sat incongruously among the pastry displays and cake stands. It was a beast of technology amidst the old-world charm of her bakery, commandeered for a purpose far beyond bureaucratic emails and budget spreadsheets.

"Maybe there's something we missed," she murmured, fingers dancing across the keyboard with surprising agility. She navigated through files and folders with a practiced ease, her intuition guiding her like an inner compass.

"Ah-ha!" she exclaimed, her voice ringing with triumph. On the screen, a series of deleted emails slowly resurrected from digital oblivion, the electronic ghosts of correspondence between Mayor Jonathan Bennett and Councilman Richard Cornwall. The two men's faces, usually so composed and urbane in public, now seemed to leer back at her from the pixels.

"Looks like our esteemed mayor and Councilman Cornwall were quite chummy," Olivia observed, her eyes narrowing as she scanned the cryptic messages hinting at late-night rendezvous and hushed discussions of land deals.

"Secret meetings and shadowy plots. That's straight out of a political thriller," one of her friends remarked, leaning over her shoulder to glimpse the screen.

"Except this isn't fiction," Olivia replied, her tone sobering. "This could be the motive we've been looking for—the reason behind the murder."

The room fell silent, save for the faint ticking of the antique clock hanging above the espresso machine, marking the passage of seconds that felt like hours. Olivia knew they stood on the precipice of something dangerous, a truth that someone wanted buried deeper than the foundations of the old lighthouse.

"We need to dig into these meetings," she declared, her determination flaring like the crackling hearth of her oven. "Find out what was so important that it had to be erased from history."

"Count me in," came the resolute responses, a chorus of loyalty and shared resolve.

"Good. Because if there's one thing I know," Olivia said, her lips curving into a wry smile despite the gravity of their situation, "it's that secrets are like yeast—they always rise to the surface."

Emily Pierce, known to her friends as Em, never thought she'd find herself back in Bayside Cove's town hall, a place where childhood memories of civic ceremonies mingled with the more complicated politics of adulthood. But here she was, her tall frame folded into the hard wooden bench of the public gallery, blending into the background like sugar dissolving in warm tea.

"Keep your head down and your ears open," she reminded herself, adjusting the collar of her nondescript beige jacket that made her auburn hair seem even more vibrant by contrast. Her striking green eyes, usually so full of fire, today played the role of dispassionate observers from beneath the brim of a simple cap.

Tucked away in her pocket, a small recording device – no bigger than one of the artisanal truffles from Olivia's bakery – sat primed and ready. The hum of hushed conversations around her was a cacophony of local concerns, but Emily's focus was laser-sharp, zeroed in on two individuals: Councilman Richard Cornwall and Victor Wellington, the latter standing like a sleek, predatory bird amongst a flock of pigeons.

Cornwall's athletic build and tailored suit gave him an air of casual power as he moved through the room, his dark hair perfectly coiffed, while Victor's sharp features were set in a mask of cool indifference. She positioned herself strategically, close enough to catch their words but far enough not to attract attention.

"Remember, it's all about subtlety," Emily whispered under her breath, recalling the many lessons from her years away, where every new city had been a chessboard and she a willing pawn in the game of survival.

As the meeting commenced, she noted how Victor's voice cut through the murmur, clear and authoritative, discussing zoning changes with the ease of someone who knew they held the upper hand. Emily watched as Cornwall listened intently, his piercing blue eyes scanning the room, missing nothing.

"Careful now, Emily," she thought as Victor's gaze swept past her hiding spot, "one wrong move and you're not just a pawn, but a player ousted from the game."

The clink of a water glass against a microphone brought the room to order, and Emily leaned slightly forward, the recorder in her pocket now capturing every official word for posterity – and perhaps for justice. She hoped the whispers of clandestine deals would slip from their lips, revealing the secrets that Olivia suspected were the yeast behind the murder most foul.

"Patience," she reminded herself, a smile tugging at the corner of her mouth despite the seriousness of her mission. Amidst the droning of municipal affairs, Emily waited, a sentinel among the unsuspecting, for the moment when the truth would finally come to light.

Emily Pierce perched on the edge of a stiff-backed chair, her posture relaxed to blend in with the other attendees, but her mind was anything but at ease. The bland beige walls of the council chamber encapsulated the humdrum of local politics, yet beneath that veneer lurked secrets ripe for the picking. Her fingers, concealed by the oversized sleeves of her nondescript sweater, danced over a notepad, while the small recording device, hidden in her pocket, captured the conversations around her.

The atmosphere in the room buzzed with the monotony of municipal matters until an abrupt change in pitch sliced through the drone. Emily's pulse quickened as Councilman Richard Cornwall's smooth baritone clashed against Victor Wellington's commanding bass.

"Your so-called 'development' is nothing more than a land grab!" Cornwall's accusation resonated clearly, his polished exterior barely containing the intensity within.

"Progress waits for no one, Richard. And neither will I," retorted Wellington, every inch the businessman ready to steamroll any opposition.

Emily leaned slightly forward, her green eyes sharpening as she strained to catch every inflection and nuance. She scribbled furiously, each word a potential key to unlocking the mystery that brought her back to Bayside Cove. The heated exchange between the two men was a symphony of ambition and accusation, and she listened intently, dissecting their verbal dance like a maestro studying a score.

"Your ambition blinds you, Victor! There are lives at stake here, ecosystems at risk!"

"Please, spare me the melodrama. It's all part of the grander scheme. The growth of Bayside Cove is inevitable."

Emily's heart raced, the thumping almost loud enough to drown out the words that could upend everything. Wellington's dismissive tone stoked the fire in Cornwall's eyes—a silent battle raging before the very public whose interests they were elected to serve.

"Careful, Victor," Cornwall warned, his voice low but fierce. "There are lines one should never cross, even in pursuit of greatness."

The Frosted Felony

"Lines?" Victor scoffed, a smirk tugging at the corner of his lips. "Consider them redrawn."

Their voices rose and fell, a tempest contained within the council chambers. Emily felt the weight of the moment, the gravity of the information she gathered—a puzzle piece snugly fitting into place, revealing a larger, darker picture.

She kept her gaze fixed on her notes, her presence a shadow among the crowd, but her resolve was luminous. Every argument, every pointed finger, was another breadcrumb on the trail to the truth. And Emily, with her auburn hair cascading like a waterfall of secrets down her back, knew this was just the beginning. A storm was brewing in Bayside Cove, and she would be the lighthouse guiding Olivia and her allies through the tempest.

Olivia's resolve hardened like the caramel she so expertly tempered in her bakery each morning. She could no longer stand idle, whisking theories together without tangible results. With a last glance at the assortment of evidence spread across the countertop—a collection of photos, notes, and digital breadcrumbs—she wiped her flour-dusted hands on her apron and set out for Evelyn Grant's office.

The door to the environmental campaign headquarters swung open with an assertive creak, announcing Olivia's arrival. The room was a verdant jungle of leaflets and posters proclaiming the need to save Bayside Cove's natural beauty. Amidst the chaos of conservation efforts sat Evelyn, her piercing green eyes focused on a stack of environmental impact reports.

"Good afternoon, Evelyn," Olivia greeted, her voice carrying the measured warmth of fresh bread from the oven.

"Olivia Pierce, to what do I owe the pleasure?" Evelyn replied without looking up, her tone edged with a hint of suspicion that contrasted sharply with her usual eco-friendly enthusiasm.

"Actually, I'm here about something rather... unpleasant," Olivia said, extracting a photo from her purse and placing it on the desk between them. The image, a snapshot of the crime scene, included a distinctive piece of protest paraphernalia in the background—one that mirrored the slogans adorning Evelyn's walls.

Evelyn's gaze lifted from the reports, locking onto the photo with an intensity that matched the storm brewing outside. "What is this supposed to mean?" she asked, her voice tinged with irritation as though Olivia had accused her favorite spruce tree of embezzlement.

"It means you were there, Evelyn. Near the murder site, around the time it happened." Olivia's accusatory tone sliced through the air, her usually playful banter replaced by the gravity of their discussion.

"Being near a place doesn't make one guilty of crimes committed there," Evelyn retorted, her back straightening like a sapling resisting a gale. "You of all people should know the importance of concrete proof."

"True," Olivia conceded, a flicker of humor returning to her eyes despite the tension. "But let's not pretend you wouldn't chain yourself to a bulldozer to prevent one of Bennett's pet projects. It begs the question: how far would you go to protect your cause?"

"Farther than most, but not to murder," Evelyn snapped, her ponytail swishing defiantly as if to punctuate her point. "I fight with facts and rallies, not violence."

"Then help me understand," Olivia urged, leaning forward, her expressive eyes seeking the truth amid the thicket of suspicion. "Help me see your innocence as clearly as I see the love you have for every leaf and lizard in this town."

Evelyn's fingers drummed on the desk, a staccato rhythm betraying her frustration. "I want justice as much as you do, Olivia. But my battle is for the soul of Bayside Cove, not against its people."

"Then we're on the same side." Olivia's voice softened, coaxing cooperation from the woman before her. "Let's work together to ensure that the real criminal gets his just desserts."

"Fine," Evelyn conceded, her fiery spirit simmering down to a pragmatic glow. "But if we're going to mix into this recipe of intrigue, we do it my way—sustainable and ethical."

"Agreed," Olivia smiled, standing up and smoothing her apron. "But let's not sugarcoat it. We're kneading the dough of danger now, and we'll have to bake at high heat until the truth rises to the surface."

With the conversation turning from confrontation to collaboration, Olivia sensed the layers of their investigation deepening. And as she stepped back into the coastal breeze, the scent of salt and mystery filled her senses, reminding her that the path ahead was as unpredictable as the swirl of marbled rye.

Evelyn's expression morphed from shock to indignation as Olivia's accusations echoed off the recycled-paper walls of her office. "Murder?"

The Frosted Felony

Evelyn's voice was a blend of disbelief and scorn. "You think I would kill to save a few trees? My activism is rooted in peace, not violence."

Olivia noted the tremble in Evelyn's hands despite her strong words—a leaf caught in an unexpected gust. "I have to consider every possibility," she replied, her tone a mix of apology and resolve. "This town is sprouting secrets like weeds, and I'm just trying to prune back the mystery."

The fierce glint in Evelyn's green eyes spoke of her unwavering commitment. "Bayside Cove's beauty lies in its untouched nature. The progress you speak of—it's paving paradise to put up a parking lot." She gestured fiercely toward the window, where seagulls rode the thermals above the undulating emerald landscape.

"Sure, but we can't let growth stifle us like overproofed bread," Olivia countered, leaning forward. "We need to find a balance, or the very charm that attracts people here will crumble like dry scones."

"Balance?" Evelyn scoffed lightly, though a smile teased at the corner of her mouth. "You make it sound like a cake recipe—equal parts concrete and conservation."

"Maybe it is," Olivia quipped, a wry smile playing on her lips. "But instead of baking powder, we use truth and justice to help it rise."

Their debate simmered down to a thoughtful silence—a truce baked in the oven of mutual concern for Bayside Cove.

Meanwhile, Sam was whistling a cheerful tune as he wiped down the counters, the bakery's sweet aromas lingering in the air like fond memories. He clicked off the lights and headed for the door, twirling the keys around his finger. He loved this part of the day—the quiet solitude after the oven's warmth and the satisfied smiles of customers were tucked away like fresh pastries in a display case.

As he turned the key in the lock, a sudden chill prickled his skin, the hairs on the back of his neck standing up like stiff peaks of meringue. An odd silence had settled over the street, the usual chatter of night birds absent. He hummed a little louder to fill the void, but the uneasiness clung to him like sticky dough.

"Probably just a change in the weather," he muttered to himself, forcing a chuckle.

He spun on his heel to head home, but the laugh died in his throat. A shadow loomed, swift and silent—an unexpected ingredient in the evening's recipe. Before Sam could react, something struck him hard from behind. His world went dark, and he crumpled to the ground like a deflated soufflé, the keys clattering beside him.

The assailant vanished into the night, leaving behind only the whispering sea breeze and the faintest echo of footsteps. Sam lay motionless on the cool pavement, the hum of the bakery's refrigerator the only sign that life still stirred within the walls of Olivia's cherished establishment.

Olivia's gaze locked with Evelyn's, the air between them charged with the intensity of their debate. The bakery owner's hands moved with emphatic gestures, flecks of flour from her earlier baking dusting the air like tiny ghosts. But mid-sentence, her words faltered, a strange sensation creeping up her spine.

"Are you alright?" Evelyn asked, her brows knitting in concern over her green eyes.

"I... I don't know," Olivia murmured, the warmth draining from her face. She placed a hand against her chest as if to steady a racing heart that no one else could hear. "Something's not right."

Without another word, she turned on her heel and raced through the door, her thoughts now only of the bakery—a haven of sugar and spice that suddenly felt worlds away. Her feet pounded the cobblestone street, each step echoing her growing dread.

"Sam," she whispered, a name carried away by the coastal wind.

She reached the bakery, its windows darkened and the open sign switched off—a silent sentinel awaiting its keeper. The door stood ajar, a sliver of darkness beckoning her inside. Olivia's breath caught as she pushed it open, stepping into the familiar scent of baked goods now tainted with something metallic and raw.

"Sam!" she called out, her voice shattering the silence.

Her eyes adjusted to the dim interior, and then she saw him—sprawled on the floor, his normally mischievous blue eyes closed, sandy hair framing his pale face. Olivia's heart clenched as she dropped to her knees beside him. Her fingers trembled as they found the pulse at his neck—steady, thank goodness—but panic still clawed at her throat.

"Sam, can you hear me?" She smoothed back his hair, her touch gentle yet urgent.

No response came from the fallen chef, his jokes and laughter now distant memories in the quiet bakery. Olivia fumbled for her phone with shaking hands, dialing emergency services as she fought to keep her voice steady.

"Please hurry," she implored into the receiver, her eyes never leaving Sam's still form. "My friend—he's been hurt."

As she spoke the address, her mind raced with questions. Who would do this? Why? Her bakery had always been an oasis in Bayside Cove, a place where worries were left at the doorstep. Now, the threshold had been crossed, and the sanctity of her world was shattered.

"Stay with me, Sam," Olivia murmured, her tone laced with affection and fear. She brushed a stray lock of hair from his forehead, a gesture as natural to her as kneading dough.

The wait for the ambulance stretched on, every second bloated and heavy. Olivia huddled close to Sam, her baker's hands now protectors, cradling his head. She whispered reassurances meant as much for herself as for him, her fierce loyalty to those she loved burning bright against the encroaching shadows of the night.

And as she waited, her resolve solidified. Someone had brought violence into her world, into the heart of Bayside Cove. Olivia knew, with a clarity that sharpened her every sense, that she wouldn't rest until she uncovered the truth. Her beloved bakery—and Sam—deserved nothing less.

Olivia's gaze swept the bakery, her sanctuary now a crime scene, as she crouched beside Sam. The warm scent of freshly baked bread still lingered in the air, a stark contrast to the cold dread that clutched at her heart. She adjusted the apron that had become her armor over the years, trying to find some semblance of the strength it usually gave her.

"Who would do this, Sam?" she whispered, more to herself than to him. The hum of the refrigerators provided a ghost of comfort, their steadfast rhythm a reminder of the bakery's daily life—a life momentarily on pause.

That's when she spotted it—a crumpled piece of paper lying innocently near Sam's outstretched hand. Olivia reached for it with a baker's precision, unfolding it carefully as if it were delicate pastry dough. Her eyes scanned the jagged handwriting: "This is just a warning. Stay out of it."

A chill ran through her, and not from the draft that played along the edges of her flour-dusted countertops. Olivia's heart pounded, the note's message echoing the danger that had crept into their lives. Sam's gentle teasing voice echoed in her memory, his puns and jokes a balm to her often too-serious nature. How he'd chuckle at her frown now, seeing her all worked up over a scrap of paper.

"Warnings are just another way of saying you're getting too close, huh?" Olivia muttered, folding the note with a newfound determination. It was a clue, a breadcrumb on the path she knew she had to follow. Whoever thought they could scare her away didn't know Olivia Pierce. She was made of sterner stuff, mixed and kneaded by Bayside Cove itself.

The distant wail of sirens began to rise above the town's sleepy murmur, growing louder as salvation neared. Olivia held Sam's hand, her other fist tightening around the note. She'd bake a hundred pies and decorate a thousand cupcakes before she let anyone hurt her friend and get away with it.

"Justice is on the menu," she promised the unconscious Sam, as the red and blue lights splashed against the bakery's frosted windows, painting them with urgency. The sirens crescendoed, their arrival breaking the silence like the crack of an egg against the rim of a bowl. Tonight, the sweetness of Olivia's bakery had been laced with bitterness, but she was resolved to sift through the darkness, measure the truth, and restore balance to her home, one clue at a time.

As the last of the paramedics disappeared into the ambulance, door closing with a decisive thud that seemed to echo off the cobblestones of Bayside Cove, Olivia felt the weight of the night press down upon her. The flashing lights cast long shadows across her face, deepening the lines of worry that had etched themselves there.

"Stay out of it," she murmured, the note burning in her pocket like a secret ember. "As if I'd ever back down now." Her words were a whisper lost in the symphony of urgency that surrounded her.

The bakery, once a beacon of warmth and sugary delights, stood silent—a stark contrast to the chaos that had unfurled at its doorstep. The scent of freshly baked bread still lingered in the air, but now it was tinged with the metallic hint of fear. Despite everything, a half-smile tugged at Olivia's lips as she imagined Sam teasing her about the 'dramatic flair' of it all. He'd probably say something like, "If you wanted to spice things up around here, Liv, you could've just tried a new frosting."

But humor fell flat in the shadow of the night's events. Olivia knew that the attack on Sam was more than just an act of intimidation; it was a message meant to ripple through the tight-knit community, stirring

The Frosted Felony

up whispers of unrest and suspicion. If they were willing to harm Sam, who was as much a part of this town as the lighthouse that guarded its shores, then no one was safe.

As the ambulance pulled away, its siren fading into the distance, Olivia turned back to the bakery. She pulled the door open, the familiar jingle of the bell sounding oddly defiant. Inside, the cozy interior felt hollow, the empty chairs and dimmed lights a testament to the abrupt end of tranquility. She knew that tomorrow, word would spread like spilled flour across the counter—fast and impossible to contain. People would talk, speculate, and eye each other with distrust. Bayside Cove would never be the same.

"Time to knead the dough and see what rises," she said to herself, rolling her shoulders back. The investigation was no longer just about solving a crime; it was about protecting her home, her friends, and the very fabric of the town she loved.

She glanced at the clock; it was well past midnight, yet sleep was a distant thought. There was work to be done, evidence to sift through, suspects to confront. And somewhere in the mix, a traitor was hiding, their hands dirty with more than just flour.

Olivia made her way upstairs, the creak of each step a reminder of the countless times Sam had bounded up two at a time, calling out his latest culinary experiment. Now, the silence was a heavy shroud, but her resolve only strengthened with each pace.

"Someone wants to play dirty? Well, they've clearly never seen a baker scrape burnt cookies off a tray," she mused, a spark igniting in her expressive eyes. With the dawn of a new day, Olivia Pierce would rise—armed with evidence, a loyal heart, and a dusting of powdered sugar courage.

And as the first light of morning crept through the blinds, casting a soft glow on the stainless steel and checkerboard tiles, it promised more than just the birth of a new day. It whispered of secrets unveiled, alliances tested, and the unyielding spirit of a woman determined to restore peace to her corner of the world.

Chapter 10

The Proof is in the Pudding

Olivia Pierce stood alone in the quiet of her bakery, the comforting scent of vanilla and freshly baked bread a stark contrast to the tension that knotted her shoulders. The murder board before her was an imposing mosaic of confusion, festooned with photos and notes that held more questions than answers. Her eyes, usually so bright with the joy of creating confections for her beloved patrons, now darted from one piece of evidence to another, seeking a crumb that might lead to the killer.

"An unsolved mystery is like an unfinished recipe," she muttered to herself. "And I don't do unfinished."

The bell above the door jingled, slicing through her concentration like a knife through one of her signature lemon tarts. In walked Daniel Cooper, the mayor's personal assistant, his usual reserved demeanor replaced by an urgency that matched the gravity of his tidings.

"Olivia," he began, pausing as if gathering the courage to shatter the silence that had settled between them. His voice was calm but carried a weight that seemed foreign coming from him. "I think you should know something about Mayor Bennett."

She turned, her hands instinctively wiping on her apron, flour leaving ghostly smudges on the fabric. Olivia's expression softened from focused intensity to intrigue as she took in Daniel's serious look. It wasn't like him to wear such solemnity; it clung to him awkwardly, much like his slightly too-large jacket.

"About the mayor?" Olivia echoed, her curiosity piqued, eyes widening with surprise. She leaned against the counter, crossing her arms —a shield against whatever revelation was to come.

The Frosted Felony

"Before... before he died," Daniel continued, his glasses sliding down the bridge of his nose as he looked up at her, beseeching her to understand the magnitude of his words. "I found discrepancies in the town's finances. Substantial amounts of money were being... redirected. I believe Mayor Bennett was embezzling funds."

"Embezzlement?" she repeated, her tone rising like dough in the warmth of her disbelief. "Are you sure?"

"Quite sure," he assured her, adjusting his glasses back into place with a resolute push. "I've seen the accounts, the paper trail. It's all there, hidden in plain sight."

"Daniel, if this is true..." Olivia trailed off, unable to finish the sentence, the implications of his assertion spreading out before her like the endless array of pastries in her display case. Could the murder have been tied to the mayor's financial misconduct? Was the sweet surface of Bayside Cove hiding a filling of deceit and greed?

"Olivia, I wouldn't bring this to you without being certain," Daniel said earnestly, holding her gaze. "I know what's at stake here."

"Thank you for coming to me." Olivia nodded slowly, her mind already kneading the new information into her ongoing investigation. "This could change everything."

The bakery, usually a haven of warmth and laughter, now felt charged with the electricity of a storm brewing over the horizon. And yet, amid the tempest of possibilities, there was the promise of clarity— perhaps even the key ingredient to solving the mystery that had shaken their small town to its core.

"Embezzlement," Olivia echoed again, the word hanging oddly in the air of her cozy bakery. She leaned back against the counter, its polished surface cool against her palms. The scent of cinnamon and baked apples lingered, a stark contrast to the bitter tang of suspicion now vying for attention.

"Paper trail or not, Daniel," she said, eyeing him with a mix of wariness and curiosity, "I need more than just your word on it. This is a serious accusation."

"Of course," he replied, his voice steady despite the gravity of the conversation. "I've documented everything—dates, amounts, even the discreet accounts where the funds were funneled."

"Can you show me these documents?" she asked, her gaze sharp as the paring knife she used for her tarts.

"Tomorrow morning," Daniel promised, adjusting the cuffs of his nondescript jacket. "I'll bring them by, first thing."

"Alright then." Olivia nodded, not entirely convinced but aware that dismissing him outright wouldn't serve her investigation. Trust was like a soufflé in her world—easy to deflate with the wrong move.

As Daniel excused himself, leaving the bakery with a brisk, almost mechanical gait, Olivia turned back to the murder board. Her mind churned with questions and theories—ingredients she'd have to measure with precision if she hoped to get to the truth.

"Mayor Bennett, what have you been up to?" she murmured to herself, tapping a finger against her lip. She considered each suspect in turn, their faces pinned amidst newspaper clippings and handwritten notes.

"Let's see, there's the councilman who opposed every project Bennett pitched—too obvious," she mused. "The local business owner whose shop was in the path of the new development? A possibility, but too much to lose. And then there's..."

She paused at the photograph of a woman with steel in her eyes, someone who had once been close to Bennett, before a bitter falling out over town politics. "Could she have found out about the embezzlement? Blackmail, revenge, a combination of both?"

Olivia shook her head, her curly hair bobbing with the motion. "No, no, that's the plot of last week's mystery novel, not this." But still, the pieces began to fall into place, forming a picture more complex than any of her cake designs.

"Money has a way of weaving a tangled web," she sighed, pulling her apron tighter around her waist. The warmth of the oven called to her, promising solace in the simple act of baking. Yet, she couldn't shake off the nagging feeling that something larger was at play—something that reached back into the very roots of Bayside Cove.

"Time will tell," Olivia decided, her resolve firming like set custard. "Until then, I bake—and wait."

The chime above the bakery door announced a new arrival, and Olivia glanced up from her scattered thoughts. The sight of James Holbrook's silhouette in the doorway was like a cool breeze on a sweltering day—unexpectedly refreshing and filled with the promise of change. In his hands, he clutched a manila folder that looked as out of place in the cozy bakery as a seagull in a hen house.

The Frosted Felony

"Good afternoon, Olivia," James said, his voice carrying the weight of importance. "I have something you'll want to see."

"James," she greeted, her tone balancing on the fine edge between wariness and welcome. "Please tell me it's good news, I could use some with my coffee."

"Depends on your definition of 'good,'" he replied, offering a small smile that didn't quite reach his eyes as he approached the counter. He opened the folder and slid out several sheets of paper, spreading them out with a careful precision that spoke of his meticulous nature.

"Forensics came back with something interesting," he began, pointing at a highlighted section of the report. Olivia leaned in closer, the aroma of cinnamon from her morning's baking mingling with the scent of purpose that always seemed to follow James.

"Traces of an herb were found in the poisoned pie—Glechoma hederacea, commonly known as ground ivy," he explained, his gaze locking onto hers.

"Ground ivy?" Olivia echoed, her eyebrows knitting together in confusion. She prided herself on knowing every spice in her pantry, yet this name was foreign to her culinary vocabulary.

"Exactly. It's not something you'd find in a typical kitchen," James confirmed, watching her carefully.

Olivia reached for the small plastic evidence bag James had placed on the table. Inside was a sprig of the herb in question, its delicate leaves pressed against the clear material. Tentatively, she opened the seal and took a cautious sniff. The scent was earthy, with a minty undertone that reminded her of the wild foliage that grew near the cliffs of Bayside Cove. It was a sharp contrast to the sweet and buttery smells that usually filled her bakery.

"Never used it," she admitted, her mind already racing through the possibilities. "It's not a common baking ingredient... at least not in any recipe I know."

"Nor in mine," James added, his eyes crinkling slightly as if amused by their shared ignorance of the herb's culinary uses. "But its rarity might just be what points us in the right direction."

"Or to the right person," Olivia mused out loud, her detective instincts flaring brightly under the gentle tutelage of James's steady influence.

"Indeed," James agreed, folding his arms across his chest as he regarded her with a newfound respect. "Shall we delve deeper into this botanical mystery?"

"Let's." Olivia smiled, her determination renewed. They were two kindred spirits, after all—one kneaded dough while the other sifted through evidence, but both sought the same result: the truth, served warm and satisfying, straight from the oven of justice.

Olivia bit her lower lip, a habit when the gears of her mind churned with possibility. She paced the length of the bakery, the scent of freshly baked bread wafting in the air, serving as a comforting backdrop to her tumultuous thoughts. It was the image of that locket which snagged her attention, a memory surfacing with the clarity of glass.

"James," she said, her voice low and urgent as if afraid the walls might be listening. "The historical society's archives—I saw something there once. A locket, old and ornate, with a carving on it. It looked just like this herb."

Her revelation hung between them, an invisible thread pulling taut with significance. James leaned forward, resting his elbows on the counter strewn with flour and sugar dust. His blue eyes, usually so clear and unperturbed, now reflected the flicker of intrigue ignited by Olivia's words.

"Are you saying there's history to this?" he asked, the detective in him alive and alert. "Something that ties back to Bayside Cove's past?"

"Exactly." Olivia nodded, her curls bouncing with each fervent bob of her head. "I didn't think much of it at the time, but now...it feels important. Like we're looking at a piece of a very old puzzle."

"Could be more than that," James mused, stroking his chin thoughtfully. "Maybe it's the missing link that tells us why the mayor was targeted—and possibly by whom."

"Right?" Olivia's hands animatedly gestured, mimicking the piecing together of a jigsaw. "If this herb is as rare as we think, then someone with knowledge of the town's lore could be our murderer."

"Or at least connected to them," James added, tilting his head slightly. "We should look into this locket further—discreetly. If it's as significant as you believe, we can't tip our hand too soon."

"Agreed," Olivia said, her eyes alight with the thrill of the chase. "We'll need to be careful, but I have a feeling this locket is the key. And I'm not just talking about unlocking the past."

"Then let's unlock it together," James proposed, offering a conspiratorial smile that was quickly mirrored by Olivia's own.

"Partners in crime-solving," she quipped, the warmth of her laughter softening the edges of their daunting task ahead.

"Time is slipping through our fingers, James," Olivia said, her voice laced with urgency as she wiped a fine dusting of flour from her hands onto her apron. She glanced at the clock on the wall, its ticking a reminder that they had no moment to lose. "We have to get to the society's archives before any more pieces of history—and evidence—fade away."

"Agreed," James replied, his gaze meeting hers with a shared intensity. He reached for his coat, slinging it over his arm. "Let's not waste another second."

They made swift work of closing up the bakery, the aroma of freshly baked bread lingering in the air like a comfortable memory. With one last look at the cozy haven of sweets and treats, Olivia hung up her apron behind the counter, trading the warmth of her oven for the cold trail of mystery that awaited them.

"Lead the way, detective," she said, her playful tone belying the gravity of their mission.

"Detective and baker, on the case," James retorted with an easy smile, opening the door for her as they stepped out into the chill of the evening.

The historical society was a short walk from the bakery, but tonight it seemed to stand at an immeasurable distance, each step heavy with anticipation. The building itself was a relic, its stone façade whispering tales of bygone eras from every crevice and corner.

James held the door open for Olivia as they entered the dusky interior, the scent of old paper and forgotten memories greeting them like an ancient librarian. They found themselves in a dimly lit room, the only illumination being the sparse lightbulbs dangling from a high ceiling, their faint glow casting long shadows between the aisles.

"Feels like stepping back in time," Olivia murmured, her eyes scanning the labyrinthine shelves packed with leather-bound volumes and parchment scrolls. "Every book could be a treasure chest or a Pandora's box."

"Let's hope for treasure," James quipped, his blue eyes reflecting the scant light as he pulled a slim flashlight from his pocket and clicked it on. "The right kind."

Olivia couldn't help but smile at his comment as they began their meticulous search. Her fingers, once adept at kneading dough and piping icing, now traced the spines of age-worn tomes with equal care. Somewhere among these archives lay a secret ingredient to their murder mystery—a rare herb that might just season their understanding of the crime.

"Anything?" she asked after a while, the silence punctuated by the soft thud of books being returned to their rightful places.

"Still looking," James answered, his voice low and steady. He carefully turned the pages of an old ledger, his detective's eye catching on every unusual entry.

"Wait," Olivia whispered, her breath catching as she paused over a particular passage in a dust-covered botanical compendium. "This looks promising."

James joined her side, his light guiding their eyes to a detailed illustration of a plant that bore an uncanny resemblance to the herb in question. Its properties were listed with care, its history within Bayside Cove noted with reverence.

"Could this be it?" Olivia leaned closer, her pulse quickening.

"Seems we're on the right path," James confirmed, leaning in to examine the text alongside her. "But we'll need more than a drawing."

"Then let's dig deeper," Olivia declared, her determination reigniting. "The answer is here somewhere, I can feel it."

Together, they continued their quest amidst the silent sentinels of history, every book and document a potential ally in their search for the truth.

Olivia's fingertip traced the ornate binding of a leather-bound tome, its spine creaking as she eased it open. The scent of aged paper filled the air, mingling with the musty atmosphere of the historical society's archives. She and James had been sifting through the records for what seemed like hours, the dim light casting long shadows across their focused faces.

"James, look at this," Olivia called out softly, her voice barely above a hush to respect the sanctity of the silent room.

He ambled over, his steps deliberate and quiet. As he peered over her shoulder, she pointed to a peculiar crease in the book's margin. With tentative fingers, she coaxed the hidden compartment open, revealing its secret—a yellowed photograph that crackled with age.

The Frosted Felony

The image showed a group of stern-faced individuals holding sprigs of an unmistakable herb—the very same they were searching for. Their somber expressions seemed to hint at the gravity of the plant in their hands.

"Is that—?" James started, his usual composure wavering.

Olivia nodded, her heart skipping a beat. "It is. They're holding it."

Their eyes locked, a wordless communication flowing between them. The revelation hung in the air, tangible and electrifying. This photograph was not just another brittle piece of history; it was a turning point in their investigation.

"Can you believe it?" Olivia let out a chuckle, though her laughter was edged with nerves. "We've been chasing our tails, and all along the answer was hiding in a book."

"Seems your baking intuition carries over to detective work," James remarked with a wry smile, his gaze still fixed on the photo. His compliment, rare as an unfrosted cupcake in Olivia's bakery, warmed her from the inside out.

"Let's not start celebrating with cake just yet," Olivia teased back, her wit a shield against the racing thoughts in her mind. "We've got more digging to do."

Their whispers became a conspiratorial soundtrack to the rustle of pages as they poured over the photograph, analyzing each detail—the way the individuals stood, the backdrop of their surroundings, the careful grip on the herb. Every element was a clue, a breadcrumb on the path to unearthing Bayside Cove's enigmatic past.

"Whatever secrets this town is keeping," Olivia murmured, her determination flaring bright like the oven's flame, "we're about to uncover them."

"Agreed," James said, his voice steady yet tinged with excitement. "This is big, Olivia. Really big."

They exchanged a glance, the kind that spoke volumes without a single word. Their shared resolve was a tangible force, driving them forward. Olivia could feel it, the thump of her heart synchronizing with James's, a rhythm set to the tempo of discovery.

With the photograph safely tucked away, they gathered their notes, the thrill of the chase reigniting their spirits. They left the archives, the door closing with a soft click behind them, sealing away the dusty shelves and old documents. But the secrets they sought were no longer confined to that dimly lit room—they were coming alive, breathing new life into a case that had once seemed cold and impenetrable.

Chapter 11

A Recipe for Disaster

Olivia's hands trembled as she held the newspaper, the ink of Victor Wellington's threat stark against the paper. Her heart pounded a frantic rhythm, echoing the gravity of his words – a lawsuit for defamation that could crumble Sweet Sensations like overworked dough. The walls of her bakery, once a sanctuary of sweet aromas and laughter, now pressed in with the weight of impending doom.

With each beat of her heart, Olivia felt her future, lovingly built with buttercream and determination, teeter on the edge of ruin. But the warmth that had always filled her shop didn't allow for despair, and neither did she. She took a deep breath, the familiar scents of vanilla and cinnamon bolstering her resolve.

"Okay, think, Olivia," she muttered to herself, setting the paper down on the counter with more assurance than she felt. She brushed a rogue strand of hair from her forehead, leaving a streak of flour in its wake.

Her mind, usually so occupied with recipes and decoration designs, shifted gears, sifting through legal strategies like choosing the perfect ingredients for a complex pastry. She reached for her phone, tapping out messages with flour-dusted fingers to her trusted circle of friends. If anyone knew how to navigate the choppy waters of small-town scandals, it was them.

"Hey, Jess, got a sec? Need advice on a not-so-tasty situation involving Wellington and his army of suits," she texted her friend Jessica, who had a knack for cutting through legalese like a hot knife through butter.

"Also, do we know any lawyers who aren't under Victor's thumb?" she added in another message to the group chat aptly named 'Bayside Allies'. The replies started chiming in, a symphony of support amidst the cacophony of fear.

"Olivia, breathe. We'll figure this out together," came the first response, followed swiftly by offers of help and contacts that might aid in her plight. Suggestions popped up like bubbles in a simmering pot, each one bringing Olivia closer to a plan of action.

"Thanks, guys. You're sweeter than my triple chocolate fudge," she replied, her thumbs dancing across the screen with renewed vigor. Her bakery was an extension of her soul, and she'd protect it with every resource at her disposal.

"Victor may have money and power," she spoke to the empty room, her voice steady despite the chaos brewing outside, "but he doesn't have the loyalty of Bayside Cove." A smile tugged at her lips, her natural charm flickering to life even in the face of adversity.

"Let's see if he can handle a dash of community spirit in his recipe for expansion," she concluded, the spark of humor igniting her fighting spirit. With every message of encouragement, Olivia's determination solidified like perfectly tempered chocolate, ready to stand up to the heat of Victor Wellington's threats.

The chime of the doorbell barely registered above the growing clamor outside Sweet Sensations. Olivia stepped onto the sun-warmed cobblestones, her apron fluttering against her as she surveyed the scene. A throng of townsfolk, spurred on by Evelyn Grant's fiery presence, clustered around her bakery, their hands hoisting posters that swayed like sails in the coastal breeze.

"Save our shores, not scones!" they chanted with a fervor that made Olivia's heart sink and skip in equal measure.

Evelyn, with her ponytail whipping like a flag of war, spun to face Olivia, her green eyes flashing an eco-friendly warning signal. "Your silence aligns you with the mayor's destructive policies, Olivia! How can you stand by and watch?"

"Stand by?" Olivia exclaimed, her voice rising over the chorus of protest. "My bakery has always prioritized sustainability. Our cups are biodegradable, our coffee is fair trade, and I've been composting before composting was cool!"

The Frosted Felony

"Words are just crumbs, Olivia," Evelyn retorted, stepping closer, her hand gesturing towards the signs as if they were shields of honor. "We need action, not lip service baked into half-hearted promises."

"Half-hearted?" The words stung Olivia more than she cared to admit. Her dedication to Sweet Sensations was as much a part of her as the flour dusting her skin or the warmth in her smile. "You think this is easy for me? My business, my passion—it's all on the line because of a rumor mill working overtime!"

"Then make a statement, take a stand with us!" Evelyn urged, her tone softening just enough to show the undercurrent of respect between two women fighting for their beliefs.

Olivia hesitated, the weight of the moment settling on her shoulders, heavier than any sack of sugar she'd ever hoisted. "This bakery is my life, Evelyn. I recycle, I conserve, I do everything I can to tread lightly on this earth we both love."

"Prove it," Evelyn challenged, her eyebrows arching like the wings of a bird poised for flight. "Join us, and let's send a message together."

Olivia's gaze swept over the crowd, over the faces she knew as well as her own recipes. Each one a blend of concern and conviction; each one a reminder that what she stirred into her business mattered far beyond the counter of Sweet Sensations.

"Alright," Olivia said, her decision firm like the crust of her signature apple pies. "I'll join you. But not against my bakery—alongside it. We'll show them that Sweet Sensations isn't just about indulgence. It's about being a responsible part of Bayside Cove."

Olivia stood outside Sweet Sensations, her feet planted firmly on the cobblestone street as she took in the scene before her. The protest had erupted into a cacophony of fervent voices and rustling paper—the colorful cardboard signs were waving like sails in the salty ocean breeze, each one a splash of anger or support against the backdrop of her beloved bakery.

"Save our shores, not scones!" chanted a group to her left, their words rhythmic and insistent. Another cluster of protestors responded with an equally catchy refrain: "What's baking, Bayside? Truth or lies?"

The air was thick with the brine from the sea and the earthy scent of homemade poster paint. Olivia felt the uneven rhythm of her own heart as she scanned the crowd, noting how the sun caught the vibrant hues of green, blue, and brown—colors chosen to symbolize the lush environment they all sought to protect.

As the energy of the protest pulsed around her, Olivia's pocket buzzed with the insistence of an incoming email. She stepped back into the cool shade of her bakery, away from the lively chants that now seemed to shake the very foundations of her world. With flour-stained fingers, she unlocked her phone and opened the message.

"Confidential: Mayor Bennett's Will" read the subject line. The sender's name wasn't displayed, just an enigmatic string of numbers and letters that suggested both anonymity and urgency. Her curiosity piqued, Olivia scrolled through the cryptic contents. Bits and pieces about altered clauses, unsigned addendums, and veiled references to the mayor's last wishes painted a murky picture that hinted at something far more ominous than simple policy disputes.

"Who would send this... and why now?" Olivia muttered to herself, her brows knitting together as she tried to make sense of the fragmented information. It felt like trying to read a recipe where half the steps had been smudged away. But the implications were there, lurking between the lines, suggesting that the mayor's will—and perhaps his intentions for Bayside Cove—weren't as clear-cut as everyone believed.

With the chants still echoing through the open door of Sweet Sensations, Olivia knew that this email could be the yeast that made the whole situation rise or the knife that deflated it entirely. A shiver ran down her spine, not from the draft but from the realization that she'd just been handed another piece to an increasingly complex puzzle.

Olivia's mind was a whirling dervish of thoughts as she parsed through the disjointed phrases in the email, each word a breadcrumb on a trail she knew she had to follow. With the echo of protests still seeping into Sweet Sensations, her determination rose like dough in the warmth of her resolve. She couldn't let an anonymous emailer's vague insinuations derail her; if anything, they were a clarion call to dig deeper.

"Unsigned addendums? Last wishes?" Olivia mused aloud, the gears of her mind grinding as she considered the mayor's known fondness for Bayside Cove's history. "The historical society's archives... That's where I'll start."

Her fingers danced across her phone screen with purpose, jotting down notes and potential leads. The scent of freshly baked pastries

The Frosted Felony

mingled with the salt-laden breeze, creating an oddly comforting backdrop to her amateur sleuthing. Olivia knew that somewhere amidst the musty pages and forgotten records lay the answers she sought.

As she plotted her next move, the chime of the bakery door announced Detective Holbrook's arrival. His presence filled the room like the subtle but distinct aroma of coffee beans, strong and somewhat bracing.

"Olivia," he began, his voice calm yet edged with urgency, "I need you to consider backing off from this investigation. It's not safe to stir the pot based on anonymous tips."

"Back off?" Olivia's fiery spirit flared, her words rising half an octave. "Detective, my bakery—my livelihood—is at stake here. I can't just sit and wait for another shoe to drop!"

Holbrook's eyes, deep pools of concern, locked onto hers. "I understand your frustration, but we're talking about more than pastries and protests. There are layers to this town you haven't seen."

"Then help me understand instead of keeping me in the dark!" Olivia countered, her tone a blend of exasperation and plea. She tucked a stray lock of hair behind her ear, a subconscious gesture of her inner turmoil.

"Olivia," Holbrook said, softening, "you have a good heart, and your head's screwed on right. But there are forces at play here that don't care about either."

"Exactly why I can't back off." Olivia squared her shoulders, her stance as firm as her resolve. "I'm not asking for trouble, but I won't cower from it either."

The detective let out a breath, the weight of his protective instincts etched in the furrow between his brows. "Just promise me you'll be careful."

"Careful is my middle name," Olivia replied with a hint of a smile, though her pulse thrummed with the risks she was willing to take.

"Right," Holbrook chuckled dryly, "and I'm the Tooth Fairy. Just... keep me in the loop, okay?"

"Deal," Olivia agreed, knowing full well that her search for the truth would be anything but cautious. With a nod, she watched as Holbrook exited the bakery, his silhouette momentarily framed against the setting sun before the door swung shut, leaving her wrapped in determination and the warm glow of the afternoon light.

Olivia leaned against the counter, her fingers drumming a staccato rhythm on the worn wood. The scent of cinnamon and sugar lingered in the air, a comforting blanket that contrasted sharply with the storm brewing inside her. She eyed the door where Detective Holbrook had just exited, his advice still echoing in her ears.

"Careful is my middle name," she muttered to herself, a wry twist to her lips. She pulled out her phone, her thumb hovering over the screen as she contemplated her next move. The frustration bubbled up within her like dough rising too swiftly in the oven. She was not one to cower behind the glass display of her bakery while others dictated her fate. With a determined tap, she composed a message to her most reliable source—a childhood friend who knew every whisper in Bayside Cove.

The chime above the door announced Holbrook's return before she could hit send. His brow was creased with concern, accentuating the rugged lines of his face. "I see that look, Olivia. It's the same one you get when you're about to try out a new recipe that everyone else thinks is too ambitious."

"Except this isn't about pastries, James. It's about my life, my livelihood," Olivia shot back, her voice steady despite the hammering of her heart.

"Which is exactly why you should leave the investigating to the professionals," he insisted, crossing the small space to stand beside her.

"Professionals who didn't notice someone tampering with a will?" Olivia countered, her hands flaring out as if to encompass the absurdity of it all. "No offense, but I think a fresh pair of eyes—which happen to be very good at spotting the smallest crumb—might see something you've missed."

"Olivia," Holbrook's tone was low and firm, "it's not about finding a needle in a haystack. It's about not getting pricked—or worse—while you're rummaging through it."

"Then help me," she pleaded, her gaze imploring. "Help me understand what's going on so I can protect what I've built."

"Protecting you is my priority," he said, the blue intensity of his eyes locking onto hers. "And sometimes that means keeping you from chasing shadows that might hide darker things."

"Shadows don't scare me," Olivia replied, her spine straightening. "What scares me is standing by, doing nothing, while threats loom over Sweet Sensations."

The Frosted Felony

Their voices rose, clashing like mixing bowls knocked from shelves, the energy between them electric with tension and unspoken emotion.

"Dammit, Olivia, this isn't just about your bakery!" Holbrook's restraint began to fray. "There are layers here that you don't understand, dangers that—"

"Then make me understand," she interrupted, the timbre of her voice a combination of defiance and desperation. "Involve me in the process. Because I will not be sidelined in a case that affects everything I care about."

Holbrook ran a hand through his tousled hair, the gesture betraying his inner conflict. "You're as stubborn as an over-kneaded dough," he grumbled, though there was a hint of admiration in his words.

"Comes with being a baker," Olivia quipped, refusing to let the gravity of the situation crush her spirit. "So, will you work with me, or do I have to go rogue?"

"Rogue?" He arched an eyebrow, a reluctant smile tugging at the corner of his mouth.

"Figure of speech," she assured him quickly, though they both knew it was more truth than jest. "But I'm serious, James. I need answers, and I'm not afraid of a little risk."

"Neither am I," he conceded after a moment, the weight of their shared resolve settling over them like flour dust in the air. "But we do this my way. Carefully."

"Deal," Olivia agreed, her determination burning bright in her chest. "But no holding back. If there's a secret ingredient in this mess, I intend to find it."

"Secret ingredient, huh?" Holbrook's voice softened, a gentle tease within the storm. "Just remember, some flavors are better left untested."

"Maybe," Olivia allowed, a small smile blossoming despite the tension. "But I've always had a taste for mystery."

The argument with Holbrook had dwindled to a tense silence, the air between them thick with unspoken concerns and stubborn resolve. Olivia's heart was a drumbeat in her chest, echoing her mixed feelings of determination and uncertainty. She could almost taste the tang of risk on her tongue—bitter yet strangely exhilarating.

"Olivia," Holbrook began, his tone softening—a subtle olive branch extended after their verbal sparring. "Just... be careful, okay?"

She nodded, the gesture carrying all the weight of her conflicted emotions. "I will," she promised, though the quiver in her voice betrayed her apprehension.

With one last searching glance at Holbrook, Olivia turned on her heel and pushed open the door to Sweet Sensations. The familiar scent of vanilla and cinnamon enveloped her like a comforting embrace, grounding her amidst the whirlwind of her thoughts. The bakery was her sanctuary, her canvas for creating edible masterpieces that brought joy to the townsfolk.

As she retreated further into the cozy space, her mind buzzed with plans and possibilities. She thought of the cryptic email, the altered will, and the unyielding desire to protect her life's work from being unjustly tarnished. Each step was a silent declaration of her intent to stand her ground, to sift through the murky waters of deceit and find clarity.

Behind the counter, Olivia's hands instinctively reached for a tray of pastries, aligning them with the precision of an artist arranging their paints. Her movements were methodical, a physical manifestation of her internal mantra—to keep moving, to keep fighting.

"Alright, Olivia," she whispered to herself, a flicker of humor brightening her solemn mood as she eyed the colorful array of macarons. "Time to bake your way out of this one."

With a resolute sigh, she grabbed an apron, tying it around her waist with a flourish. The fabric felt like armor, bolstering her confidence as she prepared to face whatever challenges lay ahead. She was determined, more than ever, to protect Sweet Sensations, to uncover the truth about Mayor Bennett's altered will, and to show Bayside Cove that her bakery was built on more than just sugar and flour—it was built on resilience and heart.

Chapter 12

Burnt to a Crisp

Olivia Pierce stood motionless on the cobblestone sidewalk, her gaze locked onto the once pristine windows of Sweet Sensations. Her hands trembled slightly as they hung at her sides, flour from the morning's baking still clinging under her nails. The charming bakery, a canvas of creamy whites and warm pastels, was now marred by garish spray-painted words that screamed accusations. "Thief" and "Liar" were splattered across the glass in angry, dripping letters, each one a dagger to Olivia's heart.

"Unbelievable," she murmured, her voice barely rising above a whisper. The morning sun did little to warm the chill that had settled in her bones—a coldness not from the coastal breeze but from the stark reality of her situation. The humor and warmth that typically danced in her expressive eyes were snuffed out, replaced with a haunted look of disbelief.

As the day progressed, the bell above the bakery's door remained eerily silent. Where there once was a line of customers eager for her cinnamon twists or the velvety smoothness of her chocolate éclairs, only a few solitary souls wandered in. The rich aroma of baking bread and sweet confections felt like a taunt in the void of the near-empty shop.

"Morning, Olivia," greeted Mrs. Donnelly, one of her regulars, hesitance tinging her otherwise cheery voice. She glanced around at the vacant tables before settling her purse on the counter. "Quite the mess outside, huh?"

"Good morning, Ellen," Olivia replied, managing a half-hearted smile as she slid a display case open. "Yes, quite the... artwork." Her attempt at humor fell flat, echoing hollowly against the marble countertops.

"Give me a dozen of the raspberry danishes, will you? I'll take them to the book club; maybe it'll help drum up some business for you," Mrs. Donnelly said, offering a sympathetic glance.

"Thank you, Ellen, that's very kind," Olivia said, packaging the pastries with meticulous care. The weight of gratitude mixed with a silent plea that this small act might somehow turn the tides.

With each tick of the clock, the bakery's ledger grew heavier with red ink, a stark contrast to the sugary delights that filled the display cases. Olivia found herself tallying figures in her head, each calculation another knot in her already tight shoulders. The empty tip jar sat on the counter, a mocking reminder of the financial strain tightening its grip on her livelihood.

"Should've been just another Tuesday," she sighed to herself, wiping down an already spotless counter. The laughter and chatter that used to fill the space were now distant memories, as tangible as the ghosts rumored to wander Bayside Cove's foggy shores at night.

"Things will pick up, Liv, you'll see," said Carol, her lone employee, from where she busied herself rearranging the cookie display for the third time. "Bayside Cove loves you too much to stay away for long."

"I hope you're right," Olivia whispered, taking solace in the familiar rhythm of kneading dough, letting the simple act ground her amid the chaos. Her bakery, once a hub of warmth and community, had become as hollow as the center of the angel food cakes cooling on the racks. Yet even as the worry lines deepened on her forehead, Olivia's determined spirit flickered beneath the surface, unwilling to be extinguished by the shadows that sought to envelop Sweet Sensations.

Olivia's fingers hovered over the ledger, her pen poised but unmoving. The numbers didn't add up, no matter how many times she went over them. With a heavy sigh, she pushed the book away and gazed out across the near-empty bakery. Her heart ached at the silence that had replaced the cheerful hustle and bustle.

"Maybe... maybe it's time to let go," she murmured, the words leaving a bitter taste in her mouth. "Of the bakery, of the investigation..."

"Hey, don't say that," Carol called from across the room, her voice echoing slightly more than usual in the quiet space. She stopped rearranging the pastries and fixed Olivia with a stern look. "You've got more fight in you than anyone I know."

The Frosted Felony

Olivia shook her head, trying to dislodge the doubts swirling within. "What if fighting just makes things worse? What if I can't handle the truth that's out there?"

"Then you'll handle it one step at a time, like you always do." Carol's words were meant to reassure, but they felt hollow. The truth was an elusive beast, and Olivia feared what it might reveal.

The bell above the door jingled, a sound that once brought joy now made Olivia tense. Emily walked in, her presence commanding even in her unease. Her green eyes held a storm of emotion that instantly put Olivia on edge.

"Olivia, we need to talk," Emily said, her voice a mix of guilt and urgency that sent a shiver down Olivia's spine. "It's about mom and dad—about what they knew."

"Knew?" Olivia's hands clenched at her sides, the flour dusting her apron puffing into the air like tiny ghosts. Memories flickered unbidden: hushed conversations behind closed doors, their parents' anxious glances exchanged over dinner.

"About the town's secrets, Liv. They knew more than we thought," Emily continued, stepping closer. Her voice dropped to a whisper, as if the walls themselves might be listening. "I found some of their old journals. There are things... things we never knew."

A cold knot formed in Olivia's stomach. Trust had always been hard-won between them, and this revelation threatened the fragile bridge they'd managed to build upon Emily's return.

"Things like what?" Olivia asked, her voice tight. "Why would they keep secrets from us?"

"Because sometimes people think they're protecting the ones they love by keeping them in the dark," Emily answered, her gaze unwavering. "They were wrong, but we have a chance to make it right."

Olivia took a deep breath, her mind racing. The bakery was her heart, but the truth was her soul. She looked into Emily's eyes, searching for the sister she once knew, the one who would ride bikes with her until the sun dipped below the horizon, promising adventures and mysteries yet to unfold.

"Tell me everything," Olivia decided, her resolve hardening like caramel left too long on the stove. She would face whatever came next, because that's what Pierces did—they persevered.

Emily nodded, and together they retreated to the back room, where old family photos watched silently from the walls, holding onto secrets of their own.

Olivia's fingers hovered over the aged leather-bound journal, its edges worn from years of secret-keeping. "I can't believe they never told us," she murmured, her voice a mixture of hurt and disbelief.

"Olivia, they thought they were doing what was best," Emily said, trying to bridge the widening gap between them with words that felt like hollow offerings.

"Best for who, Em? Because all I see are lies that left us unprepared for... for all of this." Olivia gestured to the empty bakery, her heart aching as much as her head.

Emily reached out, but Olivia pulled away, wrapping her arms around herself. "I needed you, Em. But you were just as in the dark as I was, or worse, you knew and kept it from me too."

The accusation stung, and Emily recoiled as if slapped. "I would never—" She stopped, her jaw tightening. "You think so little of me?"

"Right now, I don't know what to think," Olivia admitted, her eyes brimming with tears that threatened to spill over.

Their standoff was interrupted by the sound of shattering glass from the front of the bakery. They both turned their heads toward the noise to see Sam standing amidst a constellation of sparkling shards, his face the very picture of regret.

"Sam! What happened?" Olivia rushed over, her concern for the bakery momentarily overriding her distress with Emily.

"I... I was just trying to help, Liv. Trying to sort things out, and I knocked over the display case," Sam explained, his usual jovial tone replaced with one of mortification. He held up a jagged piece of glass, something paper-thin and delicate clinging to it. "This was inside..."

It was a photo, one of the few pieces of evidence that connected back to the town's hidden history—the very photo Olivia had been using to piece together clues about the murder. Now, it was ruined, the faces smeared beyond recognition.

"Sam, that was..." Olivia couldn't finish her sentence. The weight of her struggles pressed down on her, squeezing the air from her lungs. Her bakery, her family, her entire investigation—it all seemed to be crumbling around her.

The Frosted Felony

"Hey, hey, I'm sorry, Liv. I'll fix this, I promise," Sam said, his blue eyes wide with earnest concern.

"Can you fix everything, Sam?" Olivia asked, her voice small. She wasn't just talking about the photo.

"Maybe not everything," he replied gently, reaching out to steady her. "But I'm here, okay? We'll figure this out together."

Olivia nodded, drawing a shaky breath as she looked between the broken glass at her feet and the sister she no longer felt she knew. She realized then that her bakery wasn't just a place of sweet confections; it was the heart of her world, a world that seemed to be fracturing like the delicate sugar crust of a crème brûlée under the tap of a spoon.

"Thanks, Sam," Olivia managed to say, her voice steadier than she felt. "Let's start cleaning this up."

As they worked side by side, the silence between the sisters loomed large, filled with unspoken words and unresolved secrets. But Olivia knew one thing for certain—she wouldn't let the rift break her. Not when there was still truth to uncover and a bakery to save.

Olivia stood in the quiet of her bakery, the soft hum of the refrigerator now a deafening silence in the emptiness of the room. The scent of cinnamon and vanilla, once comforting and inviting, hung heavy in the air—a cruel reminder of bygone bustling mornings. She wrapped her arms tightly around herself, her hands, usually warm and steady from kneading dough, now cold and trembling.

"Maybe this is it," she whispered to no one, her gaze tracing the outlines of heart-shaped cookies in the display case, their sugar-dusted edges untouched and forlorn. "Maybe I'm meant to walk away."

She could almost hear the laughter and chatter of her customers, the tinkling bell above the door that chimed with every entrance. Now, all that remained were shadows on the walls where pictures used to hang and echoes of conversations that seemed to belong to another lifetime.

The idea of giving up gnawed at Olivia's resolve, but just as quickly as despair crept in, a spark flickered within her. It was small and fragile, like the flame of a candle in a storm, yet it refused to be extinguished. Her mind floated to the eager faces that would press against the glass each morning, their eyes wide with the anticipation of tasting her latest creation.

"Where else would Mrs. Henderson get her raspberry tarts?" Olivia mused aloud, a wry smile touching her lips despite the ache in her chest. "And little Timmy... his face when he gets a chocolate chip cookie bigger than his hand."

As she spoke, the memories began to weave themselves into a tapestry of resilience. Olivia remembered the notes of gratitude left on napkins, the warmth of hands clasping hers in thanks, the bonds formed over shared stories and secret recipes. Each recollection fortified her spirit, each act of kindness a brick in the foundation of her will to fight.

"Sweet Sensations isn't just a place; it's a community," she said, straightening her back as though the words themselves lifted the weight from her shoulders. "And I'll be darned if I let some spray paint and whispers tear that apart."

With newfound determination, Olivia reached for her apron hanging behind the counter. Its familiar fabric felt like a comforting embrace, grounding her in the purpose that had driven her to open the bakery all those years ago. She tied the strings around her waist, knotting them with the same precision she applied to her pastries.

"Okay, Olivia Pierce," she said to her reflection in the polished chrome of the espresso machine, "let's show them what you're made of." And with that, she rolled up her sleeves, ready to breathe life back into the heart of Sweet Sensations.

Olivia glanced at the clock ticking above the bakery's door. The hands moved with a slow certainty that seemed to mock her. She felt a knot tightening in her stomach, the silence of the empty shop pressing in around her. With each tick, she could almost hear the whispers of doubt creeping into her mind, questioning if she had the strength to continue.

"Sam," she called out, her voice echoing slightly in the stillness. "Can you come here for a sec?"

From the back kitchen emerged Sam, his apron smeared with flour and a hint of concern etching his brow. "What's up, Liv?" he asked as he approached her, wiping his hands on a dish towel.

She took a deep breath, the scent of sugar and cinnamon lingering in the air. "I'm not sure I can do this," she admitted, her voice barely above a whisper. "Every time I think we're getting somewhere, something else comes crashing down."

Sam leaned against the counter, offering her a lopsided smile. "Hey, remember when we tried to make that triple-layer cake and it ended up looking like the Leaning Tower of Pisa?" He chuckled, his eyes crinkling at the corners. "We didn't give up then. We just... leaned into it."

The Frosted Felony

A small laugh escaped Olivia's lips despite herself. "That was different," she said, but the warmth from his joke lingered, softening the edges of her frustration.

"Was it really? Look around, Liv. This is your dream," he gestured broadly to the bakery. "You've built something amazing here. Sure, it's more 'mystery-flavored' than we expected, but since when do you back down from a challenge?"

Olivia met his gaze, finding a steadiness there that anchored her. "I guess I just needed to hear that. Thanks, Sam."

"Anytime, boss." Sam's grin widened. "Besides, I already have plans for a new dessert menu inspired by all this drama. 'Conspiracy Crumble', 'Secretive Scones'—it'll be a hit!"

"Always the optimist," she said, though the idea brought a spark back into her eyes.

"Optimism is the best ingredient," Sam said with a wink.

With a deep breath, Olivia felt the last of her hesitation melt away. She stepped forward, her hands reaching out to straighten a pile of menus. The paper crinkled under her touch, a tangible reminder of the normalcy she yearned to return to.

"Alright, let's get back to it," she declared, her voice carrying a renewed conviction. "No more moping about. We've got a bakery to run, pastries to bake, and mysteries to solve."

"Spoken like the true pastry detective you are," Sam teased, but his admiration for her grit shone through.

Olivia smiled, tying her hair back into a neat ponytail. She rolled up her sleeves, revealing arms dusted with flecks of flour—a badge of her dedication. Her movements were deliberate, each step she took towards the kitchen filled with purpose.

"Let's turn up the heat and show them what Sweet Sensations is really made of," she said, her tone ringing with the promise of fresh beginnings.

As she passed the threshold into the kitchen, the familiar clatter of pans and the hum of the oven greeted her like an old friend. Here, amidst the organized chaos of baking sheets and frosting nozzles, was where she belonged. With every stir, knead, and whisk, Olivia reaffirmed her commitment—not just to her bakery, but to the truth she sought.

In that moment, as she prepped the dough for a new batch of her signature chocolate chip cookies, Olivia Pierce knew one thing for certain: she wasn't just surviving the storm; she was learning how to dance in the rain.

The scent of freshly baked cookies wafted through the air, mingling with the subtle aroma of vanilla and cinnamon as Olivia tidied up the display counter. It was late afternoon, and golden rays of sunlight streamed in through the bakery windows, casting a warm glow over the remaining pastries. She arranged the cupcakes in neat rows, each swirl of frosting a testament to her resilience.

With every sweep of the cloth, she polished away the remnants of the day's hardships. The bell above the door jingled softly, signaling the departure of another customer — fewer these days, but cherished all the more. Olivia allowed herself a small smile, the corners of her eyes crinkling with a blend of fatigue and satisfaction.

"See you tomorrow, Olivia!" the customer called out, his voice carrying a note of encouragement.

"Take care, Mr. Jennings! Enjoy those scones," she replied, her tone light despite the weight that lingered in her chest.

Straightening up, Olivia glanced outside, where the streets of Bayside Cove were beginning to quieten. That's when she saw him — Detective James Holbrook, passing by with that purposeful stride of his. He paused for a moment, glancing towards Sweet Sensations as if sensing her gaze. Their eyes met briefly, and Olivia felt a flutter in her stomach, an involuntary reaction that caught her off guard every time.

She quickly looked away, her hands fidgeting with the hem of her apron. *Why does he always have to look so... composed?* she mused, her thoughts a tangle of admiration and apprehension. There was something about Holbrook that unsettled her, yet drew her in — like the enigmatic final piece of a puzzle she couldn't help but want to solve.

As he continued on his way, Olivia's mind raced with possibilities. The detective had become an unexpected constant in the chaos of her life, his presence both reassuring and unnerving. Could there be room for something more than professional courtesy between them? She shook her head, chiding herself for entertaining such thoughts amid a maelstrom of trouble.

Turning back to the bakery, Olivia sighed, her fingers tracing the edge of the glass where spray-painted slurs had marred its clarity days before. The vandalism was a stark reminder of the unknown adversary lurking in the shadows of their quaint town. *Who would do such a thing?

The Frosted Felony

And why now?* The questions gnawed at her, feeding the flicker of curiosity that refused to die out.

Was it merely a random act of destruction, or did it tie into the murder investigation that had taken a grip on Bayside Cove? The uncertainty of it all loomed over her, yet Olivia knew one thing — she wouldn't rest until the truth was unearthed.

"Tomorrow's another day," she whispered to herself, a silent vow to keep pushing forward. With a last glance at the empty street, she turned the sign on the door to 'Closed' and stepped back into the sanctuary of her kitchen.

Behind her, the sun dipped below the horizon, and the bakery settled into a peaceful hush, the mysteries of the day lingering just out of reach, waiting for the dawn of new discoveries.

Chapter 13

Simmering in Doubt

The brass bell above the bakery door chimed a farewell to the last customer, its familiar tinkle fading into the soft hush of evening. Olivia Pierce trudged up the narrow staircase that led to her sanctuary, the weight of the day heavy on her shoulders. Her apartment, a cozy nook perched above the sweet-smelling haven of her beloved bakery, welcomed her with open arms. She kicked off her shoes, abandoning them haphazardly by the door, and collapsed onto the plush cushions of her well-worn couch.

"Ugh," she exhaled, pressing her palms into her eyes as if she could physically push away the doubts that swarmed her mind like persistent gnats. "What were you thinking, Olivia?" she muttered to herself, the words heavy with self-reproach. "You're a baker, not a detective." The recent events had left her feeling more like a flustered amateur sleuth than the confident owner of 'Pierce's Pastries.'

As the quiet of the room enveloped her, Olivia's thoughts drifted back to a time when life in Bayside Cove was simpler, yet tinged with its own brand of complexity. She remembered vividly the morning their parents had packed up the family car, the trunk bulging with suitcases, the backseat crammed with bags filled with the remnants of their lives. They had promised adventure, but delivered absence. The two sisters stood hand-in-hand, watching the car disappear around the bend, unaware that it would be years before they saw their parents again.

"Em, do you think they'll send postcards?" young Olivia had asked, her voice barely above a whisper.

"Doesn't matter. We have each other," Emily had replied, her green eyes fierce even then, a protective arm slung over Olivia's trembling shoulders.

The Frosted Felony

With the departure of their parents, the bond between the sisters had become their lifeline, a delicate thread that tethered them to some sense of normalcy. But as they grew older, the thread stretched and frayed, strained by unspoken grievances and Emily's restless spirit that eventually pulled her away from Bayside Cove, leaving Olivia to knead her worries into dough and sprinkle her yearning into sugar-dusted confections.

Now, alone in the dimming light of her apartment, Olivia let out a long sigh. If only she could bake a solution to the riddles that plagued her as easily as she could a batch of her signature chocolate chip cookies. With a shake of her head, she tried to dispel the nostalgia that clung to her like flour on her apron.

"Time to rise to the occasion, Liv," she whispered to the empty room. "Just like yeast in the oven." It was what she did best—finding strength in the face of adversity, even if she sometimes felt like she was crumbling under the pressure. After all, wasn't it her curiosity that made her pastries famous? Perhaps it could also help unravel the mysteries that now seemed to multiply like rabbits in spring.

Olivia knew she couldn't do it alone. Despite the distance and the silence that had grown between them, she held onto the hope that Emily, wherever she was, might still find her way back to Bayside Cove. Back to the place where their story began, and where, perhaps, they could turn the page together on a new chapter.

The couch creaked softly as Olivia sank deeper into its cushions, her heart aflutter with the day's turbulence. Basil, ever attuned to Olivia's moods, leaped onto the armrest with the grace of a dancer, padding her way over to Olivia's lap. The tabby cat settled beside her, a warm, living balm for frayed nerves. She began to purr—a soft rumble that seemed to vibrate directly into Olivia's tense muscles.

"Hey there, my little dough-kneader," Olivia murmured, finding comfort in the weight of Basil against her. Her hand instinctively sought out the smooth fur, and Basil responded by nuzzling her fingers with a gentle headbutt. It was as if the cat knew exactly where Olivia's thoughts had been winding, down the dark alleys of doubt and fear, and she was here to guide her back to the light of the present.

"Your timing is impeccable as always," Olivia said, a wry smile curling the corners of her mouth. She took a deep breath, letting it out slowly, trying to synchronize her heartbeat with the steady thrumming of Basil' purring.

As the moments passed, wrapped in silence save for Basil' rhythmic song, a soft knock at the door jostled Olivia from her reverie. Her brow furrowed in surprise; visitors were rare enough during the day, let alone at this late hour. Curiosity piqued, she gently dislodged the tabby, who gave a quiet mew of protest, and stood to answer the summons.

"Coming!" Olivia called out, smoothing down her apron out of habit. She crossed the room in a few strides, the scent of vanilla and cinnamon lingering on her as an aromatic reminder of the bakery below. With a glance through the peephole, she brushed a stray lock of hair from her face and opened the door.

"Martha Caldwell, to what do I owe the pleasure?" Olivia asked, her voice a blend of warmth and bewilderment. Martha, standing on the threshold with the poise of a ship's captain braving a stormy sea, simply smiled.

The door swung open, and there she was—Martha Caldwell as timeless as the books she safeguarded, her silver hair fastened in a pristine bun that defied the hour's informality. The sharp blue eyes that met Olivia's held a depth of mystery and an undercurrent of wisdom, like ancient tomes whispering secrets through the ages.

"Martha, please, come in," Olivia said, stepping aside to allow the town's esteemed librarian entry into her personal haven. The surprise still played on her features, but it was quickly replaced by the familiar comfort she always felt in Martha's presence.

"Thank you, dear," Martha replied, her voice a soft cadence that seemed to carry with it the hush of the library's sacred halls. She stepped over the threshold, her gaze sweeping across the room with an appreciative nod toward the cozy disarray that bespoke long hours of dedication to craft.

"Can I get you something? Tea, perhaps?" Olivia offered, though the hour suggested stronger libations might be more appropriate.

"Tea would be lovely," Martha accepted with a gracious tilt of her head. As Olivia busied herself in the kitchen, the older woman found her place on the sofa, Basil eyeing her with feline curiosity before deciding she was worthy of his silent approval.

The Frosted Felony

"Olivia," Martha began, once they were both settled with steaming mugs cradled in their hands, "I've seen the toll recent events have taken on you, my dear. You must remember the strength within you—it has been your compass through many a storm."

"Strength feels a bit like a distant memory these days," Olivia admitted, tracing the rim of her mug with a thoughtful finger.

"Ah, but it's always there," Martha continued, her tone even, reassuring. "Like the lighthouse at Bayside Cove, steadfast against the tempest. You trust your instincts when you bake, when you create. That same instinct is what will guide you now."

"Instincts can be tricky," Olivia countered with a half-smile. "They're not exactly listed in the recipe."

"Perhaps not," Martha chuckled softly, "but they are written in the heart, and you, Olivia Pierce, have one of the truest hearts in all of Bayside Cove."

Olivia let out a breath she hadn't realized she'd been holding, the tightness in her chest loosening ever so slightly. Martha's words, delivered with such calm certainty, were like a balm to the chaos that had been whirling inside her.

"Thank you, Martha," Olivia said after a moment, her gratitude genuine, her humor peeking through despite the shadows. "Your faith in me is more comforting than this tea—and considerably less likely to scald."

Martha's laughter, light and knowing, filled the room, mingling with the scent of chamomile and the persistent purring from Basil' contented slumber.

Olivia leaned back against the plush cushions, her hands clasped around the warm ceramic of her tea mug. Martha's presence was like a gentle anchor in the stormy sea of Olivia's thoughts. The librarian's words, steeped in wisdom and delivered with serene conviction, wove through the air, stitching together the frayed edges of Olivia's resolve.

"Remember, dear, you have an inner compass. It has guided you before; it will not fail you now," Martha said, her voice a soft melody against the backdrop of the small apartment.

The normally bustling space above the bakery felt hushed and sacred in that moment, as if even the walls were leaning in to absorb the comfort offered by the wise librarian. Olivia's eyes, usually so bright with curiosity and mirth, now shimmered with unshed tears—not of sadness, but of gratitude.

"Martha, I can't tell you how much this means to me," Olivia murmured, her voice thick with emotion. "It's like you always know just when I need a bit of... well, Martha magic."

A twinkle lit up Martha's sharp blue eyes, and she reached across the space between them to pat Olivia's hand reassuringly. "No magic, my dear—just years of reading people instead of just books."

Their laughter mingled, light and easy, but beneath it ran a current of newfound determination. Olivia felt it, a steady flame rekindling within her chest—a sense of purpose reignited by the kindling of Martha's words.

"Thank you, truly," Olivia added, standing and walking Martha to the door. She felt steadier on her feet, her mind clearer than it had been all day.

"Always here for you, Olivia," Martha replied, stepping into the hall. "And remember—Bayside Cove has more secrets than my library has books. Trust yourself to uncover them." With a final nod, she turned, her cardigan swaying gently as she walked away.

Olivia lingered in the doorway, watching the retreating figure of a woman who held more stories within her than any novel on her library's shelves. A mix of gratitude for the wisdom imparted and curiosity for the untold tales Martha carried with her filled Olivia's heart.

"Goodnight, Martha," Olivia called softly, though the librarian was already rounding the corner. Her words floated down the empty hallway, a silent promise that she would indeed trust her instincts, come what may.

Olivia settled at her kitchen table, the light from the lamp casting an intimate glow over the scattered papers and photographs that chronicled the peculiar events of Bayside Cove. Her fingers, still lightly floured from a day's work at the bakery, traced the edges of notes as she gathered her thoughts. With the quiet night wrapping around her like a shawl, she took up her pen and began to list the unanswered questions that prickled at her curiosity.

"Alright," she murmured to herself, "let's see what we've got." There was a warmth in her voice, a companionable sound in the silence of her apartment. It was just her, the evidence, and the soft tick-tock of the clock on the wall—a metronome for her deductive symphony.

The Frosted Felony

Her expression was the very picture of determination, eyebrows knitting together as she scribbled down queries and suspicions. "Who would benefit from the old lighthouse's destruction?" she pondered aloud, her tone threaded with intrigue. "And those strange lights by the shore, coincidence or...?"

The clock chimed softly, pulling Olivia's attention away from her sea of paper. She glanced up, her expressive eyes widening slightly at the late hour displayed. "One o'clock already?" she said, a note of surprise coloring her words. The moon outside had climbed high, a silent witness to the passage of time.

For a moment, Olivia considered the allure of her soft bed waiting just down the hall, the call of dreams yet unexplored. But the flicker of dedication in her gaze outshone the weariness that tugged at the corners of her eyes. She leaned back in her chair, arms crossing as she weighed her options, her humor finding its way to the surface despite the gravity of her task.

"Sleep is for the unhaunted," she quipped with a wry smile, brushing a stray lock of hair behind her ear. And with that, her decision was made. She pulled the evidence closer, her hands moving with renewed vigor as she dove back into the mystery, letting the rest of the world fade away into the whispers of the night.

Olivia pushed back from the table, her body protesting the long hours of scrutiny she had already endured. But as she stared at the scattered papers and the cryptic notes scrawled in her neat hand, resolve hardened within her like tempered chocolate. She couldn't give up now, not when the answers were surely hiding just beneath the surface, like the subtle flavors in one of her signature pastries.

"Alright, Olivia," she muttered to herself, cracking her knuckles with a determined grin. "Let's find you some truths."

She stood up for a moment, stretching languidly before gathering her hair into a loose ponytail. With a swift movement, she cleared a space amidst the chaos on the kitchen table, methodically aligning the papers into neat stacks. Each article, every photograph, and all her handwritten notes became part of an intricate dance, choreographed by Olivia's experienced hands.

Her eyes, once heavy with fatigue, now sparkled with an investigative fervor that reflected the moonlight streaming through the window. She leaned in, her nose nearly brushing against an old map of

Bayside Cove as she traced a line along the shore where the mysterious lights had been seen.

"Patterns, patterns everywhere, and not a drop to drink," she quipped under her breath, a smile playing on her lips despite the seriousness of her quest. Her fingers danced from one piece of evidence to another, tapping here, pausing there, as if conducting an orchestra only she could hear.

The antique clock ticked away obliviously, its rhythmic sound lost to Olivia's focus. It was as though time itself had curled up beside Basil and dozed off, leaving Olivia in a bubble of concentration that stretched the minutes into hours unnoticed.

Every now and then, she'd pause to sip from a cold cup of coffee, grimacing at the bitterness but welcoming the jolt. She shuffled photographs, lined up witness statements, and circled dates on calendars, her brow furrowed in intense contemplation.

"Connections, my elusive little friends, show yourselves," she whispered, leaning back to regard the sprawling network of information. A satisfying sense of progress enveloped her, even as the night deepened, shrouding Bayside Cove in its silent embrace.

And so, Olivia continued, the keeper of secrets in a sleepy town that was more awake than it seemed, her dedication a beacon that burned brighter as the world around her slumbered.

Olivia's pen came to a rest, the last of her unanswered questions neatly bullet-pointed on the page. She leaned back in her chair, her gaze lingering on the list that was both daunting and invigorating. With a sigh that had far more contentment than weariness, she closed her notebook with a soft thud—a punctuation mark on the night's efforts.

"Alright, team," she addressed the quiet room, a wry smile touching her lips as she glanced at the slumbering form of Basil, "we've got our work cut out for us." Her words were met with nothing but the gentle snore of her feline companion and the distant lull of the ocean outside.

She stretched, feeling the satisfying pull of muscles that had been hunched over mysteries for too long. Olivia stood up, rolling her shoulders, and turned off the lamp, casting the kitchen into moonlit shadows. The evidence sprawled across the table seemed less intimidating now, like puzzle pieces waiting patiently for her to fit them together.

The Frosted Felony

"Tomorrow," she promised herself, her voice a determined whisper, "the pieces will fall into place."

With renewed purpose steadying her steps, Olivia moved towards her bedroom, pausing only to cast a fond look back at the table that held the keys to secrets untold. The investigation was a bakery case of its own sort—full of hidden ingredients and complex recipes that only she could decipher. She chuckled softly, imagining her detective work as an elaborate cake she was destined to bake to perfection.

"Sweet dreams, Bayside Cove," she murmured, brushing a strand of hair from her face. "Your secrets won't stay hidden for long."

As Olivia slipped beneath the covers, the list of questions in her notebook seemed to glow with potential in the darkness of the room. They beckoned her onward, promising that answers lay just beyond the horizon. And with that thought cradling her mind, Olivia let sleep claim her, ready to rise with the sun and meet the challenges ahead with the same tenacity she kneaded into her dough every morning.

"Watch out, world," she thought, a grin curving her lips even as she drifted off. "Olivia Pierce is on the case."

Chapter 14

Rising to the Occasion

Olivia sat at her antique oak desk, nestled in the cozy corner of her beloved bakery. The scent of freshly baked bread mingled with the sweet fragrance of vanilla and chocolate, a symphony of aromas that usually brought her comfort. Today, however, her attention was elsewhere, fixated on the crinkled 'cupcake notes' spread out before her. Her fingers traced the edges of the paper as if they could coax secrets from the fibers.

"Symbols... patterns..." she mumbled to herself. The mayor's cryptic messages had always been an enigma, but Olivia's determination had sharpened into a fine point, as keen as the edge of her favorite icing spatula. She jotted down a recurring sequence of letters, her brow furrowing in concentration. "What are you trying to tell me, Mayor Bennett?" she whispered, half expecting the notes to answer back.

The bell above the bakery door jingled, a familiar sound that usually signaled the arrival of a customer or a friend. But today, it heralded Emily's hesitant entry. Olivia didn't need to look up to know who it was; Emily's presence seemed to charge the air itself with a blend of apprehension and hope.

"Hey, Liv," Emily greeted, her voice laced with a careful neutrality that belied the turmoil Olivia knew must be brewing beneath the surface.

"Em." Olivia's acknowledgment was terse, her eyes not leaving the notes. Trust was a delicate pastry, easily spoiled, and Emily's sudden return to Bayside Cove had left a bitter taste that lingered.

They stood there, the space between them charged with unsaid words, until Emily took a tentative step forward. "I think I might have an idea about the code," she ventured, her green eyes locking onto Olivia's.

Olivia's hands stilled, her pen hovering above the paper. She glanced up, meeting Emily's steady gaze, and saw not just her sister but the ally she needed. The past clawed at her, but the urgency of their task overshadowed old grudges.

"Fine," Olivia relented, the word feeling like a mixture too stiff to whisk. "We can try. Together."

With a nod, Emily pulled up a chair, the wooden legs scraping gently against the floor. Side by side, they bent over the notes, the bakery enveloping them in its reassuring warmth. A sprinkle of humor dusted their conversation as they began to work through the symbols, a silent truce forming like dough rising in the oven.

"Maybe it's an anagram? Or some sort of substitution cipher?" Emily suggested, her finger tracing a line of letters.

"Could be," Olivia replied, her skepticism softening. "Or maybe Bennett's just messing with us, and it's actually his order for next week's catering."

A short laugh escaped Emily, genuine and shared, bridging the gap between them like the sweet glaze that sealed a fruit tart.

"Let's figure it out then, Detective Pierce," Emily said with a playful smile.

"Right behind you, Watson," Olivia quipped back, a smile tugging at her lips despite herself.

Together, they delved into the mystery of the cupcake notes, their combined resolve turning each clue over like the pages of a recipe book, each eager to discover what secret ingredient lay hidden within.

Olivia's expressive eyes darted between the lines of cryptic text, then to Emily's furrowed brow, and back again. The bakery's scent of vanilla and cinnamon lingered in the air, a comforting backdrop to the intensity of their task. Their heads bowed together in concentration, they sifted through the notes like searching for a rare spice lost in a pantry.

"Look at this," Olivia murmured, pointing to a sequence. "Every third word, there's the same symbol."

Emily leaned in closer, her green eyes catching the light as she examined the pattern. "You're right. It's too consistent to be coincidence." Her voice, usually laced with an edge of mystery, now carried the thrill of the hunt.

"Could it be some kind of code within a code?" Olivia speculated, her curiosity piqued.

"Exactly what I was thinking," Emily agreed, tapping the paper with determination.

Their excitement swelled with each connection made, their skills blending like the perfect balance of sweet and savory. Each revelation was a step closer, a sprinkle of sugar on the path to uncovering the truth.

As they were piecing together another string of letters, the bell above the bakery door jingled, heralding Sam's arrival. His sandy hair was tousled more than usual, as if he had been running his hands through it in frustration or excitement.

"Guys, you won't believe what I've found," Sam announced, his upbeat tempo matching his quick pace towards them. His blue eyes sparkled with the promise of a breakthrough.

"Spill it, Sam," Olivia said, her wit momentarily set aside by anticipation.

"Margaret Foster," Sam began, pausing for effect, "isn't just the charming philanthropist everyone thinks she is."

"Go on..." Emily urged, her adventurous spirit evident in her attentive posture.

"Turns out, she and Daniel Cooper share more than just office space at town hall," Sam revealed, his words like the first bite into a mystery-flavored jelly bean.

"Are we talking shared interests? Shared secrets?" Olivia prodded, her hands unconsciously wiping flour onto her apron.

"Shared bank accounts, shared trips, and—get this—shared property," Sam said, laying down documents that rustled like leaves in the autumn breeze.

"Joint ventures in corruption, perhaps?" Emily mused, her green eyes scanning the papers with expert speed.

"Looks like our investigation just got a sprinkle of intrigue," Olivia commented, her gaze moving from the papers to her allies. "And possibly a dash of danger."

"Sounds like a recipe for disaster—for them," Sam quipped, grinning at his own play on words.

"Or the perfect blend for us to expose what's really been baking in Bayside Cove," Olivia concluded, her resolve firm as a well-set custard.

Together, they turned back to the cupcake notes and the fresh evidence, the bond of their shared purpose growing stronger with every secret uncovered.

The bell above the bakery door jangled softly, marking the late hour as Olivia and Emily hunched over the mysterious cupcake notes.

The Frosted Felony

Olivia's hand paused mid-scribble as her eyes widened, a pattern emerging from the frosted glyphs before her. "Emily, look at this," she whispered, her voice laced with triumph. "These aren't just random sequences; they're coordinates and... a combination."

"Coordinates?" Emily leaned in closer, her green eyes reflecting the dim light of the desk lamp. "To where?"

"To the town hall." Olivia pointed to a series of numbers that matched the building's address. "And I'd bet my secret chocolate ganache recipe that this combination opens a safe hidden somewhere inside."

Emily's lips curled into a smile as adventurous as her spirit. "Then it's settled. Tomorrow night, we search for the safe."

"Agreed," Olivia replied, her heart fluttering like a butterfly in a jar. "We may just crack this case wide open."

***

Under the cloak of evening, the trio approached the grand facade of Bayside Cove's town hall. Shadows danced across the stone steps as Olivia, Emily, and Sam ascended them, their footsteps muted by shared resolve.

"Remember, keep your voices down," Olivia cautioned, her fingers brushing the cool metal of the door handle. "We need to be as inconspicuous as a vanilla cupcake in a batch of red velvet."

"Got it," Sam replied with a nod, his blue eyes alight with the thrill of the caper. "In and out like whipped cream on a hot pie."

Quietly, they slipped through the entrance, the heavy door closing behind them with a soft thud. The familiar scent of polished wood and aged paper filled Olivia's nostrils, grounding her in the reality of their mission.

"Split up, but stay within whispering distance," Olivia instructed, scanning the ornate hallway for any sign of movement. Her baker's precision now served a more clandestine purpose, each sense sharpened in the search for clues.

"Meet back here in ten minutes," Emily added, her figure disappearing around a corner with the stealth of a cat on the prowl.

Sam gave a thumbs-up, already blending into the shadows as he ventured toward the mayor's office. Olivia moved with silent grace, every creak of the floorboards under her feet making her heart race.

Each second was an eternity, yet time seemed to hasten its pace as they combed through the town hall's secrets, inching ever closer to the hidden truth nestled within its walls.

Olivia's fingertips brushed against the cool, varnished wood of the town hall's inner sanctum. The hushed whispers of her companions were ghosts in the grandeur of the dimly lit corridors, as they split their attention between the task at hand and the need for secrecy. She could almost taste the dusty air, thick with history and the faintest hint of intrigue.

"Anything?" Sam's voice was a low murmur, barely disturbing the silence.

"Nothing here," Emily responded from behind a towering grandfather clock, her voice holding the same steadiness that marked her every deliberate move.

Olivia squatted down, examining the floorboards near the mayor's office. Her keen eyes, so accustomed to spotting the smallest imperfection in her pastries, now searched for any sign of disturbance. A small, irregular gap between the planks caught her eye, and her heart skipped a beat. "Over here," she hissed, beckoning her allies with a flour-dusted hand still speckled from that morning's baking.

Emily and Sam converged beside her, their movements fluid and silent. Together, they wedged fingers into the narrow opening. With a collective effort, they lifted, and the floorboard yielded to their insistence, revealing the hidden safe nestled below like a secret ingredient tucked away in a recipe.

"Okay, here goes nothing," Olivia murmured, crouching before the safe. Her hands trembled slightly—not from fear, but from the electric thrill of being so close to the truth. She wiped her palms on her apron, leaving white smudges on the dark fabric, then reached for the dial. Each number was a step closer to vindication, each tiny click a heartbeat in the quiet room.

"Left to 15," she whispered, mostly to herself, "right to 7, left again to 22..."

The last number fell into place, and after a breathless pause, there it was—a soft but resolute click that felt like victory. Olivia's pulse thrummed in her ears as she swung the safe door open. Stacks of documents, thick envelopes, and files teetered on the brink of freedom. It

The Frosted Felony

was all there—the proof they needed, the hope of Bayside Cove in manila and paper.

"Would you look at that?" Emily leaned in, her green eyes reflecting the triumph that shone in Olivia's own gaze.

"Better than finding a forgotten batch of cookies in the oven," Olivia quipped, the corners of her mouth tilting up in a smile that mirrored Emily's. Their shared success seemed to stitch together the frayed edges of their sisterhood, even if just for this stolen moment.

"Let's gather these up and get out before—" Sam started, but Olivia was already scooping up the files with the care of a baker arranging her finest pastries in a display case.

"Before this place closes and we're stuck spending the night with the ghost of mayors past," Olivia finished for him, her voice light despite the gravity of their discovery.

Together, they bundled the evidence, their hearts buoyed by the weight of what they held in their hands. It was more than just paper; it was hope, it was justice—it was the sweetest icing on the most unexpected of cakes.

Margaret Foster's eyes glinted with the cold precision of a woman who knew how to get what she wanted as she leaned across the mahogany table that separated her from Daniel Cooper. The dim light of the secluded coffee shop they chose for their clandestine meeting cast subtle shadows on their faces, creating an air of mystery and urgency.

"Daniel," Margaret began, her voice a melodious whisper laced with steel, "we cannot afford any loose ends. It's time we take decisive action to secure our position."

Daniel regarded her with a mix of admiration and apprehension, his fingers tapping a silent rhythm on the tabletop. "Margaret, I understand the stakes, but are you sure there's no other way? We're already walking on thin ice here."

"Darling," she cooed with a sly smile, reaching out to still his nervous hand with her own perfectly manicured one. "Sometimes, the ice needs to be broken to catch the fish. Trust me; I've navigated these waters before."

Unseen by them, Olivia, Emily, and Sam were huddled together in the town hall, hearts racing as their hands worked swiftly to gather the evidence that could unravel Margaret's carefully spun web. Olivia tucked a stray lock of hair behind her ear, a habit when she was focused, and glanced at her companions. "This is it, guys. Everything we need is right here."

"Let's not celebrate until we're clear of this place," Emily cautioned, her gaze flitting to the door then back to the documents in her arms.

"Agreed," Sam added quietly, his eyes scanning the room one last time.

Their moment of victory was cut short by the soft echo of footsteps approaching. Olivia's pulse quickened, and a finger flew to her lips, signaling silence. In unison, they ducked behind a towering bookshelf filled with dusty tomes on Bayside Cove's history, barely daring to breathe.

The footsteps grew louder, more pronounced, and Olivia strained her ears, trying to discern if the intruder was friend or foe. Every creak of the wooden floorboards sent a jolt through her nerves, and the faint scent of lemon oil polish that permeated the air now felt suffocating.

"Did anyone see us come in?" Emily's whisper was so faint it nearly blended with the shuffling of papers in their arms.

"Shh," Olivia breathed out, her eyes locked on the sliver of space between two leather-bound volumes where she could just make out the gleam of shoes pacing outside their hiding spot.

"Stay calm," she mouthed to her friends, her mind racing with potential escape plans. But even as fear threatened to choke her resolve, Olivia couldn't help but feel the smallest surge of adrenaline. After all, wasn't this the kind of suspenseful moment that would make her bakery's patrons gasp over their morning coffee and scones?

The shoes halted, and for a heartbeat, everything stood still. Then, as quickly as they had come, the footsteps receded, leaving behind a heavy silence that blanketed the trio in both relief and dread.

"Close call," Sam exhaled after a moment, his words puncturing the quiet.

"Too close," Olivia agreed, her heart slowly resuming its regular rhythm. She flashed a grin that didn't quite reach her worried eyes. "But hey, what's a little breaking and entering without a dash of danger, right?"

Emily chuckled softly, the sound tinged with nerves. "Next time, let's stick to cupcakes and frosting. They're less likely to walk in on us."

The Frosted Felony

With a collective nod, they stepped out from their temporary refuge, ready to navigate the treacherous path that lay ahead, united by determination and a shared love for their small coastal town.

Huddled behind the towering bookshelf, Olivia stilled as a voice cut through the silence like a knife. It was smooth, almost sweet, but laced with venom—one she'd heard in council meetings and polite, treacherous small talk. Margaret Foster.

"Daniel, we need to tie up loose ends before this spirals out of control," Margaret's voice drifted over, each word chillingly precise.

"Loose ends?" Daniel's replied, a tremor of unease in his question.

"Olivia Pierce and her little band of amateur sleuths," Margaret said with a dismissive laugh that didn't quite mask the danger behind it. "They've become more than a nuisance."

Olivia felt Emily's hand grip her arm, a silent solidarity in the shadow of threat. Even Sam, ever the optimist, had lines of tension etching his youthful face.

A moment passed and then another, the words 'eliminate Olivia' echoing in Olivia's mind like an ominous refrain. She knew the weight of them; they were no idle threats. The resolve within her crystallized, sharp and unyielding. Justice for Bayside Cove wasn't just a quest—it was a necessity.

Without a word, Olivia gestured towards the exit, her fingers steady despite the adrenaline coursing through her veins. They moved as one, silent shadows slipping between moonlit columns and dusty archives, the gravity of their discovery propelling them forward.

"Can you believe this?" Sam whispered once they were safely outside, his voice barely audible. "Margaret Foster, the town's darling, is actually..."

"Let's not dwell on that now," Olivia interrupted, her tone low but firm. "We need to focus on staying ahead of them."

"Right," Emily agreed, her gaze fierce. "We've got work to do."

"First thing tomorrow, we go through everything we found," Olivia said, already plotting their next steps. "We lay it all out, make sense of it—"

"And take down the queen of cupcakes turned queen of corruption?" Sam offered, trying to lighten the mood.

"Exactly," Olivia said, with a ghost of a smile tugging at her lips. Despite the danger, there was something invigorating about standing up for what was right, especially with her sister and friend by her side.

"Let's head back," Emily said, her eyes reflecting the resolve that had brought them this far. "We have a long night ahead of us."

Back inside the comforting embrace of her bakery, Olivia Pierce ran a flour-dusted hand through her hair, strands catching between her fingers as she surveyed her sanctuary. The familiar scent of sugar and vanilla hung in the air, mingling with the sharper tang of adrenaline that still clung to each of them after their stealthy exit from town hall. Sam Turner leaned against the polished countertop, his blue eyes serious despite the playful quirk of his lips. Emily Pierce stood by the window, her posture rigid, like an unyielding sentinel guarding against unseen threats.

"Okay," Olivia began, her voice steady as she pulled out a notepad scattered with crumbs from its hiding place beneath the cash register. "We've got enough evidence to start a storm, but we need a plan."

"Right," Sam agreed, crossing his arms. "And we need to stay one step ahead of Foster and Cooper." His usual lighthearted demeanor was replaced by a focused intensity that only surfaced in times of crisis.

"First things first," Emily cut in, her emerald eyes scanning Olivia's notes. "We need to sort through this mess. Figure out what's relevant and what's just icing on the cake."

"Speaking of cake...," Sam muttered, eyeing the leftover pastries.

"Focus, Sam," Olivia chided, though she couldn't suppress a fleeting smile at his attempt to bring levity to their situation.

"Right, sorry," he said, but the twinkle in his eye suggested otherwise.

They gathered around the large oak table at the center of the bakery, where Olivia often hosted cake decorating workshops. Now, it served as their war room. Spread out before them were pages of scribbled notes, coded messages, and copies of financial records—all pieces of a puzzle they were determined to solve.

"Look at us," Olivia said, her voice infused with warmth as she took in the sight of her closest allies. "The baker, the chef, and the adventurer, all huddled together, trying to save the town."

"Sounds like the beginning of a bad joke," Emily retorted, though her lips twitched in amusement.

The Frosted Felony

"Or a great adventure," Sam countered, winking at her.

"Both, probably," Olivia concluded. She took a deep breath, feeling the gravity of their task settle upon her shoulders like a cloak. "But seriously, I can't thank you both enough. We might have our quirks, but there's no one else I'd rather have by my side right now."

"Olivia, come on," Emily said softly, reaching across the table to squeeze her sister's hand. "You know we're in this together."

"Always," Sam added, his grin returning as he placed a gentle hand on Olivia's shoulder.

"Right. Together," Olivia echoed, strengthened by their solidarity. "And together, we'll get through this. We'll expose every last secret Bayside Cove has been hiding."

"Even if it means flipping this town upside down like a pineapple upside-down cake," Sam chimed in.

"Please, no more cake metaphors tonight," Emily groaned, but her smirk betrayed her appreciation for the sentiment.

"Alright, team," Olivia said, looking from one to the other, her gaze fierce yet filled with unmistakable affection. "Let's get to work and show this town what we're made of."

And with that, they dove into the sea of documents, their camaraderie an anchor in the tumultuous waters they were about to navigate.

Olivia turned the sign on the bakery's front door to 'Closed', a final click resounding in the dimming light of evening. She wrapped her scarf tighter around her neck, bracing against the cold that seeped through the glass. Emily and Sam fell into step behind her, their breath visible in the frosty air.

"Feels like the whole town is holding its breath," Emily murmured, her eyes scanning the quiet streets of Bayside Cove, the fading sunset casting long shadows between the buildings.

"Or maybe it's just waiting for us to stir things up," Sam replied with a mischievous glint in his blue eyes. His words were muffled slightly by the scarf he'd haphazardly looped around his neck.

"Either way, we're in for one heck of a night," Olivia said, unlocking her car, the beep echoing off the nearby storefronts. They loaded their precious cargo of documents carefully into the backseat, the evidence of corruption nestled among boxes of unsold pastries.

"Speaking of stirring things up," Emily began, leaning against the car as Olivia made sure everything was secure, "Do you think we'll actually find anyone at town hall this late?"

"Only one way to find out," Olivia answered, securing the trunk with a satisfying thud. "But if there's even a chance to get ahead of Margaret and Daniel, we need to take it."

"Plus, I've always fancied a bit of late-night sleuthing," Sam quipped, jumping into the passenger seat and rubbing his hands together for warmth. "It's like being in one of those detective novels, minus the trench coat and fedora."

"Let's just hope our story has a happier ending," Emily said as she climbed into the backseat, her tone serious despite the smile tugging at the corners of her mouth.

"Happy endings are our specialty," Olivia assured her, starting the engine. The bakery receded in the rearview mirror as they drove away, leaving behind the scent of sugar and spice for the promise of justice and truth.

"Alright, team," Olivia said, glancing at her companions through the mirror. "Time to bake a new future for Bayside Cove."

With nods of agreement, they set off into the night, the chill of the air no match for the fire of determination burning within them. Their journey had only just begun, but together, they felt unstoppable.

Chapter 15

Turning Up the Heat

The town hall doors groaned open as Olivia, flanked by Emily and Detective Holbrook, stepped into the hushed foyer. The stale air hung heavy with tension, mingling with a faint scent of aged mahogany and dust. Olivia's warm brown eyes swept over the gathered suspects, each figure casting an uncertain shadow in the dim light filtering through the stained-glass windows.

"Alright, folks," Olivia said, her voice echoing slightly off the high ceilings, "let's not dance around the maypole any longer than we have to."

Victor Wellington stood up, straightening his tie, the lines on his face deepening like trenches as he sized up Olivia. His dark eyes gave away nothing, but Olivia could almost hear the cogs turning behind his polished facade.

"Victor, your passion for progress in Bayside Cove is no secret," Olivia began, her words carefully dispensed like measured ingredients in a recipe. "But this?" She held up a sheaf of papers, evidence that fluttered like a white flag. "This suggests your vision might include lining your own pockets."

"Olivia Pierce," Victor replied, his tone smooth as aged whiskey, "You bake delightful pastries, but I'm afraid you're half-baked on the facts."

Emily's eyebrow arched at his retort, but she remained silent, a pillar of calm beside her sister.

"Except these numbers don't lie," Olivia continued, unfazed. "Bank transfers, property acquisitions well beyond a councilman's salary... It seems our little town's revitalization funds have been diverted to more personal ventures."

"Allegations," Victor countered, every inch the businessman on trial, "require proof, Miss Pierce."

"True," Olivia conceded, tucking a rebellious auburn lock behind her ear, "and here it is." She laid out photographs, bank statements, and emails methodically across the oak table that separated them. "Not to mention a motive tied up prettier than a bow on a birthday cake."

Detective Holbrook watched the exchange, his lips twitching into an almost imperceptible smile; it was hard not to admire Olivia's gumption. She had a way of making even the most damning evidence seem as palatable as her bakery's signature cherry pie.

"Let's just say, Victor," Olivia concluded, "your scheme has more holes in it than the potholes you promised to fix on Main Street."

A murmur rippled through the room, the townspeople's attention fixed on the confrontation unfolding before them. Victor's confident mask showed its first crack, a slight shift in his stance betraying his unease.

"Charming analogy," he managed to say, though the charm was clearly beginning to curdle.

The tension in the town hall was palpable, a thick fog of suspicion that clung to every wood-paneled wall and whispered through the rafters. With Victor Wellington's confidence now taking on water, Emily Pierce stepped forward, her athletic frame cutting through the unease as she approached Councilman Richard Cornwall.

"Richard," she began, her voice the perfect blend of steel and silk, "you've been playing chess with this town's livelihood." Her green eyes locked onto his blue ones, unflinching and confident.

Cornwall, standing tall and impeccably dressed in a suit that screamed authority, attempted to parry with his usual charm. "Miss Pierce, surely you jest. I serve at the pleasure of the people."

"Then your definition of 'pleasure' must include manipulating the mayor for your own gain." She placed her hands on her hips, as if bracing against the gale force of political duplicity.

A ripple of murmurs spread through the assembled crowd, their attention shifting like leaves in an autumn breeze. Cornwall's lips tightened, his calculated demeanor fraying at the edges. "I assure you, any decisions made were for the betterment of Bayside Cove," he deflected, but his gaze darted away, betraying a crack in his façade.

It was then that Detective James Holbrook saw his opening. He moved toward Evelyn Grant, who stood quietly, her presence almost ethereal with her earth-toned attire blending into the surroundings. "Ms. Grant," he said, folding his arms as he regarded her with his piercing gaze, "tell us about the environmental violations you've been investigating."

Evelyn's posture straightened, her green eyes alight with a fire that matched her passion for nature. "The marshlands," she began, her tone clear and assertive, "are home to endangered species, yet I found evidence of illegal dumping—chemicals that could devastate the ecosystem."

Holbrook nodded, appreciating her directness. "And your motives?"

"Simple. To protect what can't protect itself," Evelyn stated emphatically. "Here." She handed over a folder stuffed with photos, reports, and notes scrawled in margins. "Documentation of everything."

"Thank you, Ms. Grant." Holbrook took the folder, flipping it open to scan the contents, while the townspeople leaned in, trying to catch a glimpse of justice being revealed.

Emily turned back to Cornwall with a knowing look, while Holbrook continued to peruse the evidence from Evelyn. The pieces of a larger puzzle were beginning to slot together, each revelation casting a new light on the shadows that had long lingered over Bayside Cove.

The air in the town hall was thick with tension, a tangible force that clung to every wood-paneled wall and whispered through the rafters. Olivia's eyes swept over the suspects, her gaze lingering on Margaret Foster. The woman's polished exterior, usually so immaculate, was fraying at the edges.

"Margaret," Olivia said, her voice steady but warm, "we know about the vandalism. Why don't you tell us your side of the story?"

Margaret's lips quivered as she looked up, her angular features softening into something akin to grief. "Yes, I defaced Olivia's bakery sign," she admitted, her voice barely above a whisper, each word like a crack in a dam holding back a reservoir of emotions. "But murder? That's madness! I would never—"

"Nobody's accusing you of being a saint, Margaret," Emily interjected with a wry tilt of her head, "but there's a chasm between petty sabotage and killing someone."

Detective Holbrook's blue eyes watched the exchange, his stance relaxed yet alert. He cleared his throat gently, drawing attention without raising his voice. "Let's remember, we're here for the truth, not a witch hunt."

As if his words were the strike of a match, accusations began to fly like sparks among the gathered townsfolk. Victor Wellington jabbed a finger towards Margaret, his face contorted into a mask of indignation. "She's capable of more than she admits!" he barked, only to be met with a chorus of retorts from others.

"Enough!" Olivia raised her hands, flour dust still clinging to her skin despite the gravity of the situation, a reminder of the life interrupted by this chaos. Her eyes danced with humor despite the seriousness of the moment. "This isn't a bake-off, people. Let's keep our cool."

"Olivia's right," Detective Holbrook stepped forward, his tousled hair catching the light as he moved. "We need to sift through the facts, not hurl baseless claims."

"Speaking of sifting," Emily said, her eyes narrowing playfully at her sister, "you'd think with all the baking you do, Liv, you'd have a better method for filtering out lies."

A ripple of mild laughter eased some of the room's stiffness. Even Margaret managed a weak smile, the corners of her mouth twitching in reluctant amusement.

"Alright, let's get back to it," Olivia said, her tone friendly but firm. "Margaret, can anyone vouch for your whereabouts on the night of the murder?"

Margaret's shoulders slumped, her earlier sarcasm dissolving into despair. "No, I was alone, working late on a batch of pastries. But I swear on my mixer, I didn't kill anyone."

"Your mixer?" Emily raised an eyebrow. "That's sacred territory for a baker."

"Indeed," Olivia agreed with a nod, casting a glance at James, who gave a subtle, approving tilt of his chin. They were a team, united in their quest for the truth.

"Let's move forward," Detective Holbrook suggested, his gaze methodically sweeping the room. "We've got more ground to cover."

The suspects shuffled nervously, their unease a silent symphony playing beneath the hum of conversation. Olivia caught Emily's eye, and they shared a look of determination, their bond as sisters silently reaffirmed. A gentle nod from James sealed their alliance as they prepared to delve deeper into the secrets of Bayside Cove.

The Frosted Felony

The clamor in the town hall reached a fever pitch as accusations were hurled like daggers through the thickening air. In the midst of the chaos, Daniel Cooper saw his chance. His eyes darted to the door, and with a sudden lurch, he bolted from his chair, his disheveled hair bouncing as he made a desperate dash for freedom.

"Daniel, stop!" Olivia's command sliced through the cacophony, but her words fell on deaf ears.

Sam Turner's chef instincts kicked in as he sprang into action, his movements swift and sure like a cleaver through soft dough. He sidestepped a toppled chair, his blue eyes locked onto the fleeing figure of Daniel, who was now fumbling with the door handle, his trembling hands betraying his cool facade.

"Nice try, Danny boy," Sam called out, the faintest trace of humor still clinging to his voice despite the gravity of the situation.

At the same time, James Holbrook's detective strides were measured and purposeful. He closed in from the opposite direction, his analytical gaze predicting each of Daniel's frantic twists and turns. "You won't get far," he intoned, his voice a low rumble of certainty.

Cornered between Sam's nimble agility and James' unwavering resolve, Daniel skidded to a halt, his back pressing against the cool wood of the closed door. His glasses askew, he looked from one determined face to the other, his chest heaving as if he had run a marathon rather than a few panicked steps.

"Going somewhere?" James asked, an eyebrow arching just so, as he and Sam flanked Daniel like bookends of justice.

Meanwhile, at the center of the room, beneath the flickering lights of the town hall chandelier, Olivia, Emily, and Detective Holbrook regrouped. Their attention turned to the object that seemed almost alive in Olivia's grasp – the ancient locket she'd found earlier. Its surface, a tapestry of intricate metalwork, pulsed with an eerie luminescence that grew brighter with each heated exchange that passed among the townsfolk.

"Does anyone else feel that?" Emily whispered, her fingers hovering over the locket but not daring to touch it.

"Feel what? The fact that we're in the middle of a small-town showdown, or that you've got a piece of history glowing like a Halloween decoration?" Olivia replied, half-joking, half-serious, her heart racing.

Detective Holbrook leaned in closer, his eyes narrowing thoughtfully. "It's reacting to something... emotions, maybe?" he mused. "Or perhaps it's more than just a pretty trinket."

"Guess we'll find out," Olivia said, her baker's hands steady despite the unnerving glow of the locket. The warmth of their shared mission seemed to wrap around the trio as they faced the unknown together, the light of the locket casting long shadows across their determined faces.

As the echoes of Daniel's thwarted escape attempt settled into a heavy silence, Olivia exchanged a glance with Emily and Detective Holbrook. The trio stood like sentinels among the scattered chairs and whispered rumors, their eyes locked on the luminescent artifact in Olivia's hands.

"Think this little gem is more than just an accessory?" Olivia murmured, her voice a steady thrum amid the tension.

Emily nodded, the corners of her mouth lifting in a wry smile. "It's not every day you see a locket doubling as a mood ring."

"Could be our best lead yet," Holbrook added, his tone a mix of professional curiosity and reluctant wonder. "It's been here all along, hiding in plain sight."

Olivia gave the locket a gentle shake as if willing it to divulge its secrets, the soft clinking sound a stark contrast to the cacophony of accusations that had filled the room moments before.

"Alright, everyone!" Olivia's commanding voice cut through the chaos, bringing a hush over the crowd. "Let's take a deep breath. We're going to figure this out, together." Her gaze swept across the townspeople, her warm eyes radiating sincerity and command in equal measure.

There was a collective exhale, the townsfolk responding to Olivia's presence like sails billowing under a calming wind. Trust hung in the air, tangible and sweet, much like the scent of freshly baked bread that often wafted from her bakery.

"Nobody's leaving until we get some answers," she continued, her tone firm yet reassuring. "And I promise you, we will get to the bottom of this murder."

Murmurs of consent rippled through the crowd, a testament to the faith they placed in Olivia's capable hands. She had become more than just a purveyor of pastries; she was their beacon in the fog of mystery that had settled over Bayside Cove.

The Frosted Felony

The room had settled into an uneasy silence, with only the creaking of old wooden floorboards beneath shuffling feet and the distant sound of waves crashing against the Bayside Cove shoreline. Olivia stood at the center, her shoulders squared and her expression a blend of resolve and compassion.

Emily glided through the crowd, her presence almost ethereal amid the tension. As she reached Olivia, their eyes locked in a communication that transcended words. A shared history, once frayed with distance and misunderstanding, now wove itself back together in the space between them.

"Em," Olivia began, her voice softer than the flour-dusted apron she wore like armor.

"Olivia," Emily replied, the corners of her mouth lifting in a smile that mirrored her sister's. They exchanged a nod, the unspoken promise to see this through together as potent as any spoken vow.

"Looks like we have quite the recipe for mystery on our hands," Emily quipped, the humor lightening the gravity of the situation.

"Seems so," Olivia agreed, a chuckle escaping her lips. "But I've always been good at following recipes to a T."

Detective Holbrook observed their exchange from a respectful distance, his perceptive blue eyes absorbing the scene. He approached, his footsteps deliberate but unhurried, a subtle fragrance of sea salt mingling with his cologne as he neared.

"Ms. Pierce," he said, offering Olivia a small, appreciative nod. "I must say, your knack for piecing together clues is almost as impressive as your reputation for crafting exquisite pastries."

"Detective Holbrook," Olivia replied, her eyes sparkling with a hint of mischief. "Are you saying my talent for solving mysteries might rival my lemon meringue?"

"Perhaps," James conceded, his lips curving into a rare half-smile. "Though I'd argue they both require a keen sense of detail and a certain... finesse."

Their banter was a surprising splash of color on the canvas of their investigation, painting a picture of camaraderie amidst the shadows of uncertainty. It was clear that beneath the professionalism, there was a budding respect, maybe even something more tender—a connection not yet fully defined, but impossible to ignore.

"Thank you, Detective," Olivia said, her tone sincere. "Your support means a lot. We'll need all the sharp senses we can get to unravel this one."

James's gaze lingered on Olivia a beat longer than necessary before he turned his attention to the locket still glowing faintly in her hand. The object seemed to hum with secrets, and it was clear that the answers they sought were locked within its ancient metalwork.

"Whatever the truth may be," James murmured, "we'll uncover it. Together."

"Agreed," Olivia and Emily said in unison, sealing the pledge with determined nods.

The trio stood united, a beacon of hope in the dimly lit town hall. With renewed purpose, they faced the gathering crowd, each person there silently acknowledging the strength of the bond that had formed in their midst. And with the ancient locket as their guide, the path forward seemed a little less daunting.

Olivia glanced around the town hall, her eyes settling on the faces of the townspeople scattered like leaves in an autumn wind. The weight of their gaze felt heavy, but it was nothing compared to the responsibility that now rested on her shoulders. Taking a deep breath, she turned to Emily and Detective Holbrook, who stood by her side, an unlikely trinity against the brewing storm of secrets.

"Looks like we've got quite the puzzle to piece together," Olivia quipped, a wry smile tugging at the corner of her mouth as she attempted to cut through the tension.

"More like a labyrinth," Emily added, her green eyes flickering with the flame of challenge that had always driven her.

Detective Holbrook folded his arms, nodding solemnly. "And every labyrinth has its minotaur. We'll find ours."

The simple act of solidarity seemed to cast a spell over the room. An unspoken agreement passed between them, each one acknowledging the others' strengths: Olivia's meticulous eye for detail, Emily's tenacious spirit, and Holbrook's analytical mind. They were ready to delve into the heart of Bayside Cove, to navigate the twisted corridors of deception that lay hidden beneath its quiet façade.

"Then let's not waste any more time," Olivia declared, her resolve hardening like setting caramel. "We have truths to unearth."

"Agreed," Emily said, her posture straightening like a mast bracing against the wind. "This town needs us."

"And I believe this town couldn't ask for better," Holbrook remarked, his tone a blend of admiration and confidence.

As they turned to leave, the locket glinted ominously from within Olivia's grasp. It was as though it sensed the determination in the air, its glow pulsing like a heartbeat quickened by the thrill of the hunt. The artifact held memories, and perhaps even more—mysteries that would soon unfold before them.

"Whatever lies ahead," Emily mused, "we'll face it as a team."

"Indeed," Holbrook concurred. "Bayside Cove is full of surprises, some darker than others. But together, there's no shadow we can't light up."

Their footsteps echoed across the wooden floor, a steady drumbeat promising action. As they exited the town hall, the twilight breeze whispered of challenges yet to come, carrying with it the scent of salt and secrets. In the distance, the coastal cliffs stood watch, guardians of a story still being written, while the waves below murmured of revelations waiting just beyond the horizon.

With the chapter closing on their unified front, the trio stepped out into the evening, the warmth of their newfound alliance a beacon against the encroaching night. And somewhere in the depths of Bayside Cove, the truth waited, patient and silent, ready to be awakened by the light of their resolve.

As the evening sky painted itself in strokes of lavender and dusky rose, Olivia, Emily, and Detective Holbrook huddled outside the town hall, their shadows stretching long across the cobbled square. The last whispers of sunlight kissed the ancient bricks, casting a soft glow that belied the turmoil within.

"Are you sure it's safe to go back in there?" Olivia asked, her fingers absently playing with the apron strings tied around her waist. Her flour-dusted hands were a stark contrast against the darkening fabric.

"Safe? Probably not," Emily replied, her green eyes reflecting the last rays of day like two secret emeralds. "But necessary? Absolutely."

Holbrook rubbed his chin, the stubble there making a soft scratching sound. "The night's only going to get deeper, and our suspect isn't going to find themselves."

"Right." Olivia straightened her shoulders, baking battle-ready. "Let's do this."

They re-entered the town hall, the door creaking ominously behind them as if protesting their return. Inside, the air felt charged, heavy with expectation and the scent of old wood and secrets. Their footsteps were muffled by the thick carpet as they navigated through the corridor, the locket from earlier now tucked securely in Olivia's pocket, its presence a constant reminder of the mystery at hand.

"Wait," Emily suddenly said, halting. She pointed toward the end of the hallway where a faint glimmer caught their attention. It was coming from beneath the mayor's office door.

"Is that...light?" Olivia whispered, squinting. "Wasn't that room pitch-black when we left?"

"Stay behind me," Holbrook instructed, moving forward with silent steps, his detective instincts kicking in. They approached the door with bated breath, listening for any sound that might give away an intruder's presence. But there was nothing—just the soft hum of the building and their own quickened heartbeats.

Olivia's warm brown eyes met Emily's, a shared spark of adrenaline passing between them. Holbrook reached for the handle, his blue eyes intense and focused. He turned it slowly, the click echoing louder than it should have in the silence.

They stepped into the room, and the source of the light became clear—a computer screen, left on and displaying a document so shocking that all three of them gasped in unison.

"Is that..." Olivia couldn't finish her sentence, her voice trailing off as she read the header of the document: 'Confidential - Project Leviathan.'

"Someone is here," Emily breathed out, her tone a mix of awe and trepidation.

"Or was," Holbrook added, scanning the room for any sign of movement.

Suddenly, the computer screen flickered and shut down, plunging the room into darkness. A chill rushed through the space, and the locket in Olivia's pocket throbbed with a cold intensity.

"Did you feel that?" Olivia asked, clutching her pocket.

"Feel what?" Holbrook asked, but before anyone could answer, a muffled thump came from the closet to their right.

The Frosted Felony

Without hesitation, Holbrook strode over and flung open the closet door. Inside, bound and gagged, was Councilman Cornwall, his eyes wide with fear and pleading for help.

"Good lord," Emily exclaimed, rushing to assist the councilman.

"Someone's trying to frame him," Olivia realized, her baker's intuition mixing oddly with her amateur sleuthing skills.

"Or silence him," Holbrook added grimly.

As Emily untied the councilman, Holbrook picked up a piece of paper that had fallen from his pocket. It was a cryptic note with a single line:

"Follow the trail before it goes cold."

"Looks like we've got a new breadcrumb," Holbrook said, his voice tinged with both frustration and excitement. "And this one's leading us straight into the belly of the beast."

"Whatever 'Project Leviathan' is, it's just the tip of the iceberg," Olivia murmured, the locket now burning against her skin through the fabric of her apron.

"Come on," Emily said, determination lighting her gaze. "We've got a trail to follow."

The three of them stood in the dark room, the weight of their next steps heavy in the air—an alliance of baker, wanderer, and detective, poised on the brink of a discovery that could change Bayside Cove forever.

As they moved toward the exit, the moon rose high above the coastal cliffs, casting a silver gleam that seemed to beckon them onward. And somewhere in the depths of the night, a truth lay buried, ready to shake the foundations of everything they thought they knew.

With hearts racing and the promise of danger lurking at every turn, they stepped out of the mayor's office, leaving the chapter—and the reader—hanging on the edge of a revelation yet to come.

Chapter 16

The Moment of Truth

The fluorescent lights of the interrogation room hummed overhead, casting a stark glow on the trio seated at the metal table. Olivia Pierce's fingers drummed an erratic rhythm against her knee, the only outward sign of the storm brewing within. Across from her, Detective James Holbrook sat with an unwavering gaze fixed on Daniel Cooper, his expression as stern as a headmaster's before delivering a verdict.

"Feels a bit like waiting for a pot to boil, doesn't it?" Olivia tried to lighten the mood, but her words hung in the air, dissolving into the tension that cocooned them.

Daniel, sandwiched between anticipation and dread, offered a weak smile, though it failed to reach his eyes. His hands were folded neatly on the table, yet they betrayed him with the slightest of trembles.

"Sometimes the truth takes its time," Holbrook replied, his voice steady as the ticking of the clock on the wall. His eyes, those deep pools of blue, never strayed from Daniel, as if trying to coax the confession through sheer will.

Olivia shifted in her chair, the cool metal pressing against her back. She could almost smell the sea salt on the breeze through the closed window, a reminder of the quaint charm of Bayside Cove waiting outside. Her bakery, with its sweet aromas and flour-dusted counters, seemed miles away from this cold, sterile place.

"Daniel, you've always been the kind to dot your i's and cross your t's," Olivia ventured, hoping to break through the young man's reticence. "I can't imagine you'd leave us hanging without a good reason."

The Frosted Felony

"Olivia's right," Holbrook chimed in, his tone firm but not unkind. "We're here to listen. It's just us and these four walls."

The room remained silent, save for the tick-tocking clock that echoed Olivia's heartbeat. She glanced at Holbrook, noting the subtle clench of his jaw—a fortress of calm in their midst. Even in the face of the unknown, he stood as a pillar of rationality, much like the lighthouse that guided ships safely to Bayside Cove's shores.

"Would anyone like some water?" Olivia asked, peering at the one-way mirror, knowing that someone was observing their little tableau. "Or perhaps something stronger to loosen the lips?"

It was an empty offer in the confines of the law, yet it coaxed a chuckle from Daniel, a small victory against the silence.

"Water will be fine, thanks," Daniel said, his voice barely above a whisper.

"Coming right up," Olivia said, rising to fetch the pitcher on the sideboard. The liquid poured into the glass with the softest splash, a soothing sound amidst the cacophony of nerves.

She returned to her seat, sliding the glass across to Daniel. As he reached out, his fingers brushed hers, and she felt the chill of his anxiety. Olivia caught Holbrook's eye, both sets of brows raising in silent understanding—they were on the cusp of something pivotal, a moment that would forever alter the fabric of their cozy coastal town.

Detective Holbrook leaned back in his chair, the leather creaking under his weight, a stark contrast to Olivia's rigid posture on the edge of her seat. His gaze pinned Daniel like a butterfly in a collector's case.

"Daniel," he began, each word deliberate, "I need you to talk to me about the mayor. The poison found in his system—it's not something you come across by accident."

Olivia watched as Daniel's Adam's apple bobbed with a hard swallow. She wished she could offer him some of her freshly baked comfort—perhaps a cinnamon roll might sweeten the truth from his lips. But this was no time for pastries.

"Detective, I..." Daniel's voice trailed off. He looked down at his hands, now trembling on the cold metal table.

"Look at me, Daniel," Holbrook said, a gentle firmness in his tone. "Look at me and tell me what happened."

It was as if time itself held its breath. Olivia's heart pounded a rhythm that seemed to resonate through the room, a silent yet insistent drum calling for the truth.

Finally, as if the words were being coaxed from the depths of his soul, Daniel lifted his head, his eyes glassy with unshed tears. "I did it," he confessed, and the tremor in his voice mirrored the shaking of his hands. "But you have to understand—it was to protect the mayor's secret."

"Go on," prompted Holbrook, his blue eyes never leaving Daniel's face.

"His embezzlement scheme," Daniel continued, the words spilling out like a dam broken by the weight of water. "He was funneling money, and if it came out, it would ruin everything he's worked for. Everything we've worked for."

Silence filled the room, heavy and palpable. Olivia felt the air thicken with implications, as if the very walls were leaning in to listen. Daniel Cooper, the unassuming man with a meticulous eye for detail, had risked it all—not for greed, but loyalty. It was a twist Olivia hadn't seen coming, one that no amount of sleuthing in her cozy kitchen could have prepared her for.

Olivia's mouth went dry, and the interrogation room shrunk to the size of her bakery's walk-in freezer—a tight space where every breath felt visible. The detective's words had been a mere formality; it was Daniel's admission that sent a shock wave through her. Protecting embezzlement? This wasn't the simple mishap of a batch of burnt scones; this was a crime with ingredients far too bitter for her taste.

"Embezzlement?" she echoed, her voice a strange whisper amidst the rising tension. "Daniel, how could you—" But her question dangled in the air, half-baked and unfinished. The implications kneaded into her thoughts like tough dough. If the mayor's dirty secrets crumbled, so would Bayside Cove's trust in its leaders. And her bakery—people came there for comfort, not to digest the town's latest scandal.

As if on cue, the locket she'd found earlier, now warm against her chest, vibrated with an urgency that mirrored her racing heart. It was a quaint piece, as mysterious as the spice blend she kept locked away from prying eyes. With a sound like sugar glass shattering, the locket burst open.

A pulse of energy cascaded through the room, as tangible as the shock of biting into a hidden jalapeño in a chocolate truffle. It left

The Frosted Felony

Detective Holbrook, Daniel, and Olivia momentarily suspended in disbelief. Papers fluttered to the floor like fallen leaves, and the light above flickered, casting shadows that danced along the walls with more grace than Olivia at the town's annual bake-off.

"Wha—what was that?" Detective Holbrook stammered, his stern façade showing cracks.

"Was that the locket?" Daniel asked, his fear momentarily overpowering the guilt that had lined his face moments before.

"Seems even antique jewelry has its secrets," Olivia managed to say, forcing a wry smile that didn't quite reach her worried eyes. In the wake of the locket's outburst, the tension that had enveloped them seemed to dissolve like sugar in hot tea, leaving a new flavor of uncertainty that no one had anticipated tasting today.

The energy released from the locket rippled through the interrogation room's walls and out into the hallway, where a small crowd of townsfolk had gathered. They were the curious sort, drawn to the police station by the scent of scandal like bees to an overturned jar of honey. But what they encountered now was no ordinary town gossip—it was laced with an undercurrent of something far more enigmatic.

"Did you feel that?" one woman asked, her voice trembling as much as the hand that clutched her cardigan tighter around her shoulders. Her companion, a retired fisherman whose face told tales of squalls weathered at sea, stared at the door with eyes wide enough to rival the full moon.

"Like a gale force wind, but not a window open," he muttered, his astonishment echoing down the corridor.

Another onlooker, a young man who'd been leaning casually against the wall, lost his balance as the pulse hit, sprawling onto the floor in a tangle of limbs. "Whoa, what was that?" he exclaimed, picking himself up. "Someone playing with fireworks indoors?"

The whispers grew louder, weaving together theories and questions, each more incredulous than the last. A supernatural event wasn't just rare in Bayside Cove; it was unprecedented, save for the whispers of old legends long thought to be mere bedtime stories to encourage children to behave.

Inside the interrogation room, Olivia and Detective Holbrook shared a glance over Daniel's slumped figure. It was a look that transcended words, bridging the gap between rational skepticism and the irrefutable evidence of the mystical. Olivia's expressive eyes, usually so adept at reading her customers' unspoken pastry preferences, now reflected the turmoil of this new reality.

Detective Holbrook cleared his throat, regaining a semblance of composure. "Seems we're not alone," he said, his voice a mix of awe and dry wit. "And I don't mean the audience outside."

"Guess Bayside Cove is full of surprises," Olivia quipped, her attempt at levity falling a little flat in her own ears. The locket's legacy, whatever it may be, was woven into the very fabric of their lives now, as inseparable as chocolate was from cocoa beans.

"Surprises indeed," Holbrook agreed, his blue eyes scanning the room as if half-expecting a ghostly apparition to appear. He offered a hand to help Olivia to her feet, their partnership solidifying in the face of the unknown.

"Should we tell them?" she nodded towards the door, where the murmurs of the crowd had reached a crescendo.

"Let's take it one mystery at a time," Detective Holbrook suggested, his tone as steady as his gaze. "Starting with the one we just survived."

"Fair enough," Olivia conceded, dusting off her flour-speckled hands. As they edged closer to the door, the hum of the townsfolk's speculation buzzed in their ears—a reminder that Bayside Cove was, perhaps, more magical than any of them had dared to believe.

As Olivia and Detective Holbrook moved toward the door, the charged whispers of the townsfolk seeped through the cracks, wrapping around Olivia like a cloak woven from the very essence of Bayside Cove's enigma. The murmurs were laced with uncertainty and fear, but beneath it all, the unmistakable undercurrent of wonder hummed, alive as the sea breeze that swept through their streets.

"Olivia, the town... if they know what's really going on," Holbrook began, his brow furrowed in concern, "it could change everything."

Olivia's gaze drifted over to the window, where the first evening stars were just beginning to prick the velvet sky. Her heart was a tumultuous sea, waves crashing against the cliffs of decision. To reveal the secret would be to invite chaos, to tear open the fabric of a community that thrived on its quaint charm and closely guarded mysteries. But to conceal it...

"Daniel's confession is one thing," Olivia said softly, her voice steady despite the storm inside her. "But this," she gestured vaguely towards the shattered locket on the floor, "this is heritage. It's magic." Her eyes met Holbrook's, flickering with the reflection of a shared burden.

"Exactly. Magic," Holbrook echoed. "And once word gets out, people will come. Not just curious tourists, but those who... might not respect what Bayside Cove stands for."

She nodded, weighing his words. The bakery, her sanctuary of sugar and flour, came to mind. A place where secrets were shared over steaming cups of coffee and where every crumb told a story. The thought of her haven being overrun by thrill-seekers and opportunists sent a shiver down her spine.

"We'd have reporters camped out by the lighthouse, paranormal investigators poking around every corner..." Olivia trailed off, imagining her regulars displaced by strangers with cameras and questions. Her friends, her neighbors—who looked to her for comfort in the form of confectionery delights—might find themselves lost in the spectacle.

"And our residents," she continued, her throat tight, "they've lived with these secrets, protected them. Daniel's one of them, too. He did what he did thinking he was protecting something bigger than himself."

"Olivia," Detective Holbrook said gently, placing a reassuring hand on her shoulder, "whatever you decide, I'm with you. We'll figure it out together."

A breath she didn't realize she'd been holding escaped Olivia's lips in a quiet sigh. Together. That word held more weight now, tethered as they were to a truth that danced just beyond the realm of the ordinary.

"Thank you, Detective," she said, offering a small, wry smile. "I guess we're more than just a sleepy coastal town with a killer blueberry pie, huh?"

"Seems so," he replied with a chuckle that didn't quite mask the gravity of their situation. "Though I'd say your pie alone could put Bayside Cove on the map."

"Let's hope it doesn't come to that," Olivia mused, her resolve hardening. Protecting the town's secrets wasn't just about preserving its charm; it was about safeguarding a way of life—for her fellow townspeople and for the generations to come.

"Come on," Detective Holbrook said, nodding toward the door that led back to the rest of the station. "Let's face our public."

"Right behind you," Olivia affirmed, stepping forward with newfound determination. As they emerged from the interrogation room, the air crackled with unanswered questions. But for now, the secrets of Bayside Cove remained safe within its borders, guarded by those who loved it most.

Olivia Pierce's fingers danced restlessly along the cool metal of her grandmother's locket, a talisman of Bayside Cove's unspoken legacy. The room was silent except for the muffled sounds of the precinct outside —footsteps, distant chatter, the mundane hum of everyday life that stood in stark contrast to the supernatural storm they had just weathered.

"Alright then," Detective Holbrook finally broke the silence, his voice steady but laced with the same uncertainty that clouded Olivia's thoughts. "What's our next move?"

The locket ceased its movement between Olivia's fingers as she met the detective's gaze, her decision carved into the lines of her face. A soft crease formed on her brow, signaling the weight of the choice she bore. Her lips parted, at first hesitant, but then firm and resolute.

"We protect it," she declared. "We protect all of it—the secrets, the charm, the whispers of magic that breathe life into this town."

"Keep it under wraps, you mean?" Holbrook's eyebrows arched slightly, the question hanging between them like the delicate balance they sought to maintain.

"Exactly," she nodded. "Bayside Cove is more than just streets and storefronts. It's an identity, a living storybook where every page whispers a new enchantment."

Her eyes flitted across the room, landing on the remnants of the shattered locket, now just glints of silver and dust. She could almost hear the hushed gasps and rumors that would stir if the veil lifted even an inch. They were not ready—not her town, not the world beyond.

"Keeping this quiet won't be easy," Holbrook cautioned, his tone mirroring the gravity of their pact. "There will be questions, suspicions... We'll need to tread carefully."

"Understood," Olivia replied, a playful yet serious glint in her eye. "But hey, I juggle hot pans and sugar rushes daily; how much harder can this be?"

A chuckle escaped them both, dispelling some of the tension that clung to the air. Yet as the laughter died down, Olivia felt the invisible threads of consequence weave around her heart. To protect Bayside Cove

The Frosted Felony

was to embrace its mysteries fully, to stand guard over stories untold and powers unseen. She knew there would be moments when the truth clawed at the edges of silence, when the allure of revelation would test her resolve and perhaps threaten the very fabric of her beloved town.

"Ready to step back into the ordinary world?" Holbrook asked, motioning towards the door that led to the rest of the station.

"Let's do it," she replied, taking a deep breath as she prepared to walk alongside the fine line separating their hidden world from the one outside. "After all, we've got a reputation to uphold—even if it's built on more than just my blueberry pie."

With each step they took, Olivia felt the weight of her decision anchoring her to the ground, a reminder that she was now a keeper of secrets, a guardian of the extraordinary masquerading as the everyday. Bayside Cove depended on her discretion, her courage, and yes, her baked goods, to remain the charming enigma it was meant to be.

Olivia Pierce stepped out of the interrogation room, her mind a whirlwind of thoughts that seemed to echo the hushed chatter of the precinct outside. The musty scent of old coffee and worn leather mingled with the sharp tang of printer ink, grounding her in the reality of the station—a stark contrast to the mystical chaos they had just experienced.

"Did you ever think we'd be dealing with... whatever that was?" Olivia asked, casting a sidelong glance at Detective James Holbrook, who closed the door behind them with a quiet click.

"Can't say it was on my detective's bingo card," he replied, the corners of his mouth twitching upward in a half-smile that didn't quite reach his eyes. "But then again, Bayside Cove does have a knack for the unexpected."

She nodded, the sound of their footsteps on the linoleum floor punctuating the silence as they moved through the maze of desks and filing cabinets. She noticed how Holbrook's gaze seemed to linger on the officers and clerks they passed, as if searching for any sign that the supernatural energy had leaked beyond the confines of the interrogation room.

"Any idea how we're going to explain the... energy burst?" Olivia finally broke the silence, her voice barely above a whisper.

"Technically speaking, we're not," Holbrook said, stopping by a window that framed the darkening sky outside. "Some things are better left unexplained—at least until we've got a handle on what we're dealing with."

"Right," she murmured, peering out at the town's quaint streets that now harbored an untold number of secrets. "Just another day in paradise."

"Exactly." Holbrook turned to face her, his eyes reflecting sincerity. "And I trust that you'll keep the town's interests at heart?"

"Always," Olivia affirmed, finding strength in his trust. "Bayside Cove's charm is worth protecting, even if it means keeping a few ghosts in the closet."

"Speaking of which," Holbrook began, a lightness entering his tone, "I suppose you'll be heading back to your bakery? I imagine there's a batch of scones that needs rescuing from the clutches of overbaking."

A genuine smile tugged at Olivia's lips. "You know it. Can't let those scones down—they're the real pillars of the community."

"Then I won't keep you," he said, stepping aside to let her pass. "But Olivia, be careful. We don't know what else might come to light."

"Understood," she replied, feeling the reassuring weight of her decision settle around her shoulders like a cloak. "And James, thank you—for believing in more than just the evidence."

"Thank you for giving me something to believe in," he countered, and with a final nod, they parted ways, their steps echoing through the halls of the precinct.

Olivia walked away, the comforting smell of the ocean breeze beckoning her home. As she left the police station, the flickering street lamps cast dancing shadows across her path, reminding her that the line between the ordinary and the extraordinary was thinner than ever. With each step, she embraced her role as a guardian of Bayside Cove's hidden magic, ready to face whatever the future held.

Chapter 17

Cooling Down

Olivia stepped up to the creaky wooden podium, the floorboards of the town hall emitting a familiar groan under her feet. The murmurs in the room hushed as all eyes turned to her. She surveyed the faces before her—neighbors, friends, and the pillars of Bayside Cove—all united by a common thread of uncertainty about their beloved town's future.

"Good evening, everyone," Olivia began, her voice steady and clear, "I stand here before you, not just as the owner of Sweet Sensations but as someone who loves this town with every fiber of her being." A few nods rippled through the crowd, encouraging her to continue.

"Recent events have shaken us, made us question the integrity of our community. But let me be clear—it is during these trying times that we must band together." She paused, locking eyes with Mrs. Henley, who ran the flower shop, then with Mr. Jacobs, the local librarian, both offering silent support.

"Your trust means everything to me, and I am determined to restore it. We are more than just a picturesque spot on the coast; we are a family. And like any family, we will face our challenges head-on and come out stronger on the other side."

A gentle murmur of agreement fluttered around the room, and Olivia felt a warmth spread through her chest. She took a moment to let her gaze wander over the old town hall, its familiar scent of polished wood and history hanging in the air, reinforcing the gravity of her commitment.

"Many of you have stood by me, showing support in ways that fill my heart with gratitude," she continued, her hands instinctively brushing flour from her apron—a habit she found comforting. "Whether it was a smile, a friendly wave, or just popping by the bakery for your daily treat, your gestures have not gone unnoticed."

In the soft glow of the overhead lights, she saw heads nodding, faces softened by her words. The simple yet profound acts of solidarity they had shown were the threads that wove the fabric of their small-town life.

"Let's not forget why we're here tonight," Olivia said, her tone shifting as she approached the crux of her message. "The embezzlement scheme has cast a long shadow over Bayside Cove, but I promise you this—we will get to the bottom of it. I've been working tirelessly, poring over accounts and records, because the truth matters. Our future depends on it."

The crowd leaned in, their attention tethered to her every word. A sense of resolve hung tangible in the air, like the aroma of freshly baked bread wafting from the kitchen of Sweet Sensations itself.

"Thank you for standing with me. Together, we will heal, we will rebuild, and we will enjoy many more sunny days by the cove." Her voice echoed against the walls, wrapping the townsfolk in a blanket of reassurance.

And as she stepped down from the podium to a round of heartfelt applause, Olivia knew that no matter what lay ahead, the spirit of Bayside Cove was indomitable, much like the crisp crust of her signature apple tarts—golden and unyielding.

The meeting hall, usually a sanctuary of communal warmth, suddenly seemed to shrink as the door swung open with an authoritative push. Victor Wellington entered, his lawyer in tow, both of their silhouettes stark against the soft glow of the overhead lights. A ripple of tension passed through the gathered townsfolk as murmurs and sideways glances filled the space.

Olivia's hands, still faintly dusted with flour from her afternoon baking, clenched at her sides. She stood firm, the embodiment of Bayside Cove's resilience. "Victor," she began, her voice steady but laced with an unmistakable edge, "I see you've received my invitation."

"Olivia," Victor replied, his tone smooth like the polished leather of his shoes. He surveyed the room with those piercing blue eyes, every inch the titan of industry he was groomed to be. "I wouldn't miss it for the world. After all, it's not every day one gets to witness firsthand the... quaint concerns of small-town life."

The Frosted Felony

"Concerns that have everything to do with your revised plans for the waterfront," Olivia countered, stepping into the center of the room where the townsfolk could witness this pivotal exchange. "We're asking you to consider more than just profit margins. Our town has charm, history—qualities that need to be preserved, not bulldozed for another concrete monstrosity."

"Charm doesn't pay the bills, Olivia." Victor's gaze locked onto hers, unyielding. "Progress is inevitable. It's not personal; it's business."

"Business?" Olivia's laugh was a short, humorless burst. "Bayside Cove isn't just a ledger entry, Victor. It's home. People here aren't data points."

"Ah, but without growth, even the most charming of homes falls into decay," Victor countered, though the set of his jaw hinted at some internal struggle.

"Adaptation, Victor, not annihilation," Olivia insisted. "There's a way to develop without stripping away the soul of the place. Think green spaces, sustainable materials. Progress that respects the past."

Victor's lawyer whispered something in his ear, likely a reminder of public image or perhaps the legal quagmire they could face if the town rallied against them. Victor's expression softened fractionally, the businessman's armor cracking ever so slightly.

"Make the changes," Olivia pressed on, sensing the shift. "Show us that there's a heart beating in that chest of yours, not just a calculator."

"Fine," Victor relented, his words clipped. "I'll instruct my team to review the plans. But don't mistake this for sentimentality, Olivia. It's simply good strategy."

"Call it what you will," Olivia said, a smile playing on her lips. "But know this—the heart of Bayside Cove beats stronger than any machine, and that's something worth investing in."

As Victor nodded curtly and turned to leave, the townsfolk erupted into subdued applause, their hope rekindled by the promise of a compromise. Olivia watched him go, knowing that the real work lay ahead but buoyed by the knowledge that even the strongest tides can be turned when a community stands together.

The town meeting had dissipated, leaving a sense of unity hanging in the salt-tinged air of Bayside Cove. Olivia, her pulse still dancing with the victory over Victor Wellington's plans, found herself wandering to the pier where tranquility wrapped around her like a well-worn quilt. She was joined by Emily, who seemed to materialize from the seaside mist, her green eyes reflecting the coastal twilight.

"Em," Olivia began, her voice softer now that the crowd had dispersed, "I've missed this—just us."

Emily leaned on the weathered railing, the ocean's rhythm syncing with her contemplative nod. "Me too, Liv. It feels like we've lived a dozen lifetimes since we last really talked."

"More like a baker's dozen," Olivia quipped, brushing a stray lock of hair behind her ear, flour dust sparkling against the darkening sky.

Emily chuckled, and there it was—the sound that once filled their childhood home with warmth. "Remember how Mom used to say we could solve any problem with enough sugar and a pinch of patience?"

"Patience," Olivia echoed, laughing. "Something I ran out of with Victor today." She looked at Emily, her smile lingering. "But sugar, I have plenty of."

"Good, because I think Bayside Cove needs your pastries as much as it needs healing," said Emily, her tone laced with sincerity. "So, what's next for you? For us?"

"First, we rebuild," Olivia mused, her gaze trailing over the glimmering water. "Sweet Sensations, our family ties... Maybe even some bridges I thought were burnt to ash."

"Count me in," Emily replied, her athletic frame leaning in closer, a silent vow to stand by her sister.

Their shared laughter mingled with the call of seagulls overhead when Olivia recounted the time they'd tried to bake cookies without preheating the oven, resulting in an infamous batch of what they lovingly dubbed 'cookie blobs'.

"Cookie blobs that Dad ate with such gusto," Emily chimed in, "as if they were the finest delicacies in the world."

"Because to him, anything made by his girls was a Michelin-starred dessert," Olivia added, her heart swelling with the memory.

The past and present interwove as they stood side by side, the lighthouse beacon guiding ships in the distance just as their renewed bond promised to guide them through whatever lay ahead. It was the simplicity of the moment, the shared history, and the quiet resolve to step into tomorrow together that enveloped Olivia and Emily in a sense of rightness, a feeling long overdue.

The Frosted Felony

Olivia stood in the doorway of Sweet Sensations, a paintbrush in one hand and a vibrant sense of hope lighting up her expressive eyes. The early morning sun poured its golden hue over the freshly painted walls, as if blessing the new beginnings. Volunteers, each one a familiar face bound by shared history, moved around with an infectious energy that mirrored her own.

"Careful with that trim, Jack!" she called out, her voice ringing with laughter as Jack, a retired fisherman with hands as steady as his boat on a calm sea, wielded his brush with surprising delicacy.

"Wouldn't dream of messing up your ship, Captain Olivia," he shot back, winking before returning to his meticulous work.

The bakery's exterior was coming to life under their collective touch; a tapestry of care that extended well beyond the building itself. Shutters were being realigned, the signboard polished until it gleamed, and every stroke of paint felt like a tender caress on the old structure's skin.

"Olivia, you've got more helpers here than there are seashells on the beach," Emily observed, stepping beside her sister with a tray of homemade lemonade.

"Seems like it, doesn't it?" Olivia replied, her heart swelling with gratitude at the sight of neighbors working alongside each other. "This place is more than just walls and an oven—it's a piece of all of us."

As the morning unfolded into afternoon, townsfolk drifted in and out, drawn by the buzz of activity and the scent of baking that wafted from inside. Olivia greeted each person with her characteristic warmth, sharing stories and laughter over cups of coffee and slices of her famous blueberry pie.

"Olivia, this town wouldn't be the same without your pastries," Mrs. Henderson exclaimed, clasping Olivia's flour-dusted hands in her own. "You bake love into every bite."

"Thank you, Mrs. Henderson," Olivia said, touched by the older woman's words. "I'm just glad to see everyone enjoying them again."

Children darted in and out, their cheeks smeared with chocolate and their giggles harmonizing with the rhythmic sound of hammers and saws. It was a symphony of community spirit, each note resonating with the promise of a restored haven.

"Look at them go," Emily mused, leaning against the counter. "You've made quite the impact, Liv."

"Couldn't have done it without this bunch," Olivia responded, her gaze sweeping across the scene. "It feels like...coming home."

"Because you are home," Emily smiled, and Olivia felt a surge of contentment warm her from the inside out.

"Hey, Olivia!" called out Mr. Thompson, a local schoolteacher, waving a paint-streaked hand. "When's the next batch of cinnamon rolls coming out? My taste buds are staging a protest!"

"Give me ten minutes, and I'll quell the uprising," Olivia declared, tying her apron tighter and heading back to her sanctuary—the kitchen.

As the day drew to a close, the bakery stood renewed, its walls echoing with a cacophony of voices that spoke of resilience and unity. Olivia leaned against the newly fitted doorframe, her eyes reflecting the hues of the setting sun, the corners crinkling with joy.

"Sweet Sensations is back," she whispered to herself, savoring the truth of those words. The bakery, much like her heart, had been fortified by the hands of those she'd grown to trust and cherish—proof that even the most delicate pastry could withstand the pressures of the oven and emerge, transformed and ready to be savored.

In the dwindling light of the early evening, as the last volunteer locked up their paintbrushes and stepped out of Sweet Sensations, Olivia found herself alone amidst the gently settling dust. She brushed a rogue strand of hair from her forehead, leaving a smudge of blue paint in its wake, and turned to see James leaning against the doorway, his arms folded across his chest.

"Quite the day, huh?" he said, an easy smile playing on his lips as his gaze took in the refurbished interior.

Olivia chuckled, a hand self-consciously smoothing down her apron. "I think I've inhaled enough sawdust to bake a lumberjack's loaf," she quipped, her eyes twinkling in the low light.

"Sounds... appetizing," James replied dryly, pushing off from the doorframe and taking a few steps closer. The air between them was charged with something more than just the excitement of the day's work.

"James, I—" Olivia began, but hesitated. Her heart hammered in her chest, not unlike the way it did when she piped the perfect frosting rose.

"Hey, it's alright." His voice was soft, reassuring. "You don't have to say anything you're not ready to."

The Frosted Felony

She met his gaze, finding a calm harbor in the stormy sea of her emotions. "No, I want to. Today was... it was more than just fixing up the bakery. It felt like we were mending more than just walls."

He nodded, understanding flickering in his eyes. "We've been through quite the whirlwind, haven't we? From strangers to... whatever this is."

"Partners in crime-solving?" she offered, a tentative smile forming.

"More like accomplices in creating a future," James corrected gently. "Speaking of which, what are your hopes for that future, Olivia?"

"Besides a fully functional oven and a line out the door for my pastries?" she asked, biting her lip.

"Besides that," he affirmed, taking another step closer, close enough that she could see the specks of gold in his eyes.

"I hope for trust," Olivia confessed, her voice barely louder than the hum of the refrigerator in the background. "To build relationships that can weather any storm. Like what we've started here."

"Olivia, I—" James mirrored her earlier hesitation but then seemed to gather his resolve. "I don't want our story to be just a chapter about an investigation. I want to keep turning pages with you."

"Is that your subtle way of saying you're sticking around Bayside Cove?" she teased, though her heart fluttered with hope.

"Subtlety isn't my strong suit," he admitted, a rare vulnerability crossing his features. "But yes, I'm staying. For the quiet charm of the town, the thrill of untangling mysteries, and..." He paused, glancing at her lips before meeting her eyes again. "...for the chance to see where this connection between us might lead."

"Sounds like we have a lot of pages to fill together then," Olivia said, her voice steady even as her pulse raced. There was a promise in his words, a tentative sketch of a shared path emerging between the lines.

"Starting with dinner tomorrow night?" James asked, his tone hopeful, the invitation hanging in the air like the fragrance of fresh-baked bread.

"Only if it's not at Sweet Sensations. My next batch of cinnamon rolls deserves my undivided attention," she replied with mock seriousness.

"Deal," he said, laughter warming his eyes. "Nothing competes with your cinnamon rolls, anyway."

"Good answer, Detective," Olivia said, her laughter mingling with his as they stood there, in the heart of her bakery, on the precipice of an unknown but hopeful future.

As the last customer of the day waved goodbye, Olivia flipped the sign on Sweet Sensations' door to 'Closed.' The golden rays of the setting sun streamed through the windows, casting a warm glow over the now quiet bakery. She turned to find James leaning against the counter, an amused twinkle in his eye as he watched her meticulously straighten a stack of menus.

"Ever consider that those menus might have enjoyed their disarray?" he mused, pushing off from the counter and sauntering closer.

"Disorder in my bakery? Perish the thought," Olivia retorted, her tone light and teasing. She brushed away a rogue flour smudge from her apron, the soft fabric whispering against the calm silence enveloping them.

"Perfectionist," he teased gently, standing close enough now that she could catch the faint scent of his cologne, a subtle mix of cedar and sea air that seemed to embody Bayside Cove itself.

"Detective," she countered, a knowing smile playing at the corners of her lips. There was something undeniably comforting about this banter, a dance they had come to know well.

The soft light caught the edges of his hair, turning it into a halo of dark copper. He reached out, his fingers trailing along the countertop before coming to rest just shy of her hand. It was a simple gesture, but charged with the promise of what could be. Olivia's breath caught in her chest, anticipation tingling through her veins like the fizz of champagne.

"Olivia," he began, his voice low and earnest, "this town... it's got more layers than your richest tarts. And you—"

"Am I the filling or the crust in this metaphor?" she interjected, unable to resist the pull of humor even in a moment as tender as this.

"Definitely the filling," he replied without missing a beat. "Sweet, complex, and absolutely essential."

Their eyes locked, and for an infinite second, the world outside ceased to exist. It was just Olivia, James, and the unspoken words hanging heavy between them. Then, in a movement as natural as the ocean's ebb and flow, he closed the distance and pressed his lips to hers. It was a gentle kiss, a whisper of contact that spoke volumes, conveying years of longing and the thrill of new beginnings.

The Frosted Felony

When they parted, there was a softness in his gaze that made her heart swell. This was the start of something beautiful, a journey neither of them expected but both secretly hoped for.

"Tomorrow night, then?" Olivia said, her voice laced with newfound joy.

"Tomorrow night," he confirmed, the corners of his mouth lifting in a smile that mirrored her own.

As he walked out, leaving her alone with the fading daylight, Olivia took a moment to bask in the quiet aftermath of their shared kiss. She wandered over to the window, gazing out at the peaceful streets of Bayside Cove. The town had been through its fair share of trials, but like the sturdy oaks that lined the boulevard, it remained resolute. Her bakery, once a place shrouded in uncertainty, now stood as a beacon of hope—a testament to the resilience of community and the healing power of love.

Olivia felt a surge of optimism swell within her chest. The investigation had tested her, unraveled secrets she never knew existed, and yet, she emerged stronger. She had confronted her fears, opened her heart, and found a kindred spirit in an unexpected ally. Together, they had weathered the storm.

She glanced down at her hands, still dusted with the remnants of flour from a day's work, and smiled. Growth, like the perfect rise of dough, required time, patience, and a touch of warmth. As the sun dipped below the horizon, painting the sky with hues of pink and orange, Olivia knew that whatever tomorrow brought, it held the sweetness of possibility and the promise of fresh discovery.

Basil, with a purr as smooth as caramel cream, nudged Olivia's leg just as she was about to lock the front door of Sweet Sensations. She paused, cocking her head to one side, and met the feline's knowing gaze.

"Alright, Basil, what is it?" she asked, though she knew the tabby couldn't answer. The cat merely sauntered toward the back room, his tail high like a flag of truce waving in the quiet bakery.

Olivia chuckled and followed, flicking off lights as she went. The smell of freshly baked pastries still lingered in the air, mingling with the scent of aged paper and history that seemed to seep from the old walls. In the back room, Basil leaped onto a table where stacks of documents from the historical society's archives lay scattered—a project she had been meaning to tackle when time permitted.

"Is this your subtle way of telling me there's more work to do?" Olivia teased, her fingers tracing the yellowed edges of an old map of Bayside Cove. Beneath the surface of everyday life, there were tales untold, secrets that hummed beneath the cobblestones of the town.

She picked up a journal, its leather cover worn and pages filled with elegant script. It belonged to the town's founder, and rumors had always circled about hidden passages and forgotten lore. Olivia had laughed those stories off as fanciful myths, but now, with everything that had happened, she wasn't so sure.

"Who knows what you're hiding, hmm?" Olivia mused aloud, thumbing through the pages. She caught snippets of text that spoke of the original settlers, of bonds forged with mysterious protectors, and of a covenant that linked the town's prosperity to forces beyond their understanding.

"Perhaps it's time we took a little peek into the past," she whispered, excitement tingling in her veins. Basil purred in agreement, or so Olivia liked to think, as he settled down beside the journal.

Leaving the documents spread out for tomorrow's curiosity, Olivia turned off the last light and stepped outside into the cool evening air. She looked up at the bakery sign, now restored to its former glory, and felt a surge of pride. Bayside Cove was more than a picturesque town; it was a community bound by shared stories and united strength.

"Goodnight, Basil," she called softly, the door closing behind her. "Tomorrow we bake, and maybe, just maybe, we'll unravel a bit more of our sweet mystery."

With the promise of new discoveries on the horizon, Olivia walked home under the twinkling stars, each step echoing the transformative power of unity and the complex layers of life waiting to be tasted, savored, and explored—just like the intricate flavors of a perfectly crafted pastry.

As the first light of dawn brushed the horizon with strokes of pink and orange, Olivia Pierce was already bustling about in her beloved bakery, Sweet Sensations. The aroma of freshly baked bread and cinnamon wafted through the air, a fragrant promise of comfort to anyone who passed by.

"Nothing beats the smell of the morning bake," she said to herself, pulling a tray of golden croissants from the oven. Her movements were a dance she had perfected over countless mornings—a twirl here to grab a

The Frosted Felony

dish towel, a pirouette to reach the cooling rack, all while humming a tune that mixed with the symphony of sizzling pastries.

The bell above the door jingled merrily as the first customer of the day entered, bringing with it a cool breeze that played with the chimes hanging by the window. "Mornin', Olivia! I swear you've got some magic in these walls; it's like being wrapped in a warm hug every time I step in here," Mrs. Henderson exclaimed, her eyes twinkling with affection for the young baker.

"Only the best hugs for my favorite customers," Olivia replied with a grin, sliding the croissants into a display case. She knew every person who walked through her door wasn't just a customer but a part of the tapestry that made Bayside Cove so special.

As the sun climbed higher, painting the sky in ever-brighter hues, the bakery filled with the gentle hum of conversation. Regulars exchanged greetings and shared stories, their laughter mingling with the clatter of cutlery on plates. Olivia moved among them, serving, chatting, and sharing in the camaraderie that only a tight-knit community could foster.

"Hey, Olivia, save me one of those berry tarts, will ya? They're my grandson's favorite," called out Mr. Jenkins, waving his cane playfully as he claimed his usual seat by the window.

"Already set aside two, just for you," Olivia assured him, winking conspiratorially. Little gestures like these were her way of weaving threads of connection, reinforcing the bonds that held the town together.

In the midst of the morning rush, James stepped in, his presence a calm harbor in the lively seas of the bakery. He caught Olivia's eye from across the room, a silent message passing between them that spoke of shared secrets and whispered promises.

"Looks like another successful day for Sweet Sensations," James observed, leaning against the counter with an easy smile. His gaze lingered on Olivia, admiration clear in his eyes.

"Every day is a success when it starts with good company and ends with a full heart," she replied, her cheeks coloring slightly at his attention. Their gentle flirtation was a new layer added to the rich pastry of their lives—one they were both eager to explore.

As the chapter drew to a close, Olivia stood outside her bakery, looking at the gathered crowd of familiar faces. The warmth of the oven's glow behind her was matched only by the warmth in her heart. With each laugh shared, each secret confided, and each pastry savored, she was reminded of the strength and sweetness woven through the fabric of Bayside Cove.

"Here's to tomorrow, and all the flavors it may bring," Olivia toasted quietly to herself, her voice carrying on the salt-tinged breeze. The mysteries of the town awaited, hidden in dusty archives and hushed whispers, but for now, the simple joy of living was enough to fill the pages of her story.

With a contented sigh, Olivia turned back toward the bakery, the door closing behind her with a soft click. The sense of hope and anticipation hung in the air—a delicious prelude to the next chapter in the lives of Olivia and the residents of Bayside Cove.

Chapter 18

Home Sweet Home

Olivia Pierce pushed open the door to Sweet Sensations, and immediately, the cozy warmth of the bakery enveloped her like a familiar hug. The sweet scent of cinnamon and vanilla swirled in the air, mingling with a melody that danced softly from the hidden speakers. She paused for a moment, closing her eyes to savor the notes of her favorite song as they twined with the olfactory symphony of her livelihood.

"Ah, the magic of baking," Olivia murmured to herself, her voice tinged with the affection reserved for an old friend.

She glanced around at the pastel walls adorned with framed photographs of Bayside Cove. Each frame captured a memory; each memory was steeped in flour and sugar. With a practiced eye, she ensured everything was in its proper place before turning her attention to the day's special unveiling.

"Time to add a little mystery to the menu," she announced, despite the empty shop. It was a ritual, speaking to the room as if it were a confidant. She approached the counter, where a lineup of pastries lay hidden beneath a polka-dotted cloth, each creation waiting to tantalize taste buds and stir curiosity.

With a flourish, Olivia whisked the cloth away, revealing the new line of 'mystery flavored' pastries. Their intricate designs seemed almost too beautiful to eat—almost. The pastries bore names that winked at her recent adventures as an amateur detective: "Whodunit Walnut Whip," "Private Eye Pecan Pie," and "Secret Agent Scone."

"Let's hope these are as much a hit as the last case was a puzzle," she chuckled, arranging the treats so that each had its moment in the spotlight. Her fingers brushed against the delicate icing of the

"Incriminating Raspberry Incrusted," and she couldn't help but smile at the thought of how her sleuthing days had spilled into her baking—a blend of passion and intrigue.

It wasn't just about the flavors; it was about the experience. Olivia wanted her customers to savor the taste as much as the thrill of unraveling a good mystery. And maybe, just maybe, it would encourage them to trust in the unknown, to take a risk on a flavor they might never have chosen otherwise.

"Guess it's true what they say," she mused aloud, giving the pastries one final approving nod. "Life is short, but it's definitely sweet." Her words hung in the air, a testament to the journey she'd embarked upon, both in her kitchen and beyond its doors.

The bell above the door chimed rhythmically as a steady stream of customers filed into Sweet Sensations. Olivia stood behind the counter, her eyes sparkling with anticipation as she watched the townspeople swarm around her latest creation—the mystery pastries.

"Step right up and take a guess," Olivia beckoned, her voice lilting over the soft music that filled the bakery. "Each one's a secret waiting to be unraveled—one bite at a time."

A young woman, her hair tied back in a sun-kissed ponytail, eyed the "Covert Cherry Clue" tart. "What's the mystery in this one?" she asked, her tone equal parts curiosity and challenge.

Olivia leaned in conspiratorially. "Ah, that one's steeped in secrecy. But I'll give you a hint: it's a cherry base with a twist you'd never expect—just like the most surprising clues in any good investigation."

The customer's smile widened as she took a tentative bite, her eyes closing in delight as the unexpected flavor danced on her tongue. Murmurs of approval rippled through the crowd, each person eager to embark on their own gustatory adventure.

From the corner of the room, Sam watched the scene unfold with pride. His hands moved deftly as he replenished trays and offered samples, his cheerful presence adding to the bakery's warm ambiance. As if sensing Olivia's gaze, he looked up and caught her eye, his grin broad and contagious.

"Look at them, Liv," Sam said, gesturing towards the throng of patrons. "They're eating it up—literally and figuratively!"

Olivia laughed, her heart swelling in her chest. "Couldn't have done it without my right hand man—or should I say partner?" Her words were light, but the pride she felt was profound. Together, they had turned Sweet Sensations into more than just a bakery; it was a cornerstone of Bayside Cove—a place of comfort, creativity, and community.

"Partner has a nice ring to it," Sam replied, sliding a plate of "Lurking Lime Labyrinth" bars across the counter to an eagerly awaiting couple. "Especially when I get to celebrate your wild ideas coming to life like this."

Their shared laughter was a sweet melody that blended seamlessly with the hum of conversation and the clinking of pastry tongs. In that moment, amidst the aroma of sugar and spice, the weight of responsibility lifted from Olivia's shoulders. Trusting Sam with part of her dream had been a risk, but it was one that had brought an unexpected richness to both her business and her life.

"Here's to mystery, mayhem, and mouthwatering pastries," Olivia toasted, raising an imaginary glass before turning to greet another wave of customers, each one drawn in by the allure of the unknown flavors waiting to be discovered.

The bell above the door jingled, a familiar herald to new arrivals at Sweet Sensations. Heads turned as Emily Pierce, with her purposeful stride and the kind of determined expression that preceded significant announcements, made her way into the bakery. Olivia felt her pulse quicken, a mixture of elation and trepidation stirring within her as she watched her sister navigate through the clusters of patrons.

"Guess who's decided Bayside Cove could use a little more intrigue?" Emily announced, her voice cutting through the soft murmur of conversations and the gentle crooning of the background music. The room fell into a hush, the scent of cinnamon and vanilla now accompanied by a palpable sense of curiosity.

Olivia wiped her hands on her apron, flour dust puffing into the air like tiny clouds of suspense. "What are you up to, Em?" she asked, her tone light but her eyes searching for clues in her sister's confident stance.

Emily's smile held the promise of adventure. "I'm opening my own private investigation office," she declared, and the bakery erupted in a chorus of excited chatter.

"Here? In Bayside Cove?" Olivia couldn't mask the astonishment in her voice, nor the flicker of joy at the thought of having her sister nearby. But interlaced with the thrill was a whisper of concern, like the shadow that trails a sunny day.

"Right here," Emily confirmed, her green eyes sparkling with the ambitious fire that burned within her. "Where better to start than the place where every mystery seems to find its way to our doorstep?"

Sam leaned over to Olivia, his voice a playful murmur. "Looks like we'll be needing a 'Private Eye Pie' on the menu soon."

Olivia chuckled, her laughter mingling with the warm notes of the bakery's atmosphere, yet she couldn't shake the flutter of unease that danced in her chest. She imagined future collaborations, the intertwining of pastries and detective work, and she felt simultaneously invigorated and cautious.

"Em, that's... it's great. You're going to be amazing." Olivia meant every word, even as she pondered the delicate balance they would have to strike working together. Her sister was a force of nature, unpredictable and fierce, while Olivia's life was carefully measured in cups and teaspoons.

"Thanks, Liv," Emily replied, reaching out to squeeze her hand—a gesture that bridged past distances and reaffirmed their shared bond.

Olivia returned the pressure, letting the reassurance seep through her skin. Together, perhaps they could blend the sweet with the suspenseful, creating a recipe not just for success, but for a renewed sisterhood.

The afternoon light slanted through the bay window of Sweet Sensations, casting a golden glow over the bustling bakery. Olivia, her fingers skimming the edge of a cooling rack laden with rows of cinnamon twists and chocolate éclairs, paused to watch as customers milled about, their faces alight with curiosity at the new line of mystery pastries.

"Decisions, decisions," murmured a regular patron, eyeing the array dubbed 'Whodunit Walnut' and 'Clueberry Crumble.'

Olivia smiled, her heart swelling with pride. "Every bite is an adventure," she assured him. "Just like life, wouldn't you say?"

As Sam deftly placed a 'Secret Ingredient Scone' into a box for another eager customer, Olivia allowed herself a moment of quiet reflection. The hum of soft music blended with the murmur of voices, creating a symphony of ordinary magic that underscored her thoughts.

She had learned so much more than she had ever expected when she first donned the apron of an amateur sleuth. The flour on her hands was now mixed with the metaphorical dust of intrigue and the icing sugar of secrecy. But amid the chaos of clues and conundrums, it was trust that had risen like yeast in warm dough—trust in those around her, in the eclectic townsfolk of Bayside Cove, and, most importantly, in herself.

"Hey, Liv," Emily called from across the counter, her voice snapping Olivia out of her reverie. "I've been thinking about names for the office. What do you think of 'Pierce Investigations'?"

"Has a nice ring to it," Olivia replied, her gaze affectionate yet thoughtful as she considered her sister's question. It was trust that had stitched the frayed edges of their relationship back together. It had taken time and patience, but as they both navigated the ebb and flow of forgiveness, the bond between them had strengthened, reinforced by shared secrets and silent understandings.

Turning her attention back to her pastries, Olivia couldn't help but marvel at how her little bakery had become a nexus for the unexpected. The risks she'd taken—leaping into the unknown, chasing after shadows and whispers—had revealed layers to Bayside Cove she'd never known existed, each more intricate and fascinating than the last.

"Taking chances sure has a way of sweetening the pot, doesn't it?" she said to no one in particular, a wistful smile playing across her lips.

"Especially when there's cake involved," Sam quipped from behind her, his grin infectious.

"True enough," Olivia agreed, laughter bubbling up from within her. She glanced around the cozy interior of her shop, the scent of vanilla and spices a comforting embrace. Her journey into the heart of the town's mysteries had not only brought surprises and challenges, but also a deeper appreciation for the people and places that made up her world.

"Maybe it's time to add a 'Leap of Faith Lemon Tart' to the menu," she mused aloud, her eyes twinkling with mischief.

"Only if we can have a 'Trustworthy Tiramisu' to go alongside it," Emily shot back, leaning against the counter with a smirk.

"Deal," Olivia said, and they all laughed, the sound mingling with the clinking of cups and the rustle of paper bags. In the heart of Sweet Sensations, amidst the daily dance of sugar and spice, Olivia Pierce found herself at the crossroads of comfort and courage, ready to taste whatever mystery the future might hold.

The bell above the bakery door jingled, a familiar herald that lifted Olivia's spirits before she even caught sight of who had entered. She turned from where she stood, arranging a tray of mystery-flavored pastries, and her pulse quickened as her gaze landed on James Holbrook.

The detective's presence filled Sweet Sensations with a different kind of warmth, one that mingled effortlessly with the aroma of baked goods.

"Looks like you've captured quite the crowd," James commented, his blue eyes scanning the bustling shop before settling back on her with an appreciative smile.

Olivia's heart did a somersault, but she managed a playful grin. "All part of the master plan. Lure them in with intrigue and keep them here with sugar."

"Seems to be working," he said, his voice low and tinged with amusement. His gaze lingered on her, not just as a detective assessing a situation, but as a man seeing someone who meant more to him than just a mere acquaintance.

"Care to join me on a stroll?" James offered his arm in a gesture so charmingly old-fashioned that it coaxed a soft chuckle from Olivia.

"Are you asking me out on a date, Detective Holbrook?" she teased, her cheeks flushing with a warmth that rivaled the ovens behind her.

"Would that be such a crime?" James asked, his eyebrow quirked in mock seriousness.

"Only if you don't share your theories about the 'Enigmatic Eclair' flavor," Olivia replied, her own eyebrow raised in playful challenge as she took his arm.

"Then I'm guilty as charged," he confessed, leading her past the counter and towards the door, where the afternoon light spilled into the cozy confines of the bakery.

Hand in hand, they stepped out onto Main Street, its cobblestone path winding through the heart of Bayside Cove. The quaint town, dressed in the colors of the late afternoon sun, seemed to embrace them as they walked. Shop windows glowed invitingly, displaying everything from handcrafted jewelry to antique books, while the gentle murmur of conversations and laughter provided a soothing soundtrack to their leisurely exploration.

"Feels like we're miles away from the rest of the world," Olivia mused, taking in the picturesque scene.

"Sometimes, that's exactly what you need," James agreed, his thumb lightly brushing against her hand, sending a pleasant shiver up her arm.

The Frosted Felony

They moved with an easy rhythm, a dance they didn't realize they had mastered until this very moment. Every glance and touch, each shared smile under the watchful eyes of Bayside Cove's charming facades, wove together the beginnings of a story that was theirs alone—a tale spun from the threads of curiosity, courage, and perhaps something a little sweeter.

Olivia and James found themselves outside a cozy café, its windows fogged from warmth and conviviality that seemed to beckon them inside. The door chimed a welcome as they entered, shrugging off the crisp winter air that clung to their coats. They chose a small table tucked away in a quiet corner, where dim lighting lent an air of intimacy.

"Chai latte for me," Olivia said, her eyes scanning the chalkboard menu before meeting James's gaze. "What about you, Detective? Coffee? Tea? Or something more... incriminating?"

"Black coffee," he replied with a wry smile. "I'm a simple man with simple tastes."

"Simple, yet mysterious," Olivia teased, watching as James ordered their drinks with a nod to the barista. She liked this side of him—the part that could banter and laugh amidst the seriousness of his profession.

Their drinks arrived, steam curling upwards like whispers of secrets waiting to be shared. Olivia wrapped her hands around her cup, savoring the heat that seeped into her fingers. She took a tentative sip, the spices dancing on her tongue, and watched James do the same with his coffee, his blue eyes never leaving hers.

"Tell me, James," Olivia ventured, leaning forward, "what made you choose Bayside Cove? It must have been quite the change from city life."

James set down his cup, thoughtfulness etching his features. "Truthfully?" He hesitated, then continued, "It was the promise of a story not yet written. A chance to start fresh, away from the noise and the chaos."

"Looks like you got your wish," she said softly, "though I suspect the stories here are more complex than they seem."

"Indeed," he agreed, a warm glint in his eyes. "But I've found an excellent guide in unraveling those complexities."

Their conversation meandered through shared laughter and confessions, each revelation drawing them closer. Olivia felt layers of her guard peel away, exposing a vulnerability she hadn't realized she was ready to show. James listened, his replies thoughtful and measured, revealing glimpses of his own guarded heart.

As the café hummed around them, the world outside seemed to fade, leaving only the two of them suspended in a pocket of time. Eventually, they emerged from the cocoon of the café, stepping back into the festive bustle of Bayside Cove's Winter Festival. The town square was aglow with twinkling lights, casting a romantic hue over the cobblestones.

"Look," Olivia pointed to a stand where an old-fashioned vendor sold roasted chestnuts. "It smells like my childhood Christmas memories."

"Shall we?" James offered, leading her towards the aroma that mingled with scents of pine and peppermint.

They walked hand in hand, sharing chestnuts and stealing glances, until they reached the center of the square. Snowflakes began to fall, each one as delicate as the moments they were stringing together.

"Olivia," James murmured, his voice barely above the soft crunch of snow underfoot, "there's something rather magical about tonight."

"Is that the detective's intuition speaking?" she quipped, her breath forming a tiny cloud in the air.

"Perhaps." He stepped closer, his hands finding hers. "Or maybe it's just being here with you."

And then, as if the universe itself had conspired to create the perfect ending to their evening, Olivia felt James's lips tenderly meet hers. The kiss was a sweet culmination of their shared laughter and intimate conversations—a promise woven into the very fabric of Bayside Cove's Winter Festival. Around them, the scent of freshly baked treats lingered, wrapping the moment in a blanket of warmth and possibility.

Chapter 19

A New Recipe

The scent of cinnamon and yeast filled the air, mingling with the warmth that always seemed to envelop Olivia's kitchen. Flour dusted the countertop like a light blanket of snow, setting the stage for the Winter Festival preparations. Olivia's fingers worked the dough with practiced ease, kneading rhythmically as her laugh punctuated the cozy space.

"Careful, James," she teased without looking up, "if you keep staring at me like that, you might just fall into one of these mixing bowls."

James leaned against the counter, his coffee cup cradled in his hands. "I'm just admiring the artistry," he replied, his voice laced with a humor that reached his blue eyes. "Baking is a science, but watching you work is like witnessing a dance."

"Flattery will get you everywhere," Olivia quipped, a rosy hue tinting her cheeks as she flashed him a grin.

Just then, the bell above the bakery door jingled, heralding Emily's entrance. Her green eyes scanned the kitchen before landing on an unexpected sight—a worn spine of an old book peeking from behind a loose brick in the wall. A gasp escaped her lips, drawing Olivia and James's attention.

"Olivia! James!" Emily exclaimed, pointing excitedly. "Look what I found!"

Curiosity piqued, Olivia wiped her hands on her apron and approached, James following behind with a detective's intrigue lighting his gaze. They watched as Emily tugged gently at the brick, revealing more of the hidden treasure.

"Is that...?" Olivia began, her voice trailing off as she reached out to touch the ancient leather binding.

"An old recipe book," Emily confirmed, her words quickening with each breath. "It must have been here for ages."

"Or it could be a secret handed down through generations," James mused, ever the investigator. "Hidden right under our noses."

Olivia exchanged a knowing look with Emily, their shared history in Bayside Cove suddenly feeling even deeper. The past had a way of surfacing when least expected, and now, with the festival upon them, they were about to uncover another layer of their hometown's rich tapestry.

Olivia's fingertips danced over the cracked leather of the recipe book, her brow furrowing as she deciphered the faded ink of notes that seemed almost deliberately cryptic. She lifted the book from its dusty alcove and turned to face James and Emily, a small puff of ancient flour dispersing into the air.

"Look at this," she said, her voice laced with wonder. "It's not just recipes. There are annotations here—notes about Bayside Cove and its... its magic?"

James leaned in closer, his detective's intuition tingling. "Magic?" he echoed, skepticism softened by a playful twinkle in his eye. "In our little town?"

Emily leaned against the counter, arms crossed, but her lips curled up at the corners. "This place always had its quirks. Maybe this is one secret we've missed."

The kitchen door swung open, and Sam burst in, his eyes immediately locking onto the book in Olivia's hands. His sandy hair was tousled more than usual, likely from arranging and rearranging the festival display to perfection. Sam's bright blue eyes sparkled with curiosity as he came to a halt beside them.

"Is that what I think it is?" Sam asked, craning his neck to get a better look at the ancient tome.

"An old recipe book," Olivia confirmed, "but it might be more than just that."

"Let me see!" Sam reached out, and Olivia obliged, passing the book to him with care. His fingers flipped through the pages, reverence mixed with urgency.

"Wow, these notes... Could be clues to the real heart of Bayside Cove," Sam mused aloud, completely engrossed.

The Frosted Felony

"Maybe we should explore what it all means," he suggested, meeting each pair of eyes with infectious enthusiasm. "There could be a whole hidden magic to this town we never knew about."

James chuckled and took a sip of his coffee, the warmth of the mug seeping into his palms. "What do you say, team? Shall we become hunters of the arcane right after we finish prepping for the Winter Festival?"

"Sounds like an adventure to me," Olivia replied, the sparkle in her own eyes mirroring Sam's excitement. "I say we dive in headfirst."

"Plus, who knows?" Emily added, picking up a cinnamon roll and breaking it in half. "We might even find some new, 'enchanted' recipes to try out for the festival."

With laughter mingling in the air, the four friends gathered around the mystery of the old recipe book, ready to unravel the secrets of Bayside Cove's mystical past.

The warmth of the bakery's kitchen embraced them as they moved, a stark contrast to the crisp chill that had begun to settle over Bayside Cove. Olivia led the way to the back corner, where an antique round table sat nestled between shelves lined with jars of colorful spices and bins filled with various types of flour.

"Here we can talk without all the clatter of mixers and ovens," Olivia said, her voice tinged with excitement. She brushed a lock of hair out of her face, leaving a smudge of flour on her forehead that she didn't notice.

James set his coffee cup down with a gentle clink. "This spot has always felt like a little sanctuary," he commented, pulling out a chair for Emily before taking a seat himself.

"Perfect for unearthing ancient secrets," Sam quipped, easing into the chair next to James. His eyes were bright, reflecting the string of fairy lights that hung above their cozy nook.

Olivia carefully placed the book in the center of the table. The soft glow from the overhead lights cast shadows on the faded pages, making the handwritten notes appear even more mysterious. She opened the cover, and the smell of aged paper mixed with the comforting scent of cinnamon from the oven.

"Listen to this," she began, her finger tracing a line of cursive text, "'For a charm of powerful trouble, like a hell-broth boil and bubble.'" Her voice rose and fell with the rhythm of the words, a playful smirk dancing on her lips.

"Sounds like Shakespeare decided to go into baking," Emily mused, leaning forward to get a better look at the page.

"Or maybe it's the other way around," Sam suggested, his smile infectious.

"Look here," Olivia said, pointing to a list of ingredients. "Moon-kissed thyme, starlight-infused rosemary, and sea foam salt." She turned her expressive eyes toward her friends. "Those sound like things you'd find only in Bayside Cove, don't they?"

"Definitely not your typical supermarket stock," James agreed with mock seriousness, though the twinkle in his eye betrayed his delight. "Our little town might just be a bit more enchanted than we thought."

"Sea foam salt?" Emily picked up the phrase thoughtfully. "That's what old-timers used to call the salt we gather after high tide. And I've definitely heard Nana use 'moon-kissed' to describe her herb garden."

"Maybe our ancestors knew a thing or two about magic," Olivia mused, a note of awe threading through her words. She leaned back, absorbing the idea. "We're sitting on a gold mine of mystical ingredients!"

"Looks like we're not just prepping for the Winter Festival," Sam concluded with a grin. "We're about to bake up some real magic."

The aroma of freshly baked bread and a hint of cinnamon hung in the air as Olivia's fingers pressed and turned the dough with an almost hypnotic rhythm. Across from her, James leaned back in his chair, cradling his coffee mug like it was a precious artifact.

"Given what we've found," he said, breaking the comfortable silence, "I think we should dive into the historical society's archives. There might be records about the founding families that could shed light on these... unique ingredients."

Emily perked up at the suggestion, the green of her eyes seeming to flicker with the reflection of the bakery's fairy lights. "That's brilliant, James. I've always felt there was more to Bayside Cove than met the eye," she said, her voice humming with anticipation.

"Could be a real adventure," Olivia chimed in, dusting her hands off and looking up from her doughy creation. "We should definitely look into it."

The idea seemed to stir something within her, an inspiration that bubbled up like the yeast in her dough. With a spark of excitement, she

The Frosted Felony

glanced at the recipe book, its ancient spine cracked open to reveal secrets of the past. "And while you two are digging through history," Olivia began, her tone taking on the melody of inspiration, "I'll work on something special for the festival—a dessert that's a nod to our magical heritage."

"Something that tells a story with every bite?" James suggested, a warm smile gracing his lips.

"Exactly," Olivia replied, her mind already painting flavors and textures. "Imagine a dessert imbued with moon-kissed thyme—its fragrance releasing memories of midnight walks by the ocean." She gestured with her hands, as if she could pluck the very essence of the ingredients from the air. "And starlight-infused rosemary that whispers tales of ancient skies."

"Sounds enchanting," Emily said. "You'll have everyone believing in magic with just one taste."

"Let's hope so," Olivia said, a determined glint in her eye. "This will be more than just food; it'll be an experience that captures the soul of Bayside Cove."

She pictured the festival-goers, their faces illuminated by the soft glow of lanterns, each bite drawing them deeper into the mystery and wonder of their quaint town. Her heart swelled at the thought of bringing such joy to the community—a community woven into the very fabric of her being.

"Then it's settled," James declared, standing up and offering a hand to help Olivia to her feet. "We uncover the past, and you create the future—a perfect blend of Bayside Cove's charm and mystery."

"Couldn't have put it better myself," Olivia agreed, her laughter mingling with the comforting sounds of the bakery as they sealed their new quest with shared smiles of camaraderie and a touch of excitement for the magic that awaited them.

Sam leaned against the counter, his blue eyes sparkling like the winter frost outside as he watched Olivia sketch out her dessert concept on a scrap of parchment. "You're planning to craft an entire cosmos in a confection, Liv," he said with a grin.

"Maybe just a constellation or two," Olivia replied with a playful roll of her eyes. The kitchen was alive with the scent of cinnamon and vanilla, a sensory promise of the festivities to come. She brushed a rogue lock of hair from her face, leaving a smudge of flour on her forehead.

"Alright then, Chef Constellation," Sam teased as he stepped closer to examine her drawings. "What if we did a sugar spun halo, like a ring around the moon? I could work on that while you perfect the flavors."

Olivia tapped the pencil against her chin, considering. "Yes, and what about a dusting of edible glitter to give it that stardust shimmer?"

"Perfect. Kids will think they're biting into a piece of the night sky!" Sam's hands danced through the air, mimicking the sprinkle of glitter over an imaginary dessert.

"Exactly." Olivia's smile widened. "It'll be like serving them a slice of Bayside Cove's magic."

Their conversation flowed effortlessly into the logistics—how many they could feasibly make, the timing of each component, and the setup required at the festival grounds. It was a dance they knew well, moving around each other in the bakery's kitchen, their shared language of flavors and textures creating a symphony of ideas.

As they plotted and planned, Emily shuffled through the ancient recipe book, her green eyes scanning the cryptic notes scrawled in the margins. Her finger traced the faded ink as she murmured under her breath, deciphering the hidden meanings.

"Hey, you two," Emily called out, interrupting the brainstorming session. "There's something here—a symbol that keeps repeating. It looks almost like a family crest."

"Let me see?" Olivia peered over her sister's shoulder, her curiosity piqued by the mysterious drawing.

"Martha might know," Emily suggested, snapping the book shut decisively. "She's been the keeper of Bayside stories for longer than we've been alive. If anyone can help us decode this, it's her."

"Good idea," Olivia agreed with a nod. "We'll visit the library first thing tomorrow."

"Martha Caldwell, detective of the Dewey Decimal System," Sam quipped with a chuckle. "I bet she's got half the town's secrets tucked away between those bookshelves."

"Then it's a date." Emily stood up, brushing off the crumbs from the wooden table. "Martha, some dusty archives, and possibly the key to our town's magical history."

"Sounds like my kind of adventure," Olivia said, her expressive eyes alight with the thrill of discovery.

The Frosted Felony

The anticipation of uncovering Bayside Cove's enigmatic past filled the room, as tangible as the warmth from the ovens and the sweet smell of baked goods that lingered in the air. Together, they would delve into the unknown, drawn by the allure of secrets waiting just within reach.

Olivia's fingers paused mid-knead as James reached out, his hand brushing against hers. She looked up, her brown eyes meeting his blue ones with a spark of shared excitement. Gently, he pulled her flour-dusted hands into his own, their fingers intertwining like the twisted dough she had been working on.

"Can you believe it?" Olivia's voice brimmed with anticipation. "The Winter Festival is almost here, and it feels different this year—like we're on the cusp of something magical."

James gave her hands a gentle squeeze. "I think the magic has a lot to do with you," he said, his words carrying the weight of burgeoning affection. His gaze lingered on her face, taking in the smudge of flour on her cheek that only made her more endearing.

She laughed, the sound as light and airy as the powdered sugar that dusted her baked creations. "And what about us? Do you feel it too—the excitement of what's growing between us?"

"Every moment I'm with you," James admitted, his voice lowering to a tender timbre. "Speaking of which, how about after we close up shop tonight, we find our own little winter wonderland?" His suggestion held the promise of romance mingled with the crisp night air of Bayside Cove.

"Are you suggesting a moonlit walk by the bay?" Olivia asked, a playful glint in her eyes. Her heart skipped at the thought of spending time away from the flour and oven, wrapped up in the quiet of the evening with James.

"Exactly. Just you, me, and perhaps a few nosy stars." He winked, pulling her into a warm chuckle.

"Then it's a date," she said, her smile lingering as they reluctantly let go of each other's hands to return to the tasks at hand.

The kitchen hummed with energy as the evening wore on, the aroma of cinnamon and sugar filling the space. The recipe book lay open on the small table, its pages aglow under the soft lighting. Olivia, James, Emily, and Sam huddled around it, their heads bowed in collective focus.

"Look at this," Olivia pointed to a recipe for a cake laced with herbs found only in the deepest corners of Bayside Cove. "We could make this for the festival. Imagine the talk it would stir."

"Imagine the taste," Sam added eagerly, his blue eyes dancing with the prospect of new culinary adventures.

"First, we unravel these clues," Emily interjected, tapping a note scrawled in the margin of the page. "There's more to these recipes than just food. They're a part of our town's history—its very essence."

"Who knew baking could be an act of discovery?" James mused, his rugged features relaxed into a contented smile.

"Or that a pinch of mystery could be the secret ingredient," Olivia quipped, her chestnut hair falling forward as she leaned closer to decipher the faded handwriting.

As the four friends pored over the ancient text, the bakery was filled with more than the scent of sweet delicacies—it buzzed with the palpable excitement of possibility. Together, they stood on the threshold of uncovering the enchanting secrets of Bayside Cove, their hearts beating to the rhythm of a town steeped in magic yet to be fully understood.

The Frosted Felony

About the Author

Ladies and gentlemen, step right up to "Where the Magic Happens" - a literary circus that'll make your bookshelf do backflips!
Meet Patti, the ringmaster of this wordy wonderland! She's not just an Executive Producer; she's a word-wrangling wizard, conjuring up an animated TV series based on "ELLIOT FINDS A HOME." It's the tail-wagging tale of a thumbs-up pup and his silent sidekick, proving that you don't need words when you've got opposable digits and a heart of gold!

Hold onto your bestseller lists, folks! This Polygon Entertainment superstar has hit the USA TODAY jackpot and Amazon's #1 spot more times than a cat has lives. With 7 dozen books under her belt, she's got more genres than a chameleon has colors. From Urban Fantasy to Horror, she's been spinning yarns longer than your grandma's knitting needles!

But wait, there's more! Patti's life is like a celebrity bingo card:

She rocked "Romper Room" at 4, probably making the other kids look like amateur rompers.

She rubbed elbows with Captain Kangaroo and Mr. Green Jeans. (No word on whether the jeans were actually green.)

The Frosted Felony

She shared a train ride and a sandwich with Sidney Poitier. Talk about a meal ticket to stardom!

She high-fived President Nixon at the circus. Who knew the circus could get any more political?

She went to school with David Copperfield. We assume she didn't disappear during attendance.

She roller-skated with pre-famous John Travolta. Grease lightning, indeed!

She sipped cocoa with Abe Vigoda. Fish never tasted so sweet!

When she's not busy being a literary legend, Patti's juggling roles faster than a circus performer. Teacher, grandma, furparent - she does it all with a smile that could light up a haunted house.

Speaking of haunted houses, meet the "Queen of Halloween" herself! This Wiccan High Priestess is stirring up stories spookier than a skeleton's dance moves. Her books are flying off the shelves faster than witches on broomsticks, so follow her on social media or risk missing out on the hocus-pocus!

So, come one, come all, to Patti's phantasmagorical world of words! It's more exciting than a roller coaster, more magical than a rabbit in a hat, and more diverse than a box of assorted chocolates. Don't be shy - step into the spotlight and join the literary party where the pages turn themselves and the stories never end!

www.ingramcontent.com/pod-product-compliance
Lightning Source LLC
LaVergne TN
LVHW041804060526
838201LV00046B/1119